What the critics are saying...

☙

"If you thought Nicole Austin's Passionate Realities was hot, get out your HAZMAT suit, because Savannah's Vision is a scorcher! With so many mouth-watering cowboys, is it any wonder I'm all hot and bothered? Add a thrilling plot and four hunky cowboys to the already highly flammable Cord and Savannah, and you have a book that will make you beg for more. And thank goodness there will be more! Savannah's Vision is the first in the Corralled series. I am beside myself waiting for more cowboys, more red-hot sex and more from Nicole Austin!" ~ *Joyfully Reviewed*

"I enjoyed my time with Savannah and Cord, and believe most readers will too. They are deep characters with fears and emotions that come across as genuine. Savannah's Vision is well worth picking up for an entertaining read. Besides, did I mention the sex was hot?" ~ *The Romance Reader's Connection*

"This story is SO VERY HOT I'm surprised I didn't burst into flames while reading it. It fulfills every cowboy fantasy imaginable, especially "Save a Horse, Ride a Cowboy'. The eroticism between Savannah and Cord is so intense and so beautifully written by Ms. Austin. I can't wait to read future stories about more hot handsome cowboys, sizzling sex and wildly erotic relationships like the one shared between Savannah and Cord. I recommend this book to anyone looking for a hot read." ~ *The Road to Romance*

"The characters in this book all had a depth to them so that you felt as if you were reading about people that you have known for years! The sex is so hot that the pages will burn your fingers! Savannah's Vision has all the elements of a great book; a little suspense, a bit of mystery behind the hero, hardship for the heroine, and supporting characters that just cry out to have their own story! The cowboys of Savannah's Vision make me want to go to Montana and hunt down my own cowboys! I'm definitely looking forward to the next book in this series! Nicole Austin has done it again!!!" ~ *Erotic Escapades*

NICOLE AUSTIN

Savannah's VISION

ELLORA'S CAVE
ROMANTICA PUBLISHING

An Ellora's Cave Romantica Publication

www.ellorascave.com

Savannah's Vision

ISBN #1419954393
ALL RIGHTS RESERVED
Savannah's Vision Copyright © 2005 Nicole Austin
Edited by Shannon Combs
Cover art by Syneca

Electronic book Publication October 2005
Trade paperback Publication May 2006

Excerpt from *The Boy Next Door* Copyright © Nicole Austin 2006

Warning:

The following material contains graphic sexual content meant for mature readers. This story has been rated E–rotic by a minimum of three independent reviewers.

Ellora's Cave Publishing offers three levels of Romantica™ reading entertainment: S (S-ensuous), E (E-rotic), and X (X-treme).

S-*ensuous* love scenes are explicit and leave nothing to the imagination.

E-*rotic* love scenes are explicit, leave nothing to the imagination, and are high in volume per the overall word count. In addition, some E-rated titles might contain fantasy material that some readers find objectionable, such as bondage, submission, same sex encounters, forced seductions, and so forth. E-rated titles are the most graphic titles we carry; it is common, for instance, for an author to use words such as "fucking", "cock", "pussy", and such within their work of literature.

X-*treme* titles differ from E-rated titles only in plot premise and storyline execution. Unlike E-rated titles, stories designated with the letter X tend to contain controversial subject matter not for the faint of heart.

Also by Nicole Austin

ॐ

Ellora's Cavemen: Dreams of the Oasis l *(Anthology)*
Passionate Realities
The Boy Next Door

About the Author

ॐ

Nicole Austin lives on the sheltered Gulf Coast of Florida, where inspiration can be readily found sitting under a big shade umbrella on the beach while sipping cold margaritas. A voracious reader, she never goes anywhere without a book. All those delicious romances combined with a vivid imagination naturally created steamy fantasies and characters in her mind.

Discovering Ellora's Cave paved the path to freeing them as well as manifesting an intoxicating passion for romantica. The positive response of family and friends to her stories propelled Nicole into an incredible world where fantasy comes boldly to life. Now she stays busy working as a certified CT scan technologist, finishing her third college degree, reading, writing, and keeping up with family. Oh yeah, and did we mention all the hard work involved with research? Well, that's the fun job—certainly a labor of love.

Nicole welcomes mail from readers. You can write to her c/o Ellora's Cave Publishing at 1056 Home Avenue, Akron, OH 44310-3502.

Savannah's Vision

ॐ

Dedication

ॐ

To the ladies of ACH.

You cheer my successes, pick me up and dust me off when I fall, provide inspiration and give me a swift kick in the ass when I get lazy. For your support and dedication, I give you the cowboys of the Shooting Star Ranch.

Trademarks Acknowledgement

~

The author acknowledges the trademarked status and trademark owners of the following wordmarks mentioned in this work of fiction:

Hummer: General Motors Corporation

Jeep: DaimlerChrysler Corporation

Stetson: John B. Stetson Company

Target: Target Brands, Inc.

Victoria's Secret: V Secret Catalogue, Inc.

Wrangler: Wrangler Apparel Corp.

Boy Scouts of America: Boy Scouts of America Corporation United States

Baggies: Spotless Plastics Corporation

Chapter One

❧

Lying supine, Savannah's body was cushioned by a soft, fluffy towel. Warm golden rays of sunlight caressed every inch of her heated flesh. With knees slightly bent, she luxuriated in the cool grains of sand as they slid between her wiggling toes.

The heat pouring down over her body had long ago absorbed the salt water from the skimpy teal bikini, but a fine sheen of perspiration coated her bronzed skin. Her taut nipples stood up firmly against the thin triangles of material.

With every fiber of her being suddenly on full alert, Savannah's attention was magnetically drawn toward where the waves gently licked the sand. The blood pounding in her ears drowned out the rhythmic sounds of the surf and incessantly annoying squawking of sea gulls. Propping herself up on her elbows, she stared off into the vast enormity of the Atlantic Ocean.

Slowly, a dark masculine figure was revealed against the crystal blue horizon as he moved steadily closer. It didn't matter that she could not see him clearly because her heart knew him well. She would recognize him anywhere. He was the sultry, enigmatic man who had been the star of all her wet dreams for years.

Trying to get a better look at him, she slid her sunglasses down her slender nose, peering over the top of the frames. Backlit by the sun, it was impossible to tell the color of his hair, but she knew instinctively that it would be a shiny, deep brown. Incredibly broad shoulders arrowed down along his firm torso to trim hips. His sexy, rolling gait brought him steadily closer, each step increasing the rapid beating of her heart.

Savannah surrendered to her dark fantasies. She watched the mysterious man walking straight toward her like iron drawn to a powerful magnet. When he reached the end of her towel, the girth of his shoulders blocked out the sun. Her blood began to boil in her veins. God, how she'd longed for him.

He made her so hot.

Scorching heat shot from her curled toes to the roots of her hair. Slick moisture flooded her sex, preparing her for him. Her breasts swelled as all her erogenous zones engorged with blood and blistering heat.

Total meltdown was imminent.

Umm, but he was one cool drink of water. More than six feet of lean, muscular, sex on the beach. That thought brought a slight chuckle to her lips. Savannah wasn't kidding anyone. She'd have sex with him anytime, anywhere.

Cold droplets of water splashed down over her heated flesh as he moved over her. Not even the icy cold water could cool the fever that had seized her body.

Only he could do that.

Without a word, he covered her slender form with his much larger, stronger body. Wow! Her heart went from Mach One to a screeching halt against a solid brick wall. It sputtered for a moment, then beat fast enough to break the sound barrier.

"You're so beautiful," he whispered against her ear.

The deep, husky drawl slid over her body like velvet. The warmth of his breath over her sensitive lobe sent tremors through Savannah. With the lightest touch, his glorious chest brushed along her distended nipples. The full globes of her breasts swelled, reaching toward the source of warmth.

At the first touch of his tongue to her outer ear, she gasped. Surges of electricity raced through her body, pooling low in her abdomen.

Everything other than her dream lover disappeared as he took over her heart and soul, branding her as his possession. Warm kisses trailed down her neck, accompanied by the slight scrape of teeth. God, she was on fire. If she got any hotter, Savannah was certain to spontaneously combust.

Was that possible?

A deep moan escaped her lips. Tilting her head, she granted him access as his marvelously nimble tongue traced random patterns over her neck. Large, calloused fingers moved in wide circles around the base of her breasts. As the circles became smaller her nipples pebbled almost painfully, seeking his elusive touch.

"You taste divine," he stated in that sultry drawl. "I need to fuck you!"

Oh, hell yes!

Before she could respond his fingers traced the edge of her bikini bottoms. He slid the material to the side and plunged into her aching pussy. Strong muscles clamped down on the intruder, trying to draw him in deeper.

"Mmm. You're so wet and ready for me."

Fuck yeah!

Without realizing it Savannah began to beg. Her pride did not matter. Being in public where they could be seen did not matter. The only thing she cared about was feeling the big cock currently pressed against her belly pound into her needy cunt. *Now!*

A second finger joined the first, and he began thrusting deep. Finding her G-spot, he stroked over the supersensitive bundle of nerves with just the right amount of pressure. She arched blindly into his touch, fucking his hand. His palm pressed against the throbbing bud of her clitoris, dragging a sharp cry from the back of Savannah's throat.

Bright white streaks of light began to form at the edges of her closed eyes. Her world splintered into a million tiny sparks of light as she continued to fuck his strong hand.

Savannah woke up gasping for air, sweat soaking into her nightshirt. It took several minutes to get her breathing under control. The dreams were coming more frequently now. That was the fourth time this week she had woken up in the grips of an orgasm, dreaming about *him*.

Her stomach clenched into a tight ball, sitting in her abdomen like a rock. Moonlight danced over her exposed skin as she rose and pulled on a short silk robe. She went to sit on the cushioned window seat, drawing her legs up to her chest, wrapping her arms around them. With her cheek resting on her knees she stared out blindly into the darkness. Her hand automatically went to the crystal pendant hanging between her breasts, stroking soothingly.

The dreams had been her constant companion for longer than Savannah could remember. Their increasing frequency had her anticipating his arrival. It wouldn't be long now. She could feel him moving closer.

Her granny had called her visions and dreams "second sight". For a long time it had scared Savannah to know things before they happened—sensing the future, people's darkest secrets and their true natures. The most frightening aspect was her inability to control when and where the visions came.

Over the years she had built up mental shields to filter out many of the unwanted visions. It had been necessary for her sanity. Now there were very few times when she could ever let the barriers down and truly relax.

Simply ignoring the dreams about him did not help. When she did that they became more intense. She did not want to ignore her feelings this time. This was something she had waited on for a long time. There was no possibility of turning away.

Interestingly, she had developed a useful side effect. With just a little bit of concentration, Savannah could send images to certain people to whom she felt close. This could provide hours of wickedly good fun.

She sighed deeply, not for the first time wishing her granny were still alive. There was no one else she had ever been able to talk to about her visions since most people fear what they don't understand. Even her closest childhood friend had been scared away when Savannah had tried to explain.

After she had received visions of an abducted child and had aided in the rescue, Savannah never had any peace. Strangers would show up at her home asking for "psychic readings". Like

Savannah could just conjure up her visions at will. It just didn't work like that.

Thankfully her grandmother had left enough of an inheritance that moving away had not been a hardship. In fact, she was comfortable enough that she would never have to work for a living. And she was determined to live a quiet, private life.

Living in the West had always been her dream. She had set off in her Hummer with only some maps and a small suitcase, leaving everything else behind. The further west she'd driven, the stronger her feelings of rightness became. After two days of driving around, following her instincts, Savannah found her home in western Montana.

The owner of the ranch had been going over the property with a real estate agent when Savannah drove down the drive. Overwhelming feelings of calm and belonging flooded her as she looked out over the land. It felt like home. A place she could relax.

The ranch house looked like it was straight out of the old TV show, "Ponderosa". Right down to the sweeping staircase and large leather furniture. It was absolutely perfect. She was finally home.

One of the features she most prized was the large, in-ground, heated swimming pool, waterfall and connected hot tub behind the house. Savannah loved to go skinny-dipping late at night with the moonlight shining over the shimmering water.

It had not taken long to figure out that more than 20,000 acres was more land than she could manage on her own. She hired four hunky cowboys to take care of things. Now all she needed was someone to tell them what needed to be taken care of. It seemed that ranch work multiplied daily and was never done.

With the first rays of golden sunlight barely peeking up over the mountains, Savannah began her day.

* * * * *

What the heck did she know about hiring a foreman? Nothing! The cowboys had all given their advice, and her friend, Tamara, had come over for moral support. Still, Savannah felt overwhelmed as she looked over the numerous cowboys filling out applications in the ranch yard.

Tamara would probably not be much help in this instance, but the support was totally welcomed. Her friend owned a small bookshop in the nearest one-horse town. They had instantly become close the first time they met. Savannah had wandered into the shop praying they would have an erotica selection. She'd found not only a great selection of books, but also someone to whom she could relate.

The two women hit it off right away, finding that they shared very similar interests and views. Their yearlong friendship had helped make Montana feel even more like home. And there was only one subject Savannah did not discuss with her friend.

No matter how open-minded she had found Tamara to be, Savannah knew from experience that the visions were one thing better off kept secret. They were the one thing that kept her from becoming very close with anyone. Oh, how she ached to find someone who could understand and accept all of her.

Looking out over the ranch yard, Savannah felt deep disappointment. Although many of the cowboys were extremely attractive, they were just not *him*. She had felt certain the man from her dreams would be here today since the dreams were now coming even when she was awake.

The hairs on her neck were standing on end. That was always a sign of something about to happen. If it wasn't her dream lover, what the heck was going on? Absently, she stroked her pendant while watching the men.

Tamara's voice and ceaseless fidgeting pulled Savannah from her thoughts.

"Halloo. Earth to Van. Come in Van," Tamara said with an amused chuckle.

"I'm sorry. What did you say?"

Savannah smiled at her friend. Tamara had certainly dressed the part of cowgirl today. A red Stetson sat at a rakish angle over shoulder-length mahogany tresses. Dark sunglasses sat perched on her pert, slender nose. She wore a light blue denim shirt with pearl snaps. The first three had been left open to reveal her meager cleavage, enhanced by a push-up bra. Designer jeans hugged her petite body, and were tucked into fire engine red cowboy boots.

Savannah envied her friend's small, lithe body. Her own five-foot-ten-inch height often intimidated men. And she was way too damn curvy. She would give anything to fit in Tamara's size six jeans instead of her own size twelves.

"I don't get you, girl. Look around. This place is wall-to-wall hot cowboys. I've never seen such a fine collection of muscle wrapped in Wranglers and leather chaps. I'm on testosterone and pheromone overload here."

Savannah threw back her head and laughed. Tamara was literally chomping at the bit to get hold of a cowboy. Her radiant smile rivaled that of any child set free in a candy store. "Can't you think of anything other than sex?" she teased.

"Hah. That's an interesting statement coming from an erotica junkie." Tamara's admonishing tone was ruined by the sparkle of humor that lit up her delicate features.

Her friend's fidgeting was making Savannah crazy. Whenever they were in the ranch yard, Tamara was always looking for snakes. She had a phobia about the creatures and had become paranoid since walking up on one taking a sunbath.

"If you don't stop fidgeting, I'm gonna have to bind and gag you in one of the stalls," Savannah joked.

"Oh, hell yeah! Tie me up then send in two of these fine young studs. On second thought, make it three."

Savannah's musical laughter filled the ranch yard, drawing many a male eye. "Save a horse, ride a cowboy," she quoted from a popular country song.

"Yee-haw. Ride 'em, cowgirl," Tamara replied.

"'Scuse me," came a deep baritone voice from directly behind them.

A bright red flush heated Savannah's cheeks and spread down to her breasts. There was no way the man standing behind them had not heard their comments. And how the hell did someone sneak up on her? It wasn't like Savannah to not sense someone's presence. Damn, she really was distracted.

Biting her full lower lip, Savannah turned around quickly, then audibly gasped. Her mouth became suddenly dry. Her hand went to her heart where it pounded painfully against her rib cage.

Backlit by the sun it was impossible to see his features, but it was *him*. She had no doubt that the cowboy standing there casually was her dream lover.

Finally!

"I'm here to apply for the foreman position. Is the owner around?"

Damn, that sexy drawl went right to her head as all the blood left her brain. Savannah just stood there, dumfounded. Thankfully Tamara was there to cover for her shock. Never at a loss for words, she jumped right in to the rescue.

"You're lookin' at the owner, gorgeous," she said pointing to Savannah. "This is Savannah Thompson, and my name's Tamara Dobbs."

Linking her arm through his, Tamara walked the cowboy over to the picnic table where all the paperwork had been set up. After instructing him in the application process she stood flirting with the men.

How the hell had he gotten the drop on her? Savannah was floored. She was looking at the man she had dreamed about, anticipated his arrival for so long. He was here, at her ranch. Had walked right up behind her, and she had not even sensed his close proximity. She must be slipping.

Jealousy had her blood boiling in her veins as she watched Tamara tease *her man*. Moving casually, Savanna turned until she could get a good look without the bright sunlight ruining her view.

Bam!

She felt like she had been kicked in the chest by one of the horses. It was really him, and she was finally seeing his face. Shiny, dark brown hair on the slightly long side curled up over his collar. Mmm, how she wanted to thread her fingers through the thick, silky strands.

His face was ruggedly handsome. Wide-set, pale blue-gray eyes gave the impression of someone cold and indifferent. A small bump, from being broken, marred the bridge of his nose, lending character to his features. His strong, square jaw could have been chiseled from granite. A slight cleft divided his chin. Sensuous, full male lips drew her attention.

Savannah felt her mouth watering, wondering how he would taste. Oh, how she longed to caress those sexy lips with the tip of her tongue.

A black T-shirt hugged his broad-shouldered, muscular torso, revealing incredible strength. Blue veins stood out like thick ropes along his sculptured arms and hands. His torso narrowed down to slim hips. Faded blue jeans and scarred, black leather chaps covered his lower body. His dusty, black boots looked well worn. She imagined that the thick columns of those legs would be powerful.

Their eyes met as he surreptitiously looked out from under the brim of a black Stetson. The intensity of his sharp gaze sent heat rushing through her body. She could feel the power of those eyes reaching all the way into her soul.

"Damn, now that's one hot cowboy," Tamara commented, drawing her attention. Savannah had been so mesmerized by the cowboy that she had not noticed Tamara's return. "Wouldn't mind getting my hands inside his blue jeans."

"Mine," Savannah growled in warning. Her voice came out more harshly than she'd intended.

Tamara gave her a wide-eyed look of surprise. "What?"

"He's mine. You can have any of the others that you want, but leave him alone." The ice in her voice left no room for argument.

At first Tamara thought she was joking. After looking in Savannah's dark brown eyes, she held up her hands in surrender. "Well, it's about time. Don't just stand there with your panties in a wet wad. Go get him, girlfriend."

Her dream man turned his back. Savannah watched the play of muscles as they rippled over his broad back. Those worn jeans hugged every magnificent curve of his exquisitely shaped ass, framed so nicely by the chaps. A vivid picture of her fingers pressed into those firm cheeks as she pulled him closer flashed through her mind.

Damn, she was going to melt soon. A fine sheen of sweat broke out on her brow. Not long ago she had been enjoying the cool, spring breeze. Now her internal furnace had kicked up into high gear, raising her internal temperature.

She barely heard Tamara's words. "His name is Cord Black."

Cord. An animated video of their naked bodies moving together streamed through her head. They would fit together as if custom-made to do so. It was just something she knew without question.

The breath caught in her throat when he turned back around. Although the chaps hid some things, she could tell he had an impressive package between those muscular legs. His cock would be long and thick.

Delicious!

Her panties had become damp the second she'd laid eyes on him. Savannah could feel her pussy throb and ache. Each slight movement of her body caused the thick seam of her jeans to rub sensually against her clit.

Damn, she needed to get laid and only one cowboy was going to do.

She would not be able to wait long to claim Cord. Her new foreman would be in her bed long before he could settle into the job. Oh, and there was no second thoughts. He already had the job. The other men were just wasting their time.

As inconspicuously as possible, Cord watched the beautiful owner from under the brim of his hat. At first he had been amused listening to the conversation between the two women. He had learned long ago from his sister how women ogled men, but catching these two had been surprising.

When Savannah turned to face him, Cord could not breathe. She was too good to be true.

A navy baseball cap covered her golden hair, which hung neatly in a thick braid over her shoulder. Delicate features graced a sweet, heart-shaped face. Her eyes were the darkest chocolate brown he'd ever seen. They smoldered with a banked sensuality just waiting to be released. And he was just the one for the job.

Delicate cheekbones were set high and prominent. A straight and slender nose turned up slightly at the tip. Luscious, dusky rose lips curved in a seductive Cupid's bow. They would feel soft, yet firm under his tongue. God, how he wanted to feel those lips pressed against his.

There was something almost familiar about her, but Cord knew he'd never seen the woman before. He certainly would never have forgotten such a gorgeous sight. Dreamy curves filled out a delectable hourglass figure. Large breasts stood high and firm. He could just make out the dark shadow of the areolas through her thin, white silk shirt.

Her delectable body was poured into black stretch denim, which hugged the sensuous curve of full hips. The material clung to those extremely long legs. Cord could vividly picture them wrapped around his hips as he plunged his cock into her hot pussy.

He'd bet his prized horse that she was a real blonde, and that no surgeon had crafted those lovely breasts. She was all natural, one hundred percent woman. And she would be one hundred percent his if he had anything to say about it. The painful pressure of his cock swelling in the confining denim brought Cord back to reality.

Down, boy. As if a lady like Savannah would ever let a roughneck like him anywhere near her exquisite body. Dream on, cowboy.

Mmm. And what a hell of a body it was. Not some anorexically thin girl with her bones sticking out. No. Savannah had a woman's curves. No worrying about hurting her by holding on too tightly or fucking too forcefully. Not like with her tiny little friend.

Now he just had to land the job so he could work on landing the woman. He would find a way to be the kind of man she needed. Someone she could respect.

While he filled out the paperwork, Cord kept an eye on the elegant blonde. She laughed at something her friend said, and the musical sound was like a fist to his gut. What he wouldn't give to have a woman like that.

When the two women disappeared into the stables some of the blood flow returned to his thinking head, reducing some of the pressure in his painfully erect cock. He was now able to survey the competition while finishing up the paperwork, nodding to the few men he recognized. Jobs like this were hard to come by. They all would fight hard to obtain such a prized position as foreman of the Shooting Star Ranch.

Talking to the ranch hands, he learned great deal. They all greatly respected the owner. She treated the men like family. Her wild, tomboy ways were looked upon by the men with the indulgence of older brothers. They seemed very protective of their employer, which spoke volumes about how she ran the ranch and treated the workers.

He also learned of Savannah's love for the horses she trained and the breeding program she was beginning. Apparently the animals she had chosen so far were of the highest quality. It was speculated that her horses would be highly sought after and prized.

That would work in his favor. His experience with breeding would provide an edge over the competition. There was no way he was not walking away with this job. He'd do whatever it took to insure he won the position.

He had fallen in love with this part of the country. And working and living at the Shooting Star would give him the opportunity to look for his own piece of land, his own slice of heaven.

Of course, he also wanted the opportunity to explore the magnetic pull the beautiful owner had over him. A woman like Savannah Thompson would make a good partner and a fine wife.

Chapter Two

Alone at last.

Savannah loved Friday nights. The ranch hands were all in town celebrating a well-deserved night off and she had the entire place to herself.

All day her thoughts had been plagued by the fine, rock-hard hunk of cowboy who had finally arrived. Now that he was finally here she was filled with restless energy.

For some odd reason her senses tingled as if he were nearby. Of course, that was ridiculous. Cord was nowhere near the ranch. His application indicated that he was staying at the small motel in town. But still, somehow she felt his presence. She trusted the odd feelings, wondering what was going on.

Stepping out onto the front porch, she breathed in the clean scent of the night air. The comforting smells of horses, manure, hay and the ranch yard relaxed her. A huge, full moon hung high in the sky, sending silvery tendrils of light over the dark land. Its gravitational pull always affected her deeply.

Savannah pranced out into the yard, golden hair swinging loose over her shoulders and down her back. Its silken caress over her skin felt erotic. The night air was cool on her flesh. The skimpy tank top and bike shorts she wore left a great expanse of her skin exposed. Goose bumps popped out over her arms and legs. Her nipples pebbled against the thin cotton shirt.

Four years of ballet lessons taken as a child showed in her graceful movements. With wild abandon she danced under the moon and across the yard. Feeling free and light, she curtsied to an imaginary partner then held out her hand. Adrenaline coursed through her veins as her body moved to an exhilarating inner sound track.

Reaching the stables, she quietly moved inside to find her guy. As soon as she stepped inside he called out to Savannah. "Cool your jets, big guy. I know you're ready to play under that big ol' moon. You feel it too, don't you?"

At the stall door she reached out to run her fingers over Moon Dancer's soft muzzle. "Hey stud. How's my man tonight?"

In response, the big stallion pressed his head against her chest. After unlatching the stall, she swung the door wide then turned and walked away. The big, chocolate horse followed her without having to be led.

Playing their familiar game, Savannah stopped with her back to the big horse and stood waiting, legs spread in a wide stance. She ignored his approach, but didn't have to wait long. Dancer soon came up and head-butted her back.

"Tag, you're it."

Her laughter filled the yard as she pranced backward in a zigzagging pattern. The big horse chased after his mistress with obvious joy. Her taunting words were answered by whickers and whinnies from the stallion. When she had finally exhausted herself, Savannah collapsed against Moon Dancer's thick shoulder, hugging his neck.

"Okay, stud. You win." She knew what he wanted.

In one strong, fluid motion she fisted her hands in his thick, flaxen mane and swung her body up onto his broad back.

"Are you ready to run, big guy?"

The stallion dropped his head and pawed at the hard, packed ground. With a slight squeeze of her legs, they loped off across the countryside. Woman and beast as one.

* * * * *

After spending the day getting the lay of the land, Cord felt pleasantly tired. The Shooting Star Ranch was a beautiful spread. Tall mountains stood sentry along its western border. A small river snaked over the property, providing a natural water source. The rolling land spoke to something deep within his soul, giving Cord a feeling of rightness and homecoming.

Homecoming?

That was certainly something he'd never felt before. His entire life had been spent restlessly moving from one place to another. Never staying long enough for anywhere to become home. Yet somehow that was exactly what he felt on this land. Like he had come home, finally finding his place on this Earth. A deep connection was being formed to both the land and its owner.

With a mental shake, Cord tried to push the feelings away. Soon he would find a spread that would become his home. It wouldn't be anywhere near as large as the Shooting Star, but it would be his land. He would finally put down roots and build a home.

Stopping short just before reaching the ranch yard, Cord sensed her presence even before he heard the screen door slam shut. Savannah stepped out onto the porch and took a deep breath of the crisp night air.

Hidden in shadow, Cord watched. His cock instantly hardened. It was irrational, insane, how he wanted this woman. Never before had he felt such a deep, gnawing ache. Such a primal urge to mate.

Moonlight caressed her long, golden tresses turning them silver. The hair glowed around her head like a halo. Moving with purely feminine grace, she floated around the yard. He had to fight to suppress laughter when she curtsied to an imaginary dance partner and began twirling around gaily.

Watching the exquisite woman dance in the moonlight was the most exotic sight Cord had ever witnessed. With moonlight caressing her hair and bare flesh she looked like a mystical faerie. It was a test of his self-control, not going to Savannah, pulling her into his arms and dancing her around under the light of the moon.

Tracking her progress, he stayed close. When she moved into the stables he could hear her talking, but could not make out the words. Her voice had a husky quality that caused his already rock-hard cock to lengthen and throb.

He couldn't believe his eyes when she walked out, back turned to the horse. The stallion happily followed behind his mistress like a big puppy dog. She did not need a lead rope to control the large animal.

Cord almost rushed forward to her aid when the huge animal head-butted Savannah, but her laughter stopped him cold. Disbelief washed over him as he watched woman and beast play a rambunctious game of tag. He had never seen a horse react this way to a person. It was truly a sight to behold.

Her luscious body moved sensuously in the silvery light. The thin top and fitted shorts clung to every sumptuous curve. Firm muscles rippled with every movement. The light sound of her laughter wrapped around his heart, tugging painfully. On first sight he had sensed that she was special. But he'd had no idea what an incredibly strong, sexy, playful woman Savannah Thompson was before now.

Unfamiliar feelings of possessiveness raged through Cord. She was his woman. He would find a way to get the foreman job then stake his claim. Nothing would stop him from making the mysterious nymph his own.

His heart stopped as he watched the lithe woman swing herself up onto the big stallion and race out over the land bareback. The fiery, wild filly would be a challenge to tame, but Cord Black never walked away from a challenge.

It was several hours later when Cord finally heard the steady drum roll of hooves heading toward the stables. Climbing out of his bedroll, he set out to help Savannah groom the stallion. He moved soundlessly over the land, listening to the sounds of night creatures scurrying about.

* * * * *

Moon Dancer followed Savannah into his stall after she dismounted. He stood perfectly still as she began her ministrations. He sighed deeply when she began working the curry comb in a circular motion over his thick hide.

While working, Savannah talked to Moon Dancer. She told him all about the many applicants for the foreman's job. Then she began to talk about one Cord Black. "Mmm. If that ain't one fine hunk of handsome cowboy. He's got these sexy, stormy gray eyes. I swear, he can see right through me."

She continued to talk while working over the big horse. Savannah continued even after sensing someone drawing close. It wasn't long before he came close enough for her to pick up his overpowering scent.

Without even sparing a glance over her shoulder, she said, "Hi Wyatt. What are you doing lurking around my property in the middle of the night?"

Of course, she already knew the answer. Wyatt Bodine, owner of the neighboring Bar B, was the sleazy type of man. He only showed up when the hands were off. Then he'd come on to Savannah. Try to take something she wasn't offering.

"Damn. How the hell do you do that, Vannah?" he questioned. "It's downright creepy how you know who is close by without even looking."

Savannah chose to ignore his use of the hated nickname.

"If you didn't bathe in your cologne it would be easier to sneak up on me, if that's your goal." Her deep sigh spoke of long suffering. "Is there a reason you're here, Wyatt?" She made no attempt to hide the irritation in her voice.

Wyatt moved into the stall, crowding in close to Savannah. He loved to infringe on her personal space. She cringed as his erection rubbed over her buttocks. How many times would she have to tell her neighbor that no meant no? The creep became bolder with each encounter. She sensed that he had become obsessed with her and his attempts at seduction would only continue to escalate.

Distantly, Savannah had the feeling that once again Cord was nearby, but Wyatt remained the primary focus of her attention. Attempting to look bored she moved along Moon Dancer's big body, easily sidestepping Wyatt's roaming hands.

Wyatt grabbed her, forcefully turned her around and pinned her up against the wall. Using his considerable weight, he held her in place, trapping her hands between their bodies. His rancid breath reeked of alcohol and tobacco.

His aggressive movements took her by surprise and Savannah screamed.

"I think it's about time we got a little closer, Vannah." He leaned closer, nipping at her neck while shoving his knee between her legs. "I'm gonna fuck that fine cunt until you scream my name."

She fought against the nausea that rolled through her stomach. Between his putrid scent and disgusting suggestions, she just might lose her dinner. Biting her lip was all that kept her from laughing out loud at the image of puking all over Wyatt.

Fueled by the alcohol, he was much more aggressive than normal. Roughly, he tore open her top straight down the front. The thin cotton material gave way easily with a rough ripping sound. His hands roughly squeezed her bare breasts, painfully pinching her nipples.

Okay, she was going to have to teach this randy cowboy a lesson on how he should treat a lady. Plastering on a false smile, Savannah spoke in an intentionally deep, sexy voice. "Let go of my hands and I'll show you just how friendly I can be, Wyatt."

She didn't take time to enjoy being able to breathe once again as he shifted his bulk away. Savannah noted and promptly disregarded a shadow moving in her peripheral vision. With swift, powerful motions she grabbed his beefy shoulders and drove her knee up into his groin. The satisfying sound of all the air rapidly being expelled from his lungs was like music to her ears.

Taking advantage of his stooped position, Savannah slammed the heel of her left hand into the bridge of his nose, cringing at the sound of splintering bone. Before the blood could even begin to flow she slammed her elbow into his expansive gut.

Wyatt fell into a heap on the stall floor and rolled around cupping his balls. She couldn't help laughing when he rolled right into a steaming pile of Moon Dancer's excrement.

Moving out of the shadows, Cord rushed over to join Savannah. He stared down at the pathetic man, shaking his head. "I was about to offer you a hand but it looks like you have everything under control."

He made a brief tsking sound. "I'll just cart this manure out for you."

Before making any move toward Wyatt, he turned to Savannah. With a gentle finger under her chin, Cord raised her eyes to meet his own.

"Are you okay, sugar?"

"I-I'm fine, Mister Black. Th-Thank you for your concern."

She struggled to pull the tattered shirt over her exposed breasts. His eyes followed the movements of her slender fingers as they stroked over a long, slender piece of rose quartz nestled safely in the deep valley between the full globes.

His thick fingers trailed in a sensual caress down her cheek, sending electric currents from her scalp all the way down to her toes. She could tell he felt the electricity that arced between them too.

Removing his battered hat, Cord set it on her head. She stared in amazed silence as he pulled his snug T-shirt from his pants then took it off. Just what the hell did he think he was doing?

Cord put his hat back on then pulled the shirt over her head, covering her exposed chest. Her entire body trembled at the sensation of his warmth still held within the fabric. Each rapid breath swamped her with his heady, masculine scent.

With gentle care he helped work her arms through the sleeves. Once covered, she stood staring at him. Well, chivalry was certainly not dead.

Her mouth opened then closed again without uttering a word. There were no words. All she could do was to stare at the incredibly delicious sight before her.

Holy shitake mushrooms. The big cowboy had one incredible chest. Pale, flat male nipples tempted her tongue. Her fingers itched to feel the chiseled muscles that narrowed down to his flat six-pack abs. All that expanse of wonderful male flesh called out to be stroked, and tasted.

Unconsciously running her tongue over her lips, she imagined how his skin would taste. A light pelt of dark hair covered his chest and ran in a narrow line from his navel, disappearing below a large, silver belt buckle. The rippled expanse of tanned male flesh was nearly irresistible.

The sight of her tongue sliding over her plump lip had Cord groaning in need. "Hold that thought, sugar," he said in a lazy, sexy drawl.

God, she was melting again. His sinful voice was like a velvety caress over her flesh, burning away the chill. The heat that started low in her pelvis radiated out through her body. She must be having some kind of heat stroke.

Yeah, that had to explain what was happening to her normally cool, calm senses.

Watching the flex and play of muscles over his body mesmerized Savannah. Cord took hold of Wyatt under the arms and dragged the man out of the stables. All she could do was stand there and watch. Realizing that she was becoming lightheaded, she finally let out her pent-up breath.

Thank the Lord for delicious cowboys, she thought. She had no doubt that Wyatt would not be pestering her anymore considering the possessiveness and anger she'd glimpsed in Cord's stormy eyes.

Walking back into the stables, Cord drank in the seductive sight. Savannah still stood exactly where he had left her several minutes ago. Her breathing came in shallow pants. Her slightly swollen lips and mussed hair gave her a just-fucked look.

Damn if she didn't look sexy in his T-shirt. The material clung to her full breasts and hung down to the middle of her thighs. Umm. How he'd love to see her wearing only that shirt. Well, maybe that and his hat.

He had been surprised by her quick, powerful movements. Wyatt Bodine was taller, stronger and easily more than twice her weight. Yet Savannah had quickly flattened him into a pile of shit, right where he belonged. A tough woman like that would be the perfect life partner. She could stand and work side by side with her husband.

Whoa, cowboy. Now don't go getting so far ahead of yourself. You are a long way from capturing that quick, little filly. And where the hell are these possessive feelings coming from anyway?

Shock began to set in as Cord moved toward Savannah. A cold chill overtook her. Her body became racked by shivers, teeth clattering together helplessly.

"C'mere, sugar," he drawled.

She was pulled into his warm embrace. Cord tucked her head under his chin and wrapped his strength around her, sheltering Savannah. His large hands ran up and down her arms spreading warmth through the shivering limbs.

"It's okay now. Just let it go. I'm here," he crooned. His deep, velvety voice was soothing. She felt safe and protected by his big body.

"H-He usually isn't so…so aggressive," she stammered.

"Shh."

His big hands left her arms and began to stroke warmth into her back. "Don't worry. I'll make sure he won't be bothering you anymore, sugar."

Savannah had never been happier to see anyone as when Cord had walked into the stables, but his presence on the ranch left her with many questions. "Cord, wh-what are you doing here?" She looked up at him with wide, hopeful doe eyes.

"Just getting a feel for the land in case I get the job. You have an incredibly beautiful piece of heaven here."

Savannah sighed and rested her head against his strong shoulder. She wrapped her arms around his waist, accepting the comfort he offered. "It's my little slice of paradise." She snuggled deeper into the warmth he so generously offered. "I was going to call you in the morning. The job is yours, if you want it."

Feather-light caresses ruffled her hair. Savannah's muddled brain almost thought he was kissing the top of her head.

"Oh, I want, sugar. More than you can know."

The words whispered against her neck sent shivers of anticipation through Savannah. The double entendre was not lost on her. He tilted her chin up and stared into her eyes for several long moments.

Drawing her hands up and resting them on his chest, she was surprised by the heat pouring out of his well-formed muscles. A constant hum of electrical energy coursed between their bodies. She recognized desire in his dilated pupils, surrounded by the thinnest circle of stormy gray. Her lips parted on a sigh and it was all the invitation he needed.

Savannah's knees became weak as Cord pressed his firm lips against hers. With the tip of his tongue, he tasted the corners of her mouth. Vivid images played through her mind, telling her everything she needed to know about her dream lover.

At first his tongue stroked over her lips slowly, testing her response. He gently learned her taste and the contours of her sweet mouth. When he could no longer hold himself back, Cord took her mouth with a savage intensity that surged through her body.

Slanting his lips against hers, Cord swept his tongue deep into her mouth. He kissed her with a mind-blowing thoroughness, learning every texture. With wild need, she sucked his tongue deeper. His hands on her hips were the only thing keeping Savannah upright.

Blood pulsed heatedly through her pussy and her panties flooded with hot juices. Her nipples pebbled against his firm chest. Reckless need coursed through her blood.

Take me now, she screamed in her mind.

As if hearing her silent plea, his hands dropped along her hips and around to her ass, pulling her tightly against his huge erection.

Oh shit.

The steely length of his shaft pressed into her soft abdomen sent a flood of heat to her weeping pussy. Wrapping her arms around his neck, she pressed as closely into his powerful body as humanly possible. One leg snaked up over his lean hip, pulling him more tightly against her.

It wasn't enough. She needed to be closer. She needed his hot, thick length plunging deep into her aching depths. Her fingers tightly threaded through his silky hair. If only she could mount him as easily as she did Moon Dancer. Oh, what a ride that would be.

Cord's senses were on overload. The fresh scent of apples and cinnamon had his cock throbbing. Her warm, curvy body fit against his perfectly. The hot depths of her mouth tasted like apple pie.

And damn if the responsive little minx wasn't trying to climb him. One long leg wrapped around his hip while she pulled him closer with her hands tangled in his hair. Her fingernails massaged his scalp, sending bolts of lightning through his veins. He had to stop her now before he lost all control.

His chest heaved with the effort to get enough oxygen to his brain. Cord wanted to sink his cock into the hot juices soaking through the thin material of her shorts. The incredible heat threatened to send him up in flames.

No! He would not take her like an animal in a barn. Savannah was a lady and deserved to be romanced. She deserved to be made love to in a bed, not fucked against a stall door.

Untangling her from his body took great effort. He could easily read the questions in her melted chocolate eyes. "Damn, sugar. You drive my control to the brink. But when I claim you it won't be in the barn." He turned her away from him and headed her toward the house.

Smack.

Savannah gasped at the sting of his big hand on her ass. The cocky jerk had just spanked her. Amazingly, her pussy flooded with more hot juices.

"Move your fine ass on into that house now so I can finish taking out the trash."

When she did not move he landed another firm slap across her round cheeks.

"Get going before I forget my manners, sugar."

Oooow! Frustrated energy surged through Savannah. She wanted to scream at his daring. Of all the nerve! He'd spanked her. And then he'd sent her away sexually frustrated. Oh, Cord Black had a great deal to learn about her.

Chapter Three

❧

The past two days had gone by in a fog. All Savannah could think about was the new foreman, Cord Black. Erotic images from that night in the stables were branded into her memory.

She couldn't concentrate on anything. The cowboys were starting to tease her about the botched dinners and her mismatched clothes. Today she had put her shirt on backwards and her sweater inside out.

Several times during the night she woke up in a sweat, aching with need. Her vibrator was getting quite the workout. If things kept up this way she would have to head into town for a fresh supply of batteries.

The seductive sound of rain pounding the roof had woken her before sunrise. She had always thought there was something sexy about the rain. Sensual images of Cord making love to her while fat drops thrummed down had her pussy swelling.

She loved it when it rained. Everything on the ranch would smell fresh and clean. And the land would be soft and muddy.

Perfect.

Before the first rays of sunlight brightened the yard, her cowboys had everything ready to go. Savannah's body hummed with excitement and adrenaline. After a quick breakfast of hastily made sandwiches they anxiously headed out for the day.

Looking over her men brought a bright smile to Savannah's face. Having the cowboys around was like finally having the older brothers she had always wanted. Zeke, Riley, Jesse and Brock were very protective of her.

At first they had accompanied her during her wild games just to make sure she did not get hurt, but before long the men had gotten caught up into the play. Sometimes they just stood around shaking their heads at her crazy ideas. Not today though. Today she could feel the anticipation in the air. Her boys were ready to have some fun.

Tamara had spent the night. The two of them had stayed up late drinking wine and talking. Savannah left a hastily written note on the kitchen table so her friend wouldn't worry.

* * * * *

The absolute quiet of the ranch hit Cord immediately. Where the hell was everyone? It had rained during the night but it had turned out to be a gloriously bright, sunny day. Yet none of the hands were anywhere in the yard working. The only sounds he could hear came from the horses in the stables.

After parking his truck, Cord guided his mare out of the trailer. He settled Stormy in the stall next to Moon Dancer. She stuck her big, gray head over the door to nip at Cord's shirt. It didn't take long for Moon Dancer to stick his blocky head out to meet his new neighbor.

"You two get along really nice like and maybe I can arrange a little rendezvous later."

While he walked to the ranch house, Cord was again struck by the unnatural quiet. His knock was finally answered by Tamara who stood for several minutes looking him over before finally inviting him inside.

"Where is everyone?" Cord questioned.

Tamara didn't answer until he had followed her into the kitchen and she drank some coffee. The petite woman was obviously not a morning person. She looked grumpy. Her voice came out gruff and scratchy.

"Savannah and the cowboys took off early this mornin'." She passed Cord the note she'd found on the table.

Tam,

The boys and I are headed out to the north meadow.
Everybody needs some R&R. We'll be back by dinnertime.
Van

"Well, that's sure chock-full of information." Cord lifted his Stetson and ran a hand through his thick, brown hair. "I guess I'll go get settled into my cabin."

Tamara gave him a stern look. "Hang on a second, Tex. We need to have a little chat first."

Cord gave the petite woman a wary frown before settling into a chair across from her at the table. He could see the emotions brewing in her bloodshot eyes. If he wasn't mistaken there was a tinge of jealousy there also.

"I'll keep it short and simple. Savannah is very sensitive and vulnerable. Hurt her and I'll make sure you feel ten times the pain."

The hardness in her eyes brooked no argument, but it wasn't much of a threat coming from such a small package. He simply smiled and said, "I'll surely keep that in mind, little lady."

Cord fought not to laugh at the sweetly protective friend. He had the feeling that she was jealous of Savannah's obvious closeness with the hands. Idly he wondered which one she had her sights set on.

He walked briskly across the yard. The hands all lived in the bunkhouse, but as foreman, Cord was given a private cabin. Although not luxurious, the privacy was welcome.

The small kitchen was furnished with modern appliances. Savannah had stocked the refrigerator with basic supplies. A small dining table sat near the window. In the living room was a well-worn, dark brown leather couch and recliner. A small basket of field flowers adorned the scarred coffee table. Woven Navaho rugs were scattered over the oak floors. The bedroom had a large bed with a firm mattress. The furniture was old, but clean. Crisp, clean sheets were covered with a thick, down comforter. A chest at the foot of the bed contained several quilts.

Overall, the cabin was comfortable and suited Cord just fine. Returning to the kitchen, he discovered a foil-wrapped plate on the counter. A small note of welcome was taped to the foil. Sliding the wrap aside, he found freshly baked chocolate chip cookies. That was one of the sweetest things anyone had ever done for him. He appreciated the gesture.

After getting settled, Cord busied himself in the stables. He groomed the horses, mucked out the stalls and straightened out the tack room. It was work the hands would have been performing had they been around. Once everyone came back from the meadow he would have to find out the ranch routine. From the looks of the bunkhouse refrigerator, dinners were not fixed in the small kitchen. It was mostly stocked with snacks.

His most important task was going to be figuring out a way to tame that wild filly. Savannah couldn't be treating the men so casually. He would have to set some definite limits on *his woman's* activities.

Yeah, once she was his there would be some big changes. He wouldn't put up with wild games and running around with the hands.

* * * * *

Just the sight of the muddy meadow had Savannah smiling brightly. She was more than ready to have some fun. The cowboys quickly got to work setting up hoops at opposite ends of the mud pit.

Ah! Basketball on ATV's in a fresh mud pit with her boys. Life just didn't get to be any more fun. The teams were Brock and Riley against Jesse and Zeke. Savannah played referee and helped whichever team had fallen behind. She also rode around slinging as much mud at the men as she could manage.

Brock and Jesse pulled up facing each other at center field. She came up alongside, fighting to maintain a serious look. Anticipation thrummed through her body.

"Y'all ready?"

"Hell yes," both men hollered.

"Play nice, boys," she warned.

Stretching out the anticipation, she took her time gazing at both men. Their eyes held mirth and a mischievous gleam. This was going to be so much fun. Tossing the ball high into the air, she quickly reversed her ATV, getting out of the way. Both men jumped up to stand on the front of their rides.

It was Jesse who tipped the ball to where Zeke waited nearby. At first they took the game very seriously, each team trying desperately to win. Once Savannah started her antics however, they were all soon laughing hysterically and slinging as much mud as humanly possible.

The first time she had suggested this crazy game the cowboys had looked at her with barely concealed concern. It had only taken a few weeks of living and working closely with Savannah for them to understand her playful nature though.

Being cooped up in the rain stored up a lot of energy. Their wild play in the mud alleviated the tension. And after all, the primary purpose of the Shooting Star Ranch was to provide Savannah with happiness. Why shouldn't she enjoy herself?

Frequently they staged their own little rodeos. The boys had started out letting Savannah win. She had laid into Zeke fiercely, letting him know what she thought about that attitude. If nothing else, Savannah was a fierce competitor. She could not stand anyone letting her win.

When she played, she played hard. Since starting up the ranch she had happily suffered through several sprains and many bruises. And any time the boys seemed to be holding back, she kicked their asses.

There had only been one occasion when they turned down one of her crazy ideas. After watching a late night movie she had wanted to try jousting. The boys had quickly nixed the idea. Not only would they all most likely end up injured, but the horses could end up seriously hurt. The risks were too great. Finally she had agreed, but had been greatly disappointed.

She would never forget the looks on their faces when she had walked out of the house. It had taken quite a long time to fashion her suit of armor from pots and pans. Lord, but she must have been quite the sight rattling around like something out of the medieval times. With each movement, she'd clanked loudly. Cookie sheets were strapped to her chest and back. Pot lids covered her shoulders. A large saucepan had been worn as a helmet. She'd looked like a mixed-up tin man.

The boy's laughter had been worth the effort. For several days every time they saw Savannah they broke out into hysterical fits. She loved to see her cowboys laughing and in a good mood. It did her heart good.

Of course, anyone with such a playful nature was bound to come up with some practical jokes. She still laughed loudly every time she thought about her pranks. The best one had been the time she'd come close to losing Zeke. He was the shy, quiet one in the bunch. What she'd thought to be harmless fun had greatly embarrassed him.

The showers in the bunkhouse were similar to those in a locker room, all together in one big tiled area affording no privacy. Before going off to play she had arranged for Tamara to remove all the cowboy's clothes, towels and sheets from the bunkhouse. She had not left a scrap of material behind.

Arriving back at the ranch covered in mud they had all headed directly to the showers. Savannah then snuck into the bunkhouse and removed their muddy clothes, leaving only their boots and hats. The two women then pulled up lawn chairs not far from the front door. After setting off the fire alarm they sat back and waited for the show.

Tamara had rolled right out of her chair from laughing so hard. Four cowboys had run out into the yard, wild-eyed, buck naked and soaking wet. They wore nothing but muddy boots, holding their hats over their dicks.

Zeke had been painfully embarrassed. After she'd finally returned their clothes he'd packed his belongings and promptly quit. It had taken a great deal of fast-talking to convince him to stay.

Since then he had become much more relaxed around his playful boss. Over the past year they had become a family. It would take a great deal to drive any one of them away from the ranch now. She intended to make sure that never happened. She loved every one of her boys more than she could any blood sibling.

Mud hit her face and chest with a loud splat, pulling Savannah from her thoughts. Zeke hollered with joy at having caught her off guard. Before long the pretense of a basketball game was dropped and the primary objective became to bury each other.

By the time they headed back for the house she could barely tell one man from the other. Her mood could not have been lighter or happier. For a while she had managed to chase away the nearly constant visions which could send her into depression.

She had yet to find a way to totally control the influx of images. Often they were shadowed with pain and misery. Whatever people were feeling assaulted her senses. When Tamara's aunt had died, her friend's pain had nearly killed Savannah.

The only escape she managed was while playing hard. That was one time she could totally turn off her abilities and relax. She sought that relief as often as possible. Her cowboys seemed to understand how much their play meant to her and made sure she spent most of her time laughing.

* * * * *

The throaty rumble of several engines drew Cord's attention. He moved out to the corral and sat on the fence, waiting to see what was going on.

Several moments later, five mud-covered ATVs rolled up to the nearby barn. The riders were caked with mud. Bright white smiles shone from under the layers of dirt. They were all hooting, hollering and laughing like a bunch of loons. Apparently, mudding had been the order of the day.

Savannah's eyes locked with his the moment she rode into the yard, noting his deep scowl. He looked like a pissed-off, caged animal ready to strike out. Automatically, she stroked the pendant resting between her breasts for comfort.

Cord was only sure it was Savannah because of the luscious curves. Every inch of her lithe body was covered in mud. Even her hair was caked with the dull brown substance.

Damn, he wanted to walk right up to her and kiss away the dirt. She looked sexy as hell covered in mud, happiness and relaxation radiating off her body in waves.

Casually she called out, "Howdy, Cord."

Pointing to the muddy men one by one she said, "Riley, Jesse, Brock, Zeke, this is our new foreman, Cord Black. Cord, these are my cowboys." Her face was filled with obvious affection for the small group of mud-coated men who surrounded her protectively.

Savannah's breath caught in her throat as Cord slid off the fence and walked toward the group. His smooth, rolling gait had her heart beating double time. She wanted nothing more than to fall into his arms and taste him again. To feel the blazing heat of his hard body pressed against hers. But she could not act on her desires in front of the cowboys.

She pictured his bare chest and felt her stomach do flip-flops. She had never wanted a man this badly before. She had to have him, and soon.

Cord nodded his head to the other men.

"After y'all clean up the ATVs, get showered. I'll meet you in the bunkhouse to discuss the ranch routine and duties."

His eyes held a predatory gleam as he moved closer to Savannah. Watching the other men in his peripheral vision, he ran a finger slowly over her dirty cheek.

"Looks like we'll have to hose you off before you go into the house."

He stood so close that her breasts nearly brushed up against his chest with each breath. She felt them swelling, stretching toward his heat as a flower stretches toward the sun.

The hands watched him closely. They kept a protective eye on Savannah while they went about their assigned work. Cord was pleased with both their actions and self-control.

Linking their arms, he guided Savannah toward the house. "Do you have an outdoor shower?"

Savannah had a difficult time answering. Her entire body was on sensory overload. Just the feel of his muscular forearm bunching beneath her fingers had every nerve ending tingling. She was surprised by the husky, sultry sound of her own voice.

"Back porch," was the only response she could manage.

The large porch was covered by screens. An abundance of plants provided a measure of privacy. He noted the outdoor shower, as well as the large garden tub. A supply of clean towels sat on a nearby cart.

Desire hit him hard in the gut. Just the image of Savannah standing under that shower naked was nearly enough to drive him insane.

"Need any help with your boots, sugar?"

"Um, no. I'm fine. I'll clean up then meet you in the bunkhouse."

Cupping her cheek, Cord stared into her eyes. "No."

"Wh-what?" she asked lamely.

"I said, no. The bunkhouse is no place for a lady. I'll take care of the hands and we'll talk later."

Savannah stared at him with a defiant look, hands fisted on her hips. "I have been in the bunkhouse plenty of times. If I want to go into *my* bunkhouse and talk to *my cowboys*, I will."

His expression became hard, closed off. "You will not go into the bunkhouse, Savannah. I won't have you getting the hands all worked up. I don't care what you've done in the past. The bunkhouse is off limits."

Cord could tell from her expression that she was going to be stubborn about this. "Don't think about defying me, sugar. Not unless you want to be spanked again."

Moisture flooded her pussy as she listened to his words. She remembered the sharp sting followed by heat spreading through her ass the last time he had swatted her bottom. Savannah would have never imagined getting turned on by something like a spanking. What the heck was he doing to her?

"You need to understand the way I run my ranch, Cord. This is not your typical working ranch. It's all about pleasure and relaxation. Those cowboys are not just hands, we're family. I won't be told where I will or will not go on my own land."

The deep growl that rumbled through his chest shocked Savannah.

"I suggest you not test me on this issue. Stay out of the bunkhouse or find yourself another foreman."

Cord turned and walked away before she could get any further under his skin. Damn, she was going to make his job almost as hard as she made his cock.

Savannah stood fuming for several moments before stripping naked and showering. She'd felt so wonderful after cavorting in the mud with her cowboys, only to have Cord ruin her mood. Damn if he couldn't be infuriating. Just who the hell did he think he was, ordering her around?

She'd fix him. A delicious plan began forming in her mind.

The man was pure hell on her senses. He fouled up her intuition whenever he was near. Not to mention what he did to her body. Vivid images of rolling around in the mud with him sent heat coursing through her.

The other night in the stables, the impression of his cock had been burned into her skin. She pictured herself kneeling at his feet with her lips stretched over his thick shaft. The image gave her wicked ideas.

Her connection with Cord was tangible. She should be able to reach him easily. Standing under the water she went through her relaxation techniques. Focusing her mind on images of Cord she reached out, forming a link. She found him standing in his cabin.

"Heads up, cowboy." A wicked smile curved her lips.

Savannah dropped gracefully to her knees at Cord's feet. She ran her hands up his muscular thighs. She could see the head of his long, hard cock protruding above the waistband of his low-slung jeans. *Damn if he didn't have a huge cock.*

Reaching up she unbuckled his belt, opened the button and slid the zipper down. Sinking her fingers under the waistband, she pulled the soft denim down over his thighs, dragging his briefs along too. His big, luscious cock sprang forward at full mast and waved hello.

Savannah had never seen such a beautiful sight in her life. He was at least nine inches long, and so thick that her fingers didn't meet when wrapped around his girth.

With her hands splayed over his muscular thighs she studied his magnificent manhood. The broad, plum-shaped head had turned a deep red color. Thick veins stood out along its delectable length. Her mouth watered and she licked her lips.

"I'm so hungry," she whispered.

Cord moaned as her warm breath caressed his fevered flesh.

Savannah would not be rushed. Sliding her hands up his thighs, she cupped his balls gently, enjoying their weight in her palm. As she massaged his sac, his cock jerked toward her mouth.

"Mmm. Someone wants to play."

Trailing her fingers over his length, she enjoyed the silky feel of his skin over the hard muscle below. A small amount of pre-cum collected at the slit.

Taking him into both hands she licked the fluid and teased the slit with her tongue. "Mmm, good," she mumbled against his cock, sending vibrations through his body. Slowly she ran her tongue over the broad head, licking up more of the salty fluid as it escaped.

His gravelly moans sent shudders through her body.

Savannah frequently looked up into his eyes. The intimacy of the act let her feel even closer to Cord. Wrapping one hand around the base of his cock, she stretched her lips over the rigid shaft. As she moved him deeper she swirled her tongue over his length.

"Oh yeah, sugar. Take it all."

She could hear the strain in his voice. Applying suction, she swallowed as much of his length as she could while stroking her tongue over the sensitive underside. Continually changing her rhythm kept him in a state of anticipation. She stroked her tongue along the thick ridge and then the sensitive tissue below. His deep rumbling moan showed how much he liked what she was doing.

"Oh fuck."

Oh fuck, indeed.

Her saliva coated his cock and she made slurping noises as she moved up and down its length. As his scrotum began to draw up tight and close to his body, she released him from the warmth of her mouth. Trailing her tongue down his shaft she moved lower.

After licking over his sac, Savannah took each ball into her mouth, swirling her tongue over the soft skin. The hand still wrapped around his shaft stroked slowly up and down. With her other hand she slid two fingers over the sensitive little groove between scrotum and anus.

"Damn, woman. Suck my cock," he demanded.

Returning his throbbing shaft to her mouth, Savannah sucked vigorously, hollowing out her cheeks with the effort. Sliding her hand between her legs she ran her fingers along her slit, collecting the juices pooled there.

She pushed his legs wider apart. Rimming her fingers around his anus, she spread her cream over the puckered opening.

"Ahhhh," Cord groaned.

"You taste so good. You're so big and thick."

Her words had him growling from deep in his chest.

Keeping her eyes on Cord's, Savannah slowly sunk the tip of her index finger into his anus. His eyes widened drastically and his breathing became a harsh rasp.

Moving with a steady rhythm, she sucked deeply as her head bobbed up and down. Cord thrust his hips forward to meet each stroke, fucking her face. Wiggling her finger in his tight ass had Cord losing control. He thrust deeply with each bob of her head.

Sucking as hard as she could, Savannah plunged her finger forward to the second knuckle and was rewarded with a string of hot curses. Wiggling deeper she buried her finger in the hot, narrow channel.

She hummed against his flesh, sucked and bobbed. When her finger found his prostate she rubbed the hard little ball firmly. The sensitive tissues tightened on her finger as it slid in and out, matching the rhythm of her mouth.

"Oh shit, sugar. I'm gonna come."

He tried to pull back, but Savannah was having none of that. Relaxing her throat and tilting her head back she took even more of his shaft until he was pounding down the back of her throat. Hot jets of his seed poured into her throat while she swallowed his cock. She continued sucking, bobbing and rubbing until she milked every drop of the salty fluid from his body.

Leaning back, she licked him clean while watching his eyes. Her finger pulled from his anus with a pop. Savannah smiled as his legs gave out and he dropped to the couch in a boneless heap. Feminine triumph surged through her. She'd just taken the tough cowboy down a notch.

"Don't think you're gonna be ordering me around on my ranch, cowboy."

She laughed heartily as he mumbled, "Damn, woman."

Now maybe he would think twice before trying to mess with her. Of course, he wouldn't know she had shared the experience with him. To Cord it would just be a really powerful sexual vision that came over him out of the blue.

Problem was, now Savannah was incredibly horny and unsatisfied. Her pussy ached to feel the incredibly yummy, huge cock she had explored and devoured.

Her thumb stroked her clit as two fingers drove deeply into her vagina. She was so hot and wet. It didn't take long to drive herself to orgasm, flooding her hand with a hot gush of juices.

Chapter Four

ഇ

Cord was flabbergasted. What the hell was happening? All of a sudden he had a vivid image of Savannah on her knees at his cock. He had never before experienced such an erotic wet dream, and while wide awake for that matter.

The images, sounds and sensations had been so real Cord thought he could smell their sex in the air. Her hands and mouth had felt so wonderful on his body. He'd shot off like a rocket when he climaxed. It was the most mind-blowing orgasm he'd ever experienced.

Every stroke of her tongue, lips and naughty fingers had felt so real. Hell, he had even felt the wetness of her saliva on his cock and the wiggle of her finger in his ass. In fact, that tight, virgin channel still throbbed from the stimulation.

What an incredible sight to look down and see her luscious, naked, wet body. Water sluicing over bronzed skin. Her golden hair, wet and clinging to her shoulders and back. Full, rosy lips stretched around his cock while she attempted to swallow him whole. Damn if he wasn't getting hard again just thinking about her full breasts and curvy body.

He'd had plenty of women give him head before, but nothing could compare. No real woman had ever sucked him like that. It had been even better than his most vivid, wet dreams.

How had that little witch gotten into his mind? The pleasure had been beyond description. Like a randy teenager, he had shot his load into his jeans then collapsed onto the couch. If the real thing was anything like his wild fantasy, Cord would surely die of pleasure.

After changing his soiled clothes, Cord headed to the bunkhouse. He still felt shaken and distracted from the intense, wet orgasm. After reeling in his crazy thoughts, he attempted to focus on the hands.

The men moaned and fidgeted while he explained how he expected things to be done. By the time he finished, Zeke sat holding his head in his hands. What was up with these guys?

"Do you have a problem with what I just outlined?" Cord made eye contact with each of the four men.

"Yeah, a big one! That's not the way things are done here on the Shooting Star. This is primarily a pleasure ranch, not a working one. Until you showed up this was a dream job," Riley complained.

"I'll tell ya right now, Van will never go for this. I'm thinking you might wanna talk to her before you go changing everything. Otherwise, you might not have anything to change," Brock stated.

"You're gonna find yourself out of a job," Jesse added.

"And what do you have to say?" Cord asked Zeke.

"Van's not gonna like this. She won't agree with what you wanna do."

Cord paced across the plank floor, taking stock of the four men. They were all muscular, fit and capable of performing the duties he expected. He didn't understand why they were trying to get out of performing an honest day's work for their pay.

"Tell me a little bit about how y'all do things now. Start with today. What did you do today?"

Brock smiled broadly. "It rained last night so the north meadow was nice and muddy. We played basketball."

Cord was beginning to get a headache. "I must be missing part of the story here. You played basketball in a muddy meadow?"

Riley took a shot at explaining. "Van likes to play. She invented some ranch games. Today was ATV basketball in the mud. A few days ago it was bareback relay races."

The men all laughed at the memory.

"Yeah, that was fun," Zeke said.

"I liked snowmobile hockey on the frozen lake a few months ago," Brock stated.

Cord just shook his head. He couldn't believe what he was hearing. "Let me get this straight. Y'all were hired on to play games with Miss Thompson? What about running the ranch?"

"Oh, we still clean out the stables, take care of the horses, mend the fences and do other chores. It's not like we don't work. But the primary goal around here is to have fun," Jesse explained with a smirk.

Cord just shook his head again. What the heck had he gotten himself into? This was the most lackadaisically run ranch he had ever encountered. No wonder she needed a foreman to run things.

"Look, Miss Thompson hired me to direct the work of this ranch. I plan on doing that in the best way I know how. And Miss Thompson is not your sister, friend or girl. She is the owner of this ranch. The way you address and treat her should reflect that."

Zeke dropped his hands. "But she told us to call her Van," he protested.

Cord raked his hands through his hair in frustration. "I think we may need to involve her in this discussion. It's almost chow time anyway. Let's head over to the house."

* * * * *

Sitting on the porch, Savannah went over her plans to surprise Riley. She'd made his favorite dinner. The fried chicken, garlic mashed potatoes, sweet baked beans, corn on the cob and biscuits were all prepared. Her famous holy cow cake sat in the refrigerator. The presents sat on the sideboard. Streamers, balloons and shiny confetti covered the dining area.

She couldn't wait to see the look on his adorable face.

When the bunkhouse door opened she looked over in that direction. She almost fell out of the chair.

Life is good.

Five tall, broad shouldered, muscular, drop-dead gorgeous cowboys were walking across the ranch yard straight toward her.

Her cowboys.

Riley, the prankster of the group. His dark good looks always made her think of a fallen angel. Shiny tendrils of his jet-black hair dropped down rakishly over his deep blue eyes. His dark complexion and angular jaw made him look grim, but he was one of the most fun-loving men she had ever known.

Brock, on the other hand, was the group's father figure. He kept everyone in line and kept his protective green eyes on everything. She had always wanted to run her fingers through his sable hair with its unruly waves. When he smiled, his full lips made his bushy mustache quiver.

Zeke was the shy, quiet one of the group. His beautiful sandy hair and cornflower blue eyes gave him an almost feminine beauty. Umm, but when you saw the muscular package it was all attached to there was no doubt he was all man. His quiet innocence touched Savannah's heart.

And Jesse, the baby of the group. She liked to tease him by calling him Jesse James. That devilishly handsome cowboy was sure to steal a lot of women's hearts. His light brown hair was always perfect, even when he'd been wearing his hat. His glittering amber eyes were filled with passion. She thought that maybe it was Jesse that Tamara had her sights set on.

Umm, and her newest cowboy. Savannah did not have adequate words to describe how perfectly yummy Cord looked. She wasn't sure yet how he would fit in with the other boys, but he sure as heck fit in with her. Mmm, mmm, mmm.

As they drew closer she could tell something was bothering her boys. Tension rolled off the group of men in waves. Well, not tonight. Tonight she had a celebration planned. She would not allow them to be in a glum mood.

Putting on a bright smile, she stood at the top of the steps. As they got closer, she launched herself at Riley and he caught her easily. Wrapping her arms and legs around his big body she squealed with delight as he twirled her around in circles. When the world finally stopped spinning, Savannah planted a loud, wet kiss on his cheek.

"Happy birthday, Riley! We're having a party tonight in your honor."

A fierce growl rumbled up out of Cord's chest. "Put her down, *now*." His eyes held a dangerous gleam.

Cord could not believe the jealous rage he felt watching Savannah held so close in Riley's arms. What the hell was wrong with him? It wasn't like she was his woman, *yet*.

She looked so damn good in her sundress, boots and Stetson. The way the dress swirled around her thighs as she moved had him hard in an instant. He couldn't help but to be jealous seeing her long, bare legs wrapped around the other man's waist.

Riley sat her aside, but held onto her arms until she was steady on her feet.

Whipping her head around, Savannah stared. Her dark, angry gaze shot daggers at him. "Is there a problem?" she asked through clenched teeth.

"Nothing we won't get straightened out, Miss Thompson."

Savannah's laughter held no note of humor. "Name's Savannah, but you can call me Van. I hate formality. We have a casual setup here. I prefer to be on a first name basis with my boys."

Reaching out she ran her fingers lovingly over Zeke's cheek. The tender look of caring she gave him made Cord's blood boil. He just didn't understand what was happening to him. How the hell could he feel so jealous and possessive over a woman he barely knew?

Cord barely heard the words she whispered to Zeke.

"Its okay, honey. You can relax now."

He was amazed to see the tension instantly leave the other man's big body. Just a gentle touch and soft word from her and the big cowboy melted.

Turning back to the others she said, "Come on inside now. We have a birthday to celebrate. Just ignore the big grump. He'll figure out how things work around here soon enough." She easily herded the big men into the house.

"I made all your favorites, Riley. You sit down at the table while Brock and I bring in dinner."

Savannah seated Riley in a place of honor at the head of the table. The festive decorations did nothing to lighten Cord's mood. He was ready to stomp on anyone who came near the witchy woman.

"Sit down, Brock. I'll help Miss Thompson."

Brock looked torn between whose instructions he should take. Savannah tenderly patted his arm. "That's fine. Sit down and relax boys. Cord and I will have dinner on the table in a jiffy."

Moving over to Cord, Savannah linked her arm in his. "Come on, cowboy. Let's see if you know your way around a kitchen."

She quickly maneuvered him away from the other men. Once they were out of earshot she turned on Cord, dropping the false smile and his arm simultaneously.

"Let me explain again the way things work around here. This is my retreat. I like things to be light and relaxed. Your job is to organize the work and become part of the ranch family."

Cord started to interrupt, but she stopped him cold with a hard glance.

"I'm not finished. We are not formal here. Every one of those boys is like a brother to me. We have a lot of fun playing. The primary work around here revolves around taking care of my horses and keeping the place up. The rest of the time we play."

Turning her back to him, she began pulling pans from the oven.

"If you can't fit into the relaxed atmosphere around here, this is not going to work out." She handed him a large, cloth-covered bowl. "I wouldn't have hired you if I didn't think you'd fit in. You will just need to put out a little effort."

Savannah made quick work of putting the rest of the meal into serving dishes.

"Now, we're having a party tonight. Relax and have fun. And for heaven's sake, stop scowling at me."

The food was delicious. Everyone relaxed as they talked about the rowdy basketball game from earlier in the day. After they cleared the table, Riley opened his presents. Savannah appeared delighted by his boyishly exuberant reaction to the small gifts.

Cord sat back and watched the group interact. They were much more like a family than any ranch owner and hired hands he'd ever seen. Savannah's affection for the men was clear. It was also clear that they were very protective of her.

They sang a pitifully off-key version of "Happy Birthday". Everyone laughed when Riley couldn't blow out all the candles and he waved his hat over the cake to put them out. Then Savannah served large slices of the rich dessert to each of the men.

"Holy shit," Cord mumbled around his first bite of the delicious confection.

Everyone laughed at that.

"Actually, it's called holy cow cake," Savannah corrected with delight.

"That too," Cord said with genuine laughter.

Savannah could not believe how young and carefree he looked while relaxed and laughing. The lighthearted look took years off his face and gave him a softer appearance. When his laughter reached those cold, blue-gray eyes his entire appearance changed. He went from hardened man of the world to a sweet, shy little boy in the space of a heartbeat.

Oh, and the things that change did to her heart. She had found him handsome before, but now he was devastating. That small glimpse into his soul touched her in ways she couldn't even fathom.

After filling up on the sugary dessert, they all went into the living room.

"I feel like dancing, Van," Riley stated.

Now there was a good idea. She needed to work off some of the sugar overload from the cake. Maybe it would help dissipate some of her restless sexual energy too. "You heard the man," she said. "Come on boys, roll up that rug. Let's slide the furniture out of the way."

Quickly they created a makeshift dance floor. Turning to the stereo, Savannah put in a Kenny Chesney CD. She twirled around several times then stood swaying to the beat. Then she crooked her finger seductively at Riley.

"C'mere, cowboy."

Cord saw red. He wanted to run all those boys out of the house and claim *his woman*. And he had no doubt she would be his woman. They belonged together.

As if hearing his thoughts, Savannah turned to Cord. "Hold that thought, big boy. Right now its time to celebrate Riley's birthday. No party poopers."

She gave him a stern look and something passed between them. He sensed a promise of things to come in that look.

"Yes, ma'am." He sat back on the couch and held his tongue.

Savannah and Riley two-stepped around the room to an upbeat tune. She smiled brightly with joy clear in her eyes, making Cord's heart soar. She looked so beautiful and happy dancing with the big cowboy.

The firm muscles in her long, tanned legs flexed with each movement. She seductively swayed those curvy hips. Oh, and the way her full breasts freely jiggled against the thin material of her sundress.

Damn, doesn't the woman own any bras?

Each man took a turn dancing her around the room. When it was Cord's turn he was thrilled to hear a slow song start up. Holding her luscious form within inches of his body, Cord moved her slowly around the room. Heat radiated from Savannah and her cheeks held a bright flush from exertion.

It felt so right to hold her in his arms. Sensual heat sizzled between them. Electricity hummed in the air. He felt the intense currents arc between them like heat lightning. They were linked together in a way he could not understand, but was impossible to deny. From the look in her eyes, Cord knew she felt it too.

Locking his gaze on those big, soulful brown eyes, he brought the slender hand held within his own to his lips. Brushing a soft kiss across her knuckles, Cord drank in everything about her. As they moved he smelled apples, cinnamon and woman. With the other hand, resting at the base of her spine, he pulled her closer against his body.

He could feel his erection straining against his pants. Each slow movement had her soft curves brushing over the hard length. He wanted nothing more than to lean down and taste her lips, then sink into her sweet heat. Then he remembered the hands sitting quietly on the couch, watching every move he made. An audience was the last thing Cord wanted.

The song ended way too soon and she was swept away again by Riley. After she had a second dance with each man, Cord sent them on their way to the bunkhouse. He had a lot of work planned to zap some of that reckless energy the boys seemed to exude.

"We need to do some work on the fences tomorrow, so y'all best get some rest now." It was only with a great effort of will that he managed to suppress a smile.

The hands all groaned, but did as instructed. Savannah kissed each man on the cheek before they headed out, then grabbed Cord's hand.

"Come on, cowboy. Help me clean up."

"Be my pleasure, ma'am."

Savannah stopped short. "Look, would you stop it. Don't call me ma'am, or Miss Thompson. It's either Savannah or Van, your choice."

That wicked smile was back, lighting up his face, making him look even more devastatingly handsome.

"I guess it's Savannah then. You're way too pretty for a name like Van."

With that settled, they made quick work of loading the dishwasher and packing up the decorations. She felt very comfortable working along his side. It seemed like the most natural thing in the world.

"What are we gonna do with all these balloons?" Cord asked.

With an impish grin, Savannah yelled, "Yee-haw!" She jumped onto the pile, popping a balloon under her bottom. Her laughter bubbled up around him and Cord surprised her by quickly following suit.

Now that was a sight to see. He should have looked out of place. One big, hard, tough cowboy sitting in a pile of balloons, wearing a devilish, little boy grin. Savannah knew she was getting a rare glimpse of the man who hid deeply buried under that steely exterior.

"I knew you'd fit in fine once you relaxed a little bit."

The lustful look of yearning in her eyes did him in. Cord could hold himself back no longer. He needed to drink from those rosy lips once again. Leaning slowly forward, he gently took her face in his big hands. Staring down into her eyes, he gave her several moments to turn away.

A slow, sexy grin crossed his lips. When she gave no resistance, Cord moved slowly, brushing his lips softly over hers. Then he traced the curvy line of her lips with his tongue. His head was spinning. He felt drunk from the heady combination of the tender kiss and her feminine scent. He nipped at her lower lip and felt a spark take hold deep within his body. Her lips parted on a moan and he greedily drank in the small sound.

Pulling back he stared into heavy-lidded, chocolate eyes darkened by passion. Her kiss-swollen lips quivered as she met his heated gaze. Mmm, and her luscious breasts moved rapidly up and down with each panted breath. He had never seen a prettier sight.

"Don't...please...Cord." Savannah fought to catch her breath. "Please, don't stop."

That slow, sexy grin was back, melting her heart. And that deep growl rumbling through his chest. Oh, she was such a goner. Time slowed down, and the world melted away. All that existed was the man before her and his kiss.

Savannah's sexual experiences in the past had been disappointing. Sure, she could have hot, steamy sex with a man. Had always enjoyed it right up until he climaxed. Although she prayed it wouldn't happen with Cord, she feared it would be the same as it always had been.

Even though she could not randomly read people, something happened at the moment of climax. Feelings and release took over the person, opening them up to her abilities. Her own shields would also be weak. That was when she would see into a man's ugly soul and future. That was the moment all her previous relationships had ended.

It had been so damn long since she'd even had sex because of what happened. She just prayed that what she saw when

Cord climaxed would not be a turnoff. Somehow she felt that the innate good heart she'd sensed in him would shine through.

Heck with this, she thought. Having sex with Cord would be worth the risk. Taking the initiative, Savannah rose up on her knees and straddled his long legs. Pressing close against his chest, she took his mouth in a searing kiss. She wiggled her tongue against the seam of his lips until they parted. Then she swept into his mouth and moaned deeply. Their tongues danced around each other, mingling their tastes. She tasted the sweet tea they'd drank earlier and a warm masculine flavor that was uniquely his.

With each breath, her breasts brushed against his soft shirt. Her nipples quickly became hard peaks, which radiated tingling sensations straight to her clit. Hot juices flooded her pussy, soaking her panties.

It would be so easy to set his cock free and slide her panties to the side. She could have him where she wanted him in a matter of seconds. And oh, how she wanted him.

The hard steel of his erection pressed against her belly. Damn, but everything about the man was huge. Vivid images of him naked, moving over top of her flooded Savannah's mind, driving away any niggling doubts. In the images she looked down between their bodies, watching his cock moving in and out of her pussy.

Cord sharply drew in a breath. The images that popped into his head were so erotic and sensual. He could picture himself coming together with Savannah, turning two into one. He could feel his cock sliding deeply into her hot core. Fiery heat licked through his abdomen, his cock throbbed painfully.

She was in his head again.

Taking a deep breath, he could smell the heady scent of her arousal. He wanted nothing more than to sink into the heat of her pussy, pressed so tightly against his jeans.

"Damn, what you do to me, woman. I want you too much."

Without much effort, he lifted Savannah and set her away from himself. With a powerful surge of his muscular legs, Cord was up pacing the room.

Savannah jumped up and launched herself into his embrace. Her arms went around his neck, her legs around his hips. "I need you inside me, cowboy. Now!"

The narrow lasso Cord had on his control snapped. He turned and pinned her against the wall. Her sundress bunched up against her waist. With violent motions he jerked his shirt off over his head and threw it to the floor.

Savannah gasped when she looked down and saw the head of his cock standing up over the top of his belt buckle. Reaching between their bodies, she opened the large silver buckle, brushing her fingers over the satiny tip of his cock. She gathered up drops of pre-cum then raised her fingers to her lips, sucking them deeply into her mouth, twirling her tongue around them with a deep sigh.

"Sweet Jesus," he groaned.

Cord fumbled with the button and zipper as he watched her suck his cum from her fingers. His cock sprang free and images of Savannah on her knees, sucking him deeply into her mouth, flashed through his mind. He still vividly remembered his wet daydream.

"Oh, fuck!"

"Hurry," she whispered in a husky voice.

"Reach around to my back pocket and dig out a condom. My wallet…right pocket," he gasped out.

Her fingers trailed around his back, tracing the ladder of his spine. It was a difficult maneuver, but she managed with a few minor adjustments in position. After pulling out his wallet she quickly found a condom and ripped open the foil packet. With trembling fingers she reached down to sheath his straining cock.

Cord stared into her eyes for several long, breathless moments.

"Second thoughts?" he asked.

"No. I want you too much. It's never been like this before. Cord, hurry. I need you inside me, filling me up."

Any thoughts he had about taking her slowly flew out the window. She was trembling with need. He could feel tremors in the fingers lightly stroking his erection. No one had ever wanted him that much before.

He gripped her panties and ripped them off, then shifted her higher in his grasp. The dampness of the silky garment told him just how wet and ready she was. She guided him to her dripping opening, and with one powerful thrust of his hips, Cord plunged deeply into her liquid heat.

Damn. She would surely burn him alive. That is, if her sweet little moans didn't kill him first.

"You are so tight and hot," he gasped.

His big body held her pinned against the wall while his muscular legs began to pump with a fevered need. Savannah tilted her pelvis and met him stroke for stroke. With each powerful thrust he moved deeper, and he took her deep within himself.

"Let me in, sugar," he breathed against her neck.

Needy, soulful little noises were the only response he got. The only one he needed.

Their bodies melded together so perfectly. Cord pulled down the neckline of her dress to release her swollen breasts. When his mouth closed over a dark, rosy nipple, she cried out again. Her fingers wrapped in his hair, holding him close against her breast. After teasing the turgid bud with his tongue, he sucked as much of that plump peak into his mouth as he could. The sweetness of her soft skin went right to his head.

"Harder, please...Cord...I need..." she begged in a trembling voice.

He could hold nothing back. With each driving thrust he gave Savannah a little more of himself. He thrust harder, faster, deeper than ever. Her hot juices eased his way. The tight walls of her pussy grasped at his cock, fighting to hold onto him. Sex had never been this good before. But then again, he'd never given anything of himself. That changed the act from just being sex to making love.

The realization hit him like a two-by-four, snapping his head up to look into her eyes.

Yes, he saw it there in those dark, dilated windows of the soul. It was the same for her. They were making love, and the experience far surpassed anything they had ever felt. The connection between them was undeniable. The images flashing through his mind were reflected back to him in her eyes. He saw the two of them melding together in every way possible, but always with love.

She cried out his name as the muscles of her vagina clamped over his cock and she shattered. Cord closed his mouth over hers, drinking in her screams. They didn't need a pack of overprotective cowboys busting the door down.

The world exploded around them as wave after wave of orgasm tore through Savannah. He could feel each convulsion transmitted through her flesh into his own. Cord never paused. He thrust harder and faster as her pussy milked his cock. Her fingers fisted in his hair, her heels digging into his ass, taking him completely and demanding more.

"Oh yeah, sugar…fuck yes."

Her muscles clamped down on his shaft as she was shaken by another, more powerful orgasm which took her by surprise. Her pussy milked his throbbing cock without mercy. He felt the telltale electrical current streak down his spine, gathering in his balls, then shooting out the head of his cock. He felt his release in every cell of his body.

Cord came hard and fast, pouring what felt like endless buckets of his seed into the condom. A deep, guttural moan rose up from his chest as her body sucked him dry. His legs began to tremble, but still he held her against the wall with his weight and his semi-erect cock buried inside. He dropped his head down against her neck, tenderly rubbing his cheek against all that cool, silky blonde hair.

All his strength had left him. Depleted muscles trembled as his mind struggled to wrap around the most intense climax he'd ever had. He felt as weak as a newborn kitten. Somehow he had to harness enough energy to get them where he could sit down.

"Hang on, sugar," he spoke softly against her hair.

Savannah held tightly onto his shoulders as he made his way to the couch and collapsed back into the cushions. She sank onto his chest, resting her head in the crook of his shoulder. They both struggled for control of their breathing. A thick sheen of sweat coated their bodies.

Tremors of aftershocks still throbbed through Savannah. Amazingly, his cock began to swell again, filling her so completely.

"Again?" she asked.

"Hell yeah!"

Chapter Five

୨୦

At Savannah's suggestion, they made their way into her bedroom. Cord sidetracked into the bathroom to throw away the used condom. Returning to the bedroom, he was greeted by an incredible sight that would be forever burned into his memory.

Stretched out in all her nude glory, Savannah lay across the big bed, golden hair fanned out over the pillow. Something pulled deep inside him. He felt a deep, instinctual connection to the beautiful woman. Feelings of familiarity and belonging touched someplace deep within his soul.

A powerful sense of déjà vu stole over him. Although he had never met Savannah Thompson before the other day, it felt as if he had known her forever. Seeing her was like coming home after being lost and lonely for far too long.

Giving himself a mental shake, Cord slowly drank in the enticing sight from head to toe. Strength and femininity were the best ways to describe her. Those enormous, lust-filled, doe eyes kicked up his desire. He wanted to run his tongue over every inch of the bronze flesh so tantalizingly displayed.

Fascinating, deep rosy-hued nipples stood out proudly from large, firm breasts. The small triangles of white skin from her bikini top accented the lush globes. She lay, absently stroking the pink crystal nestled at the top of deep cleavage, while watching him.

Her long torso narrowed down to a slender waist. Her navel sported a curved gold piercing with small pink crystals dangling over her softly curved abdomen. He found the sight sexier than all get out.

Smooth, luscious curves swelled out over her hips. Her long, toned legs seemed to go on for miles. Savannah had her knees slightly bent, legs apart, revealing a tantalizing glimpse of her magnificent pussy. Dark blonde curls covered her mons, but the pink lips of her pussy were bare, glistening with her cream.

Cord licked his lips while imagining spending hours lying between her legs, licking up those hot juices. Aw, the hell with hours. Years. No, forever. He wanted forever with his lusty little filly. He had never seen a more mesmerizing sight than the seductive beauty laid out before him. Husky, sultry words finally cut through the love-induced haze that had rocked his world down to its foundation.

"Don't just stand there, cowboy. Bring that fine body on over here and fuck me."

"Yes, ma'am. I aim to please."

Savannah saw that he held something in his right hand, but she could not determine what. His hands trembled slightly as he neared the bed.

"Turn over on your stomach, sugar."

She was ready to question why, but seeing the smoldering passion in his stormy eyes took her breath. Without protest she rolled over. Anticipation of what he would do sent tingles through her body and a fresh flood of hot juices to her pussy. She realized, with a little jolt of shock, that she trusted him completely.

Of course, that was not so surprising after what they had just shared. She still had a hard time believing it. Cord had climaxed in her body and all she had seen were bright flashes of light, sparked by her own multiple orgasms. She had not received any visions or been able to read him. Finally, a man she could have sex with and not be turned off. There was no holding back her joy.

She wanted to run out on the porch, naked as a newborn, and shout loud enough for the whole world to hear. *Cord Black has a beautiful soul.* There was no darkness or ugliness in the man.

Nothing happened for what seemed like hours, but was most likely only moments. Finally, she felt the bed dip under his weight near her feet. A snapping sound heightened her anticipation.

Savannah's nostrils flared as the distinctive scent of her apple lotion filled the air, followed by Cord's strong hands on her feet. His voice was a sultry caress as he began to rub her arches. Strong fingers expertly massaged her body while his voice massaged her desire.

"Ahhhhhh. That feels wonderful!"

"Believe it or not, I was a Boy Scout. One of the first things they teach you is how to build a fire since it's essential to survival."

Why the heck was he talking about boy scouts and fire? "Say what?"

Tension from the day's work was slowly floating away to be replaced by a growing sexual tension. His strong fingers worked her flesh, creating a blazing fire within her body. He paused briefly to put more lotion on his hands then slid his slick fingers between her toes.

A deep moan rose up from the back of Savannah's throat. His fingers moved back and forth with slow, sensual movements making her toes curl into the palms of his hands. Okay, fire. She was sure feeling the heat.

"Now to build a fire you have to start with some good tinder. This first fragile layer is where you'll spark a flame."

His voice sent heat coursing through her veins. As Cord spoke, his hands moved up to caress her ankles. His calloused fingers felt incredible as they kneaded up along her firm calves. He teased the tender, erogenous zone behind her knees sending all thought swirling away. She had no idea what he was talking about and it didn't really matter.

With strong movements he massaged the backs of her thighs, fingers sinking deep into her muscles. His thumbs met at the top of her legs and moved up and out over her ass. A ball of heat formed in her abdomen and began spreading outward through her body.

"Now once you have your tinder in place, you need some kindling to nurture the flame."

Between the sensual massage and his sultry drawl, Savannah felt as though her body was going up in flames. His fingers massaged over her ass, pausing to delve into the small dimples at the top of each cheek. Strong strokes splayed over the curve of her hips. He kept his hands well-coated with the thick lotion.

His thumbs came together again at the base of her spine, fingers spread out over her back. With agonizingly slow motions his thumbs climbed the ladder of her vertebrae. The fire in her body burned hotter as his long fingers caressed the sides of her breasts on their upward journey.

For long minutes he massaged her shoulders and neck. Every bit of skin he had touched tingled. Savannah was so lost in sensation she did not immediately respond to his words until he nudged her shoulder.

"Roll over, sugar. I'm nowhere near done yet."

"I–I don't think I can. You've turned my body into jelly."

With tender hands, Cord logrolled her. Seeing the desire swirling in the depths of his gray eyes kicked the fire he had so skillfully created up into an inferno.

Cord placed a light kiss over her lips before continuing the maddening massage. His fingers caressed along her collarbones and the tender hollow in between before moving over her right arm from shoulder to finger tips. With slow motions the massage was repeated on the other arm.

"Now, once you have your kindling in place, it's time to start adding fuel to the fire."

Beginning at her breastbone, his strong fingers massaged in ever narrowing circles toward her nipples, creating an aching need for his touch. Savannah arched her back, trying to get his fingers where she needed them.

When his calloused thumbs lightly brushed over the turgid peaks she gasped. He twirled each nipple between thumb and forefinger. Electrical currents shot straight from her nipples to her throbbing clitoris.

"You're killing me," she said in a trembling voice.

"No, sugar. I'm building a fire, remember?"

"More like an inferno," she teased.

His light chuckle was like another kind of touch, wrapping her body in a silky embrace. His magical fingers moved down her rib cage and over the curves of her hips. Savannah arched up into the caress, raising her ass off the bed.

"Not yet, sugar."

She whimpered, then began to plead with him. "Please, Cord. I need you."

She felt ready to come just from his wicked fingers massaging her muscles.

"Mmm...soon. I have to finish building the fire first. After all, what kind of boy scout would stop without stoking the flames?"

Narrowly avoiding her mons, his fingers moved down her legs. When he reached her ankles, Cord reversed direction. As he caressed the insides of her thighs she rolled her hips upward. He spread her legs wider as he stroked toward the junction where her thighs met.

Yes, finally.

"Now everyone knows fire needs oxygen. Sometimes you have to fan those flames just a little bit."

Oh, God. She wanted to cry. How could he keep on casually talking about a stupid fire when she was burning alive? She was going to scream down the rafters if he didn't touch her cunt soon.

At last, thick fingers gently spread her soaked folds. Savannah nearly came off the bed as his warm breath flowed over her engorged clit, making her mindless in her need. Cord's voice dropped even lower, spreading over her like the softest silk.

"Now, once the fire is blazing strong, you can sit down to prepare a nice hot meal."

Savannah did scream as the tip of his tongue slid over her clit. Her hips bucked hard, driving her pussy more firmly against his warm mouth. Cord repositioned himself so that his muscular forearms leaned into her hips, holding her still.

Every nerve ending in her body tingled. His tongue slid over her slit all the way down to circle her anus, then made the trip in reverse again. He traced intricate patterns over her slick flesh while noisily slurping up her juices.

"You are so hot and wet for me. Damn, but you taste good. I could feast on you all night long."

With each wet lick of his tongue Cord drove her higher. Savannah felt every muscle in her body tighten. One more lick over her clit would push her over the edge. But he was skillfully avoiding letting that happen. He was slowly driving her insane.

Sensing how close she was, Cord slid down to her opening. With strong thrusts his tongue surged into her body. Hot juices gushed, dripping down over her ass. He drank greedily, licking up every sweet drop.

Cord's hands left her folds and moved to cup her full ass cheeks, tilting her up toward his feasting mouth. Strong fingers massaged, separating the soft globes. Savannah bucked against his finger as it circled the tight, puckered hole there.

"Ohmigod, ohmigod, ohmigod," she chanted repeatedly as the digit slid into the tight channel. The sensitive, virgin tissues clamped tightly over the intruder.

"Relax for me, sugar."

Relax. Yeah, easy for him to say. He wasn't the one with something stuck up his ass, and a tongue teasing…

"Ooooooh."

Her words became nonsensical moans as two fingers of his other hand slid into her pussy, stroking that sweet spot on the upper wall. With each thrust, her hips rocked to meet the dual invasions. The finger in her ass sent flames licking up her spine as it moved in counterpoint to the two in her pussy. She was held on the pinnacle of an explosion, but could not move over the summit. The multiple sensations surging through her body were just too much.

"Cord...stop...I can't. Please...don't."

A second finger joined the one already in her anus, stretching the sensitive channel. Scorching pleasure/pain spread out toward every nerve ending in her body. A third joined those in her pussy. It was too much. It was not enough. She was so overwhelmingly full.

"Come for me, sugar."

His tongue returned to her clit, circling frantically. Then he did the most amazing thing. With two fingers fucking her ass, and three fucking her pussy, Cord began sucking her inflamed clit between his firm lips. At the first nip of his teeth, bright light burst behind her eyes and Savannah shattered into a million pieces. Wave after wave of unimaginable, mind-blowing sensations scorched her body. She felt the spasms everywhere throughout her mind and body.

Cord never let up. His maniacal fingers continued to plunge into her body, lips continued to suck, tongue continued to stroke. Savannah was barely coming down from her orgasm as he built her up again, driving her to an even higher plateau. It was too much. She couldn't come like that again.

"No...stop...please. CORD!"

But her body had other ideas. She screamed his name as another orgasm claimed her, almost before the last one had completely stopped. Hot tears seared her cheeks as they spilled from her tightly clamped eyelids. Cord removed his fingers from her still convulsing flesh and gently stroked her labia as her now boneless body sank into the mattress.

He covered her with the comfort of his masculine warmth, then kissed away the tears. His weight kept her firmly tethered to the Earth once again.

"And that's how you build a proper fire."

* * * * *

Savannah's eyes snapped wide open when she felt his hard cock brush against her clit. She looked up into his mischievous smile as, inch by painfully slow inch, Cord worked his throbbing cock into her tight pussy.

He had come close to exploding just from watching her orgasm, wanting nothing more than to keep that sublime look on her beautiful face. As he watched her doze, a peaceful, angelic smile curving her lips, he was struck by such intense feelings. He had the overwhelming desire to spoil, shelter and protect his adventurous filly.

When he'd sheathed himself as deep as he could, Savannah rolled her hips, taking him further. Cord held rigidly still as the near volcanic heat of her body branded his cock. Oh, and he had no doubt. He'd been caught and branded. Savannah's mark was burned right into his flesh.

With a wicked gleam in her big brown eyes, she began to rhythmically tighten and release her pelvic muscles around him. Obviously the little witch could tell that he was riding the edge of orgasm.

"Keep that up sugar, and I won't last long," he warned.

Her feet slid up his legs as she wrapped herself around his waist. Her whole face literally radiated a combination of lust and joy. "Good. I want to watch you come as my pussy draws every drop of fluid from your big cock."

A rumbling growl issued from deep in his chest. "I wanted to take it nice and slow this time." He knew from the look on her sweet face that was not about to happen.

"Mmm, but I want it hard and fast," she pouted, sticking out her full lower lip.

"Damn, woman. You are wicked."

Cord shifted, removing her legs from his hips, folding them against her torso and resting her ankles on his shoulders. "Hard and fast is what the lady wants, then hard and fast is what she'll get. Hold on, sugar."

Her fingers sank into his sinewy biceps. Then Savannah cried out as he thrust into her body, ramming deeper yet, slamming into that little notch above her cervix. She fought to pull him closer as he drew back until only the tip of his cock remained in her pussy, teasing them both. When he thrust forward again, she could only hang on. There was no way she could meet his movements in this position.

Cord's emotions were off the chart. He wanted to bind them together in a deeply primitive, primal way so they could never again be separated. With each thrust he pushed her further up the bed, inch by inch. He pounded at her, his thrusts hard and urgent, grunting with each frantic joining of their flesh.

Savannah's primal cries only grew louder and more insistent. They were not having sex, or fucking. It was happening just as he'd imagined. They were forcefully merging into one being—one heart and soul.

Savannah fisted her hands tightly in the sheets in a vain attempt to anchor herself. Her teeth sunk into her lower lip, drawing blood. Eventually, she put her arms over her head, palms flat against the headboard for leverage and to keep from banging into the hard wood.

Cord tilted his hips slightly and her world spiraled out of control. With each punishing thrust his pelvis rocked against her clit, sending Savannah soaring, tumbling and finally free-falling. She was no longer an earthbound creature. The only things that kept her tied to this world were Cord and their wild mating. He saw it happen. Read everything clearly on her face in her heavy-lidded, bedroom eyes. Still he pounded into her flesh.

He could not get deep enough, embed himself far enough into her body. He wanted her as completely devoured by the intensity of their coming together as he was. But that was impossible. There is no way she could feel their bonding anywhere as completely as he did.

He had become relentless, a machine. He jackhammered into her warmth again and again, over and over, never stopping. Sweat poured from his skin, dripped down his face. Hell, he was probably hurting her. Certainly she would be sore after his punishing mating.

She gasped, cried, whimpered and screamed as endless orgasms washed over her body. Still he would not be sated. Cord worried that he would never be sated with this incredible woman beneath him. Yet amazingly, all it took was a few simple words from her sweet lips.

"Come for me, Cord. I need you to fill me up."

And he did. So much of his seed poured out into the condom that Cord was afraid it would burst. His climax seemed endless before he finally collapsed into her arms. He released her legs and let them slide down his sweat-slicked body.

Some time later he gathered enough strength to take care of her and dispose of the used condom. He tenderly washed her body with a warm cloth before slipping off into sleep with a sated smile on his lips.

* * * * *

Savannah woke up feeling warm, protected and horny. The masculine presence that surrounded her was overwhelming. Her head rested on a muscular arm and a large, warm leg was tucked between her own. She tentatively slid her fingers over the sinew beneath her palm.

Cord instinctively pulled her more firmly into the shelter of his big body, mumbling groggily. He felt so strong and warm, her body fit his perfectly. The scent of their sex lingered in the air as a potent aphrodisiac.

His cock woke up quickly, lengthening and swelling, and began thumping against her hip to gain her attention. It did everything but call out, "Hello sexy lady. Could you pet me for a while?"

Savannah laughed huskily. "I think someone is wide awake and crying out for attention."

"Mmm. He always wakes up first," Cord grumbled.

Pushing the sleepy cowboy over onto his back was no easy feat. Straddling his thighs, Savannah took his magnificent shaft between her hands and began slowly stroking.

His flat nipples drew her attention. Leaning forward she flicked her tongue over one soft circle, feeling a surge of feminine power as it hardened under her lips.

Cord moaned deep in his throat as cold air hit wet skin when she moved away to give the other nipple equal attention. Slowly she kissed and licked her way down his chest and over his abdomen. The firm muscles there tightened as her tongue flicked into his navel.

Each flick of her tongue brought another jerk through the rigid flesh within her hands. Moving down his body she caught his cock between her breasts. Pushing the globes together she slid his cock in the deep valley created between the two, encouraged by his moans. She almost laughed at the sight of the bulbous head poking up between her breasts with each stroke. Instead she flicked her tongue over the sensitive tip each time it appeared.

Cord's hands fisted in her hair, his hips began to thrust forward with each languid stroke. She reveled in every gravelly sound that escaped his lips as she tempted and teased him.

Taking her shoulders in his big hands Cord pulled her back up his body. "C'mere, sugar."

With her knees on either side of his chest she slid her drenched pussy over his erection. Cord's breath came out in a hiss. For several moments she rocked back and forth, coating his cock with her hot juices.

"Oh yeah! Ride me, cowgirl."

"Yee-haw!"

She couldn't help giggling at the idea of riding her cowboy. Teasingly, she slid forward until the head of his cock almost reached her opening then slid back down. Each movement slid his hard flesh over her clit, sending electric surges out to every nerve ending in her body, teasing herself at the same time.

Cord growled, "Shit, woman. We need a condom."

Savannah leaned over to his body and pulled a packet from the nightstand where he'd dropped them earlier. With quick, practiced motions she sheathed his cock, then resumed sliding up and down his steely hard shaft. Once again she paused with the head at her opening.

On the next stroke he pulled her hips forward until the tip of his cock nestled just inside her pussy. Raising her hips, she sheathed him slowly. When she had him fully enveloped in her warmth, Savannah sat perfectly still.

With her weight pushing down on Cord, she felt his cock incredibly deep inside her body. She felt full, stretched and complete. Just like she had always known would happen, Savannah's dream lover completed her. Made her whole.

"You feel so good," she whispered, her voice cracking with emotion.

"Unh. Ride me, sugar."

Moving slowly at first, she took time finding her own rhythm. Cord's fingers dug into her hips, but she would not be rushed. Leaning low over his chest she hooked her heels under his muscular thighs. With each motion her clit rocked against his pelvis. Shifting slightly brought him to the most perfect spot. As the tension slowly built in her body, so did the speed of her thrusts.

Savannah dropped even lower over Cord, her breasts brushing over his chest, the silky hairs teasing the taut peaks. With her heels she pulled his thighs higher, anchoring herself to his body. With each long thrust her moans became louder.

"Ahh, yes…ride me hard, sugar."

His fingers dug into her ass cheeks with each thrust. He lifted his hips to meet each thrust, reaching places no one before had ever come close to finding. Tremors racked her body as every nerve ending in her body tingled in anticipation of releasing the pleasure that steadily built.

"Damn, that's good."

She began to whimper as his hips circled each time he reached her sweet spot. Wild little noises erupted from her throat. Her strong thighs hugged his hips tightly.

"That's it, sugar. Take what you need."

Her fingers dug into the curves of his biceps while she took his cock deeper. Every muscle in her body tightened. She was so close to nirvana.

Cord bit his cheek, fighting to hold back his release until she could find hers. "Come for me, Savannah. I need you to come now, love," he growled from behind tightly clenched teeth.

She moaned deeply and increased her frenzied pace.

"There you go. Come for me, sugar."

Wild, animalistic noises rose from her as she fucked Cord harder and faster. Strong muscles in her legs pumped. Her breasts jiggled wildly with her frenetic movements. Cord cupped her face tenderly, staring deeply into her eyes. He took her mouth in a slow, intensely passionate kiss that sent her flying.

Her pelvic muscles clamped down rhythmically on his cock as she finally shattered. Savannah's legs lost all strength and she collapsed bonelessly against his chest. Cord wrapped his body around her and rolled them over quickly. He thrust forward three, four, five times before reaching his own throbbing release and collapsing on top of her.

After a few minutes he tried to move to the side, but she held him firmly in place. "Not yet. I need you in me. I need to feel you for just a little longer," she mumbled.

Chapter Six

ഔ

They finally surfaced as the room began to fill with sunlight. With little fuss, they moved to the shower, their hands exploring each other through the thick soap lather. Cord was astonished to find his cock beginning to rise again. His body reacted as if it had been weeks since he'd found release in her body, instead of just hours.

"Damn, sugar. You're gonna be the death of me."

Once again, Cord was taken with a sense of déjà vu as she sank to her knees, running her hands up his muscular thighs. She reenacted his wet daydream almost exactly.

He was quickly lost as she licked him like an ice cream cone. Her hot tongue stroked every throbbing inch of his cock. She slurped and sucked deeply, quickly breaking his control.

Just looking down at her plump, rosy lips stretched over his straining cock was almost enough to make him come. Water glistened on bronze skin. Her gloriously thick, golden hair brushed his thighs in a wet caress, sensitizing his skin. When she swallowed the head of his cock down the back of her throat, Cord erupted, shooting hot, salty jets of semen into her mouth as she sucked him dry.

When they finally left the shower he dressed in his rumpled clothes. Savannah slipped on a short, silk robe that barely covered her ass. Damn if she didn't look sexy as hell in that little scrap of material. She was definitely going to be hell on his self-control. Attempting to get any work done with her around would be a challenge when all he wanted to do was fall back into her bed.

"Coffee?" she asked.

Cord pulled her against him for a last, scorching kiss. Who needed coffee anyway? She was better at waking him up than any jolt of caffeine. "Umm. I need to get changed before the hands are up and about."

After several moments they finally surfaced for air. Cord set her away from him. She was just a little too tempting. "As much as I'd love to spend the day in bed with you, I've got work to do."

"Hmm. What if I write a note to your boss?"

Tenderly he ran his thumb over her cheek, chuckling lightly. "Tempting, so very tempting."

The screen door shut as she moved into the kitchen to start a pot of coffee. She felt pleasantly sore and totally relaxed until hearing loud, angry voices outside. Sure, she'd known the boys would confront Cord, she just hadn't expected it to happen so soon.

Savannah moved quietly to the screen door to get a feel for how serious this confrontation was. Cord had not even made it across the yard before her four cowboys faced off against him. She'd never seen such fierce looks on their faces. All five men stood rigid, ready for a fight.

Five fearsome warriors ready to do battle over little ol' me. Ugh, men!

"What the hell are you doing?" Riley growled.

"You got no business spending the night in that house," Zeke added, angrily pointing his finger toward her house.

Cord's voice held tightly leashed aggression. "I don't see as it's any of your business where I sleep."

Oh, that was the wrong thing to say. Savannah knew her boys would not be happy with that flippant response. *Damn, Cord. Use your head.*

"Well, that's where you're wrong," Brock spoke up. "We won't just stand back and watch you hurt Van."

"Not without a fight," Jesse muttered.

Savannah stepped out onto the porch, letting the screen door slam shut behind her. The noise echoed around the yard, loud as a gunshot. Cord kept his back to her, but she instantly held the other cowboys' attention. "What the hell's going on out here?" she asked, standing with her hands fisted at her hips.

A collective gasp went through the four cowboys. Zeke's mouth hung open. Each of the men wore identical shocked, lust-filled expressions.

"Go back inside and put some clothes on, Savannah," Cord ordered.

She moved to the top of the porch steps instead of listening to him. "I'll do no such thing until you boys tell me what's going on."

"It'd be best if you do what he says and go back inside," Brock echoed.

"Before poor Zeke here drools all over his shirt," Cord added without turning.

Savannah looked down, then turned with a frustrated stream of curses coming from her sweet lips. Okay, so standing out on the porch in the bright morning sunlight wearing only a thin scrap of silk was probably not her smartest move. She had not wanted to waste time changing while her boys tore each other apart.

Storming back into the house to get dressed, she muttered under her breath the whole way. Grabbing up the first clothes she found, Savannah pulled on shorts and a T-shirt without taking the time to find underwear or a bra. On her way back outside she grabbed her rifle from the gun cabinet. After chambering a round she moved outside to find the five men rolling in a cloud of dust. Why did they have to be so predictable?

Aiming for the sky she shot off the round before moving into the middle of the scuffle. The men quickly separated and scrambled to their feet. They all stood with astonished looks on their faces as she walked toward them.

Cord finally hazarded a glance over his shoulder. *Damn but she looks tough and sexy,* he thought. The outfit she had on was even more revealing than the robe. The tight T-shirt molded to her unbound breasts like a lover's hands. Those damn tiny shorts showed off miles of long, slender legs.

"That's quite enough of this macho bullshit," she admonished. Then she stood there shaking her head at them, rifle resting over her forearm, muzzle pointed away from everyone.

Oh, he had a long road ahead of him. Trying to tame this wild filly was going to test his patience. He had to admire her spunk though. She didn't run from anything, just marched headfirst into whatever needed to be done.

"All five of you go take cold showers and cool off. Then we're gonna have us a little talk," she ordered.

When none of them made any move to follow her instructions, Savannah gave them a stern look. "Now," she growled.

The men all turned without another word. Cord headed for his cabin. Zeke, Jesse, Brock and Riley all went into the bunkhouse. He noticed that Savannah stayed on the porch to make sure they all behaved.

Savannah sighed deeply. She had enough on her mind after a long night of hot fucking and keeping her secret from Cord. Now her boys had to go and let their testosterone-riddled macho attitudes get the better of them.

Putting an end to her train of thoughts, she shook her head. She'd learned long ago not to question what else could happen. To do so was tempting fate to throw more your way. After returning the rifle to the gun cabinet she went into the kitchen for her coffee, muttering to herself the whole time. She ate breakfast and dressed for the day before heading out, giving the boys plenty of time to cool down.

Marching into the bunkhouse, she tsked while looking over the pathetic sight she found. Zeke and Riley would both have shiners. Jesse's knuckles were torn open and his jaw swollen. Brock was in the worst shape. His lip was split open and an eye swollen shut.

Moving into the kitchen without a word, she filled plastic baggies with ice, slamming things around in her frustration. The whole damn lot of them were Neanderthals. What was it in mens' makeup that made them revert to club toting, small-brained cavemen?

"You boys are pathetic," she lectured. She passed out the ice bags, staring sternly at each of the men in turn. "What the hell has gotten into you?"

They all just sat there mutely staring anywhere except at her. Cord's deep grumble came from somewhere behind her.

"I thought I told you to stay out of the bunkhouse?"

Turning quickly she marched up to him, fire blazing in her eyes. She punctuated her words by poking him in the chest with her forefinger. "As long as this is my ranch, I'll go wherever I want."

She stood toe-to-toe with the big man, refusing to be intimidated by his size. He towered over her, but it did not matter. "Your attempts at intimidation won't work on me. Now go sit down with the other bad little boys."

Savannah waited until he complied before turning back around. It surprised her when he followed her directions without protest. She paced back and forth in front of the men trying to rid herself of the frustrated energy zinging through her system. Finally, grabbing up another ice bag she thrust it at Cord for his swollen jaw and bruised cheek.

"Why can't you boys play nice?" Standing with hands fisted on her hips she faced her cowboys.

"We were just trying to protect you from that snake," Brock complained.

She cut him off by holding her hand up for quiet. "When I need you boys to protect me, I'll let you know. Who I invite into my bed is my business. I'm a grown woman, for crying out loud."

Cord mumbled something unintelligible under his breath. She turned to face him. "This is my ranch. I'll tell you how things are going to be done. If you can't handle that, then you better go find a job somewhere else."

She glimpsed what she thought to be disbelief in his steely gray eyes. It dawned on her that when aroused his eyes were more gray. When happy or amused they turned a pale blue. When he was upset or angry those telling pools became the steely, cold color of titanium.

"Don't doubt me, cowboy. I'll fire your sorry ass so fast your head will spin."

She turned to face the other men again. "I won't put up with a bunch of Neanderthals, drunk on testosterone, striking out at each other."

By the time she finished spelling things out for the men and returned to the house, Savannah felt exhausted. Checking the caller ID display on the ringing phone, she recognized the number for Tamara's bookstore. After filling her friend in on the basics of the past few crazy days they confirmed their plans for the night.

She spent the day working with the horses and kept a close eye on the boys to make sure no further trouble erupted. Working with her beloved animals helped to relieve her tension. At the end of the long day she showered and made a simple dinner of spaghetti with meatballs, garlic bread and salad.

The boys were all on their best behavior during the meal. Zeke had brought her a bunch of wildflowers as a silent apology. They all cleaned up after the meal while she got ready to go out.

She spent extra time primping, wanting to stun her boys. After putting up her hair she put on mascara, a light sweep of blush and a deep, burnt cinnamon lipstick. Since they were going dancing she put on a thin, flirty skirt, silky Western-style top, strappy high-heeled sandals and a white Stetson.

Animated conversation in the living room let her know that Tamara had arrived and was currently flirting shamelessly with the boys.

She'd better not be flirting with Cord, Savannah thought.

When she stepped into the living room all conversation abruptly ended. The boys whistled and gave catcalls until Cord quieted them with a sharp look.

Cord felt like someone had punched him in the crotch when Savannah walked into the room. Her golden hair had been pulled into a sexy, just-fucked look topped off with a white western hat. A light touch of makeup accentuated her gorgeous features.

Shit! He wanted to kiss off all that dark lipstick.

She wore a shimmery white shirt that clung to her breasts, tucked into an obscenely skimpy denim skirt that swirled over her thighs. The short skirt revealed a great expanse of tanned, bare legs. Toes painted the same dark color of her lips stuck out of white, strappy sandals, which accentuated those luscious legs.

Damn, she looked like a spring hothouse flower.

Tamara looked incredibly underdressed in her western shirt, designer jeans and boots. He carefully watched the men's reaction to both women and considered demanding they change or stay home. Walking into a bar as sexy clad as Savannah was only asking for trouble.

"Sure, wear high heels so you really tower over short, little me," Tamara complained. Her pouty expression seemed to capture Jesse's attention.

Without a word, Savannah picked up her purse as the two women headed for the door. Tamara called out over her shoulder, "Don't wait up, boys." Soft laughter trailed after them on the crisp night air.

"Oughta be a law against two women going out looking like that," Cord growled.

The cowboys all mumbled in agreement. At least that was one thing on which they could agree.

* * * * *

By the time they left the bar, Tamara was too drunk to drive. Parking close to the porch, Savannah went to help her tipsy friend from the passenger seat.

"Hey, where'd all 'em hot cowboyz go?" Tamara asked, slurring her words.

"Shh. You'll wake up the entire ranch." Savannah supported her friend with an arm around her waist. It was no easy feat maneuvering Tamara up the steps.

"Hmm. Let's go wake up the new guy. Couldn't you just eat him up?" Drunken giggles spilled out across the yard.

"Shut up or I'll leave you in the car," Savannah threatened.

"S'okay. Jus' send one a those boyz over ta keep me comp'ny."

"She's gonna wake up half the state," Cord grumbled from behind them, startling Savannah.

He walked up and casually swung Tamara over his shoulder.

Savannah sighed in relief. "Just help me get her into the guest room and she'll settle down."

She watched in horror as Tamara dug her fingers into Cord's perfect, sculpted ass while he carried her into the house.

"Mmm. Van, found me a cowboy to ride," she giggled.

Tamara's drunken laughter rang out through the house, making Savannah feel extremely irritable. "That's my ride," she grumbled through tightly clenched teeth.

They tucked her into the bed fully dressed, removing only her boots and hat. Tamara was sound asleep before he had even pulled the covers up.

Cord shot Savannah a questioning glance. "She always get that drunk when you two go out?"

She pushed him out into the hall and shut the door. Moving into the living room, she sank down into the couch before responding. "She usually has a little more control. Her ex-boyfriend was there tonight with another woman. It sort of drove her over the edge."

Cord sat down next to Savannah and pulled her feet into his lap. Pulling off her sandals he let them drop to the floor with a loud clump. His magical fingers began massaging her aching arches.

"Ooooh, that feels like heaven." She sank even further down into the buttery leather of the couch.

After several minutes, Cord said, "About the fight this morning…"

She sat up, putting her fingers over his warm lips, stopping his words. "Let's not go there again tonight. It's been a long day."

Cord pulled her onto his lap, tucking a stray tendril of hair behind her ear. "Okay, sugar. We'll let it go."

Wrapping her hands behind his head, Savannah pulled Cord forward. "C'mere, cowboy," she whispered. "It's been way too long since you kissed me."

They spent a long time reacquainting themselves with each other's taste. The kiss started out teasing, but ended up a hungry mating of tongues. She was fast becoming addicted to his touch, his taste, his essence.

Damn, but that cowboy can kiss, among other things, she thought. He made love to her with his tongue until she was so hot she felt like she'd go up in flames. She stood up, taking his hand and pulled him to his feet. "Take me to bed, stud."

"Yes, ma'am," he replied with a devilishly sexy grin, then swept her up into his arms. He carried her into the bedroom, locking the door behind them. They landed on the bed in a tangle of needy arms and legs. He had them both undressed in no time flat.

"You are so beautiful," he praised, while stroking his fingers up her legs.

Cord could not believe the incredible sight stretched out before him. How the heck had he gotten so lucky? He stood, moving back slightly. She looked so beautiful. Her golden hair fanned out over the pillow, the heavy mass having fallen from the clip that had been holding it up. A light flush colored her cheeks a delightful shade of pink.

Just knowing how sweet her puckered little nipples would feel against his tongue was driving him crazy. Um, and how those luscious tits fit so perfectly in his hands, slightly overflowing what he could hold. Oh, how he ached to hold her again.

His eyes wandered languorously over all those lush, feminine curves. She was so fucking perfect, and perfect for fucking. He wanted to feel the soft curve of her belly against his as he lay between her lovely legs. He hungered to see those plump, pink lips of her pussy glistening with the evidence of her arousal that permeated the air.

"Spread those luscious legs for me, sugar."

The smoldering look of desire in his eyes got her juices flowing even more. Not that it was difficult for him to get her hot and ready. Pulling her forward, he knelt at the edge of the bed, draping her legs over his shoulders.

"I could spend the rest of my life between your legs and die a happy man."

His words sent visible shivers coursing through her body. His breath blew over her heated flesh, reveling in her soft whimper. For long minutes he just stared at her pussy while stroking his fingers over her inner thighs, never quite touching those swollen, pink folds.

"Cord?"

"Hmmm," his lips hummed just above her clit.

His eyes met her darkened gaze over the length of her body. Slowly he licked over her labia, avoiding where she wanted him most. His tongue slid over every tender millimeter of moist flesh, discovering every delicate fold and niche. Her cream was the sweetest nectar, exploding through his mouth.

Savannah writhed restlessly, caught in a pleasurable agony of need. She was so hot that he was surprised there was no steam rising from her sopping wet flesh. He could drink in her essence for days and never stop desiring more.

Stiffening his tongue Cord thrust into her opening, drawing more hot juices from her depths. She moaned and tilted her pelvis upward, giving him better access. His wet, slurping sounds and appreciative humming seemed to drive her to new heights. When his tongue finally slid over her throbbing clit, Savannah's hips bucked wildly, fucking his face.

"You taste so good," he mumbled. His tongue coaxed more and more fluids to gush from her writhing body. Greedily he lapped up every sweet drop.

Savannah gasped and whimpered. "Cord! I need…ahhh. I need your cock…in my mouth. Get your fine ass up here on the bed."

He sprang into action, not needing any further coaxing. Climbing up next to her, he flopped onto his back. She immediately covered him like a hot, living blanket.

"Shimmy that sexy pussy this way and sit on my face, sugar."

Straddling his head she slowly lowered herself to his mouth, searching for the feel of his lips against her pussy.

"Lick me," she whispered.

Savannah was wild with the need to taste him. Moving aggressively, she took his cock in both hands and sucked him deep into her mouth without any preliminaries. He tasted salty, wild and completely delicious against her tongue.

Cord spread her folds open and licked her pussy from clit to anus and back again. Her legs trembled above him while she eagerly sucked his cock. She found it difficult to concentrate on devouring the treat in her mouth with his nimble tongue teasing her clit.

Thick fingers massaged her ass, spreading the cheeks wide. Using her copious juices to ease the way, Cord inserted a finger in her tight back door, sliding it back and forth. She thrust her hips back against the digit, driving it deeper into the highly sensitive channel. He sucked her clit between his lips and lapped up her hot response.

She returned the favor, rimming his anus with her finger while she sucked him deep into her throat. Oh, how she loved to suck on his thick cock, not able to take his entire length, but more than enough to satisfy her voracious appetite.

He gasped as she slid her saliva-coated finger deep into his ass. As much as possible, she focused her mind on driving him over the edge. With his head pressing against the back of her throat she swallowed repeatedly while thrusting her finger in his ass. Her other hand massaged his sac, which had drawn up tight against the base of his cock. She alternated between pleasuring his balls and winding her fingers through the thick tuft of dark hair surrounding his sex.

In as coordinated a rhythm as possible while having her pussy devoured, Savannah bobbed up and down on his cock and stroked the hard ball of his prostate. She fought to keep her mind focused on her task, but it was a lofty goal when the man was nipping at her clit.

Cord moaned against the aching bud as his cum exploded down her throat in hot jets. The vibration tightened her already tensed muscles. She swallowed repeatedly, and twirled her tongue around the crown as he emptied himself, feeding her hunger. After sucking him dry, she proceeded to lick his still hard cock clean.

Savannah's body was racked by incredible wave after wave of convulsive spasms. She shrieked and bucked wildly with the force of her orgasm, grinding her pussy against his mouth. Left weak and sated she collapsed on top of him, struggling to catch her breath.

She sighed in relief that once again nothing had been revealed to her as Cord came. Finally, she had found a man she could have sex with and not have it ruined by visions. Umm, and Savannah planned on having lots and lots of sex with Cord. She had a whole lot of time to make up for with her tough cowboy.

Chapter Seven

ഇ

The two of them lay wrapped tightly around each other, breathing in harsh pants. She smiled down at his still hard cock.

"Damn, cowboy. I just can't get enough of you." She took several deep breaths. "You get me so hot and wet. The only thing I can think about is your cock deep inside my body."

A deep growl was his only response to her huskily spoken words. As soon as some of his strength came back, Cord lifted Savannah and settled her up against his body. Her back fit nicely against his chest, her ass snuggled perfectly into his groin.

His cock lay nestled between the generous, firm globes of her ass. She felt way too good against his heated flesh. He had searched so long for a woman like Savannah Thompson. She had an irrepressible spirit and fire that called to Cord on a deep level. If only he could tame a little of her wildness, then she'd be absolutely perfect. Of course, he totally embraced and reveled in that wildness when they were in bed.

Savannah wiggled her ass seductively against him, almost as if having heard his thoughts. He pulled her closer, pinning her pelvis with one arm to still her movements.

"Damn woman, give me a minute to recuperate," he chided.

She struggled to move against his cock. "Hmm. You feel pretty recovered to me, cowboy. I'm ready for another ride."

Before she knew what was happening the world tilted crazily as he positioned her on her hands and knees. Looking back over her shoulder she watched him move between her legs. He used his teeth to tear open a packet and made quick work of sheathing his cock in a condom.

"Guess I'll have to take you for a bucking bronco ride then, sugar."

He took a moment to admire her firm ass cheeks, stroking them with his big hands. Spreading her cheeks he looked longingly at her small puckered hole. Soon he would fuck her tight ass, but right now he needed to tunnel into that ultra-tight pussy.

"Cord!"

He continued massaging the firm, round globes in his hands.

"Hmm?"

"Cord, I need you. Now!"

Damn, she was demanding. "You may be the ranch boss, sugar, but not in bed. I call the shots here."

Smack.

His hand came down firmly over her left cheek, causing Savannah to shriek more from shock than the slight sting of pain. Moisture flooded her already wet slit. She seemed stunned at being turned on by a spanking.

His hand stroked over the heated flesh then dipped down to her soaked pussy. "Did you like that, sugar?"

Cord had not really expected her to respond. His thick finger slid over her clit, followed by his other hand smacking down on her right cheek. This time Savannah moaned deeply as more juices flooded his hand.

He wondered if she was even aware of her nearly constant muttered pleas for him to fuck her. His finger stroked over her slit repeatedly. As he caressed her clit he landed another firm smack on her ass. Her cheeks were becoming pleasantly pink.

Taking her hips in both hands he slid the engorged head of his cock over her slit. In moments his shaft was covered in her hot juices. "Damn, I love how you're always so hot and wet for me."

He placed the tip of his shaft at her moist opening then held still waiting for a response. Finally, Savannah pushed back against him with a cry of frustration and need. That was all the encouragement it took. In one smooth stroke, Cord buried his cock to the hilt in her throbbing pussy.

She matched his heat and passion with equal force. He lost track of how many times he sent her into orgasm, how many times she screamed his name. He felt utterly insatiable as his cock pumped into her in a steady rhythm that just might drive him insane.

Both their bodies were slicked with a thick sheen of sweat. Her muscles trembled as Savannah began rhythmically clenching her vaginal muscles around his thick shaft. Cord moaned as her muscles flexed, milking his aching cock.

"Oh God, yes. Come for me, Cord. I need you to fill me. I need your hot cum."

Her searing words drove him over the edge. As he throbbed, swelled and poured himself into his condom, Savannah spiraled into another intense, orgasmic wave. Spent, they collapsed into a boneless mass. Cord gently rolled them onto their sides and held her spooned against his body as they fell asleep.

* * * * *

Every muscle in Savannah's body protested as she worked with Star Gazer in the corral. Muscles she didn't even know existed complained with every movement, still she felt energized.

Brock sat on the fence watching the young filly go through her paces. He also watched Savannah as she moved stiffly. She felt his surreptitious, assessing glance, but ignored the attention. Hearing a commotion among the other men, his attention was drawn across the yard.

"Riley is up to something," he commented casually. A smile of anticipation kicked up the corners of his lips. His sable mustache twitched slightly with mirth.

Not for the first time, Savannah wondered how the short, coarse hairs would feel moving over her body. Maybe she should ask Cord to grow a mustache. With a quick mental shake, she dismissed the sensual images that flashed through her mind and focused on the activity taking place around the ranch. Without even realizing it, she began to speak her thoughts aloud.

"Zeke will be leaving us soon. He is being accepted into the agriculture program at Montana State University. Things just won't be the same without him here. I'm going to miss him so much."

Brock stared at Savannah with a shocked expression. He knew that she had a strong intuition, but this was something else entirely. "How can you know that? I'm the only person who even knew he applied to the program at MSU."

Savannah shook herself. She shrugged off Brock's words as if it were no big deal. "I know he's always dreamed about going to college. I don't know for sure, but that's what I feel will happen. Call it…women's intuition."

Relief washed over her when he did not press the issue further. He continued to study her as she worked with the filly. She felt the warmth of his deep green eyes like an intimate caress over her skin.

The way she was able to communicate with the animals on a level no one else understood had always seemed to fascinate him. Savannah could put the orneriest animals at ease so quickly, and get even the most stubborn mule eager to do her bidding. With a few simple touches and whispered words, she was easily able to reach an understanding that she'd never mastered with humans.

"And what about our new foreman? How long do you think he'll stay around?" Brock asked.

He watched the subtle change in her expression, those soulful green eyes seemed to drink in her unspoken emotions. She was already in too deep with Cord. She knew Brock sensed the depth of her attachment.

"You know he's going to break your heart, right?"

The confidence in his words and glance was disconcerting. Maybe she wasn't the only one that saw things. Savannah remained thoughtful for several long moments. When she spoke it was as though she had slipped into a trance again. Her voice had turned to a knowing monotone, like when she had spoken about Zeke.

"I don't know what it is. We share a deep connection that I don't understand. While he may end up breaking my heart, he's going to be the most important person ever to enter my life. I don't know where this will lead, but it will sure be an interesting trip."

The look of concern that crossed his handsome features touched her deeply. Her cowboys had become her family. Their protective actions reached a place in her heart that she'd thought had long ago been effectively sealed off from emotion. Every one of her boys would do anything within his power of ensure her happiness. She knew they felt her to be fragile and vulnerable.

Savannah stared toward the house. Suddenly she stood completely still, anticipating what was about to happen. Brock turned in that direction seconds before Tamara's shrill scream ripped through the yard.

"I knew Riley was up to something," Savannah stated knowingly. "Why can't he find another way to get her attention?" She spoke soothingly to the horse then followed the big man over the fence.

Cord was the first one to reach the house. Tamara flew over the porch and launched herself into his arms. She clung to him like a second skin, sobbing hysterically. Apparently she had just gotten out of the shower. Her tiny, little body was wrapped only in a small cotton bath towel. Water dripped off her skin.

Normally Savannah would laugh over Tamara's reaction to whatever prank Riley had played. This time she was not amused. Her almost naked friend was molded to her man, clinging like cellophane wrap. The uncharacteristic jealous rage that boiled through her blood took her by surprise.

"Brock, get her off *my* man," Savannah muttered savagely.

One look was all it took for him to understand. He quickly went to Tamara and peeled her off the big cowboy. She clung to him now instead, crying and sobbing. Through her hysterical ranting they were able to determine that she had been startled by a snake.

Cord stomped into the house with Savannah hot on his heels. "She has a phobia about snakes," Savannah stated. "It's the only thing that would have her running out of the house in only a towel. I'm sure Riley must have planted one in here somewhere."

Something about the toilet seemed to catch Cord's eye. He moved to the porcelain appliance and slowly lifted the lid. As it rose, a rubber snake moved up from the drain, surging forward menacingly.

"Son of a bitch," Cord cursed under his breath.

Savannah couldn't stop her laughter. She covered her mouth with a hand to smother her mirth, seeing that Cord's face was flushed red with anger. A vein in his forehead throbbed heatedly. She placed a hand on his arm in an attempt to calm him down.

"Now Cord, it was just a prank. Riley likes to keep things lively around here. There was really no harm done."

The prank really was very clever. Riley had attached the lifelike rubber snake to fishing line and sunk it down the toilet drain. He attached the line to the seat so that when lifted, the snake swam up out of the water toward its unsuspecting victim.

"That boy is a menace to society and I'm just the man to teach him a lesson about scaring women." Turning abruptly on his heel, Cord headed toward the front of the house. His heated rage rolled off his big body in waves.

"Cord, I think you need to calm down. It was just a joke."

She watched in growing horror as he pulled the shotgun from the cabinet on his way out the door. The laughter in the ranch yard abruptly died as he stepped out onto the porch. Savannah clearly heard Tamara's choked comment to Riley.

"You are a pathetic, immature ass."

Everyone turned and stared at Cord in disbelief. He looked like an old-time western lawman standing there with the rifle draped over one arm, not a bit of humor reflected in his cold eyes. "That he is, and it's about time he learned different. It's time to put away childish behavior and become a man, Riley."

All signs of mirth quickly left Riley's boyish features. Savannah could tell he wasn't sure what was happening as Cord advanced on him. His face turned white when the shotgun was held leveled at his chest.

This was getting a bit too real.

For each step Cord took forward, Riley took one backwards. "What are you doing, Black? It was just a practical joke. No harm, no foul." He held his hands up in surrender.

Cord's voice was cold, filled with anger. "There's nothing practical or joking about scaring a woman half to death. You need to grow up and learn some manners, boy."

Okay, there was nothing funny about this situation anymore. Cord had murder in his eyes. Savannah broke out in a cold sweat as fear coursed through her veins. Although she did not feel this would end badly, she was terrified by the hardened look that had taken over Cord as she struggled to keep up with his long stride.

Using herself as a human shield, she moved between the two men. Riley tried to push her out of the way, but she glued herself to the cowboy. Anticipating his every movement, she remained in complete coordination with his every motion.

"Go cool off, cowboy. I'll handle this situation." Her eyes never left Cord's heated gaze. She dropped her shields in an attempt to read his intentions but received nothing except cold rage.

"Cord, give me the gun."

Savannah held out her hands. She saw Brock and Jesse flanking Cord. Without looking away from his steely eyes, she spoke to her cowboys as calmly as possible. "Boys, that's not a good idea. It will just make matters worse. Take Zeke and Tamara inside."

Feeling their reluctance she continued. "Trust me," she said. "Take them inside, now." Her eyes never left Cord's. "I'll take care of this."

They reluctantly followed her suggestion, Brock carrying Tamara. Once the door closed behind them, Savannah returned her entire focus to the big, angry cowboy in front of her as he continued to advance on them.

"Savannah, get the hell out of my way." His tone was cold and fierce, leaving no room for argument.

Well, that was just tough. There was no way she could walk away from this situation. Her body jerked abruptly when she and Riley backed into a tree. Without looking back she told Riley to stay put. With painstakingly slow motions she moved toward Cord, keeping her hands in clear sight.

Using the same soothing tone that worked with the animals, she spoke to Cord. "Okay, cowboy. It's just you and me. Nothing else matters. How's about giving me that gun, then we can go somewhere and get naked."

His brutally cold tone of voice had every fine hair on her body standing on end. "Sure thing, sugar. Just as soon as I teach the boy how to behave like a man. You go on inside the house. I'll catch up with you in a little bit. Right now, Riley and I are gonna have a little man-to-man talk."

Savannah had been struggling in vain to reach into their link. Somehow Cord had her blocked. "Okay, I'll go inside, but the shotgun goes with me. Hand it over, big boy. You don't need it to settle this."

Images burst into her mind nearly driving Savannah to her knees. Cord opened the link and sent her a vision. She was stunned, having no idea how the hell he was able to send to her.

The images were clear. He had no intention of harming Riley. He only wanted to put the fear of Cord into the man and teach him what was and was not a joke.

She was in shock. How the hell had he done that? No one had ever been able to send directly to her before. They must share a deeper connection than she had suspected. But there was not time to puzzle out the how of it right now. She eyed the big man warily, sending her own question in return.

Cord reassured her that he would not harm Riley. Relief and amazement washed over her. She prayed that he knew what he was doing. With obvious reluctance she moved from between the two men as Cord handed her the rifle, then headed silently for the house.

The fear she heard in Riley's voice made her ache to turn and take him into her arms. "You're leaving me out here, alone...with him?"

Savannah didn't answer. She just continued walking until the door closed behind her. Everyone in the house stared at her in shocked disbelief. She held up her hands to stop any protests. "He won't hurt him."

"Jesus Christ. You don't know that, Van," Zeke stated.

She leaned her back against the closed door. "Boys, just relax. Everything will be fine. Sit down now. No one's going back out there. Let them work it out."

They all sat around nervously for the next hour until finally the door opened. Relief washed over the weary faces in the room. A very repentant looking, but no worse for the wear, Riley entered the house with Cord right on his heels.

Tamara had gotten dressed while they'd waited. Riley walked up to her and took her slender hand gently in his own. He stared into her eyes for several moments before speaking.

"I'm sorry for my very childish attempt to gain your attention, Tamara. I didn't mean to scare you so badly. I just wanted you to notice me." The fingers of his other hand stroked tenderly down her cheek. "Are you okay?"

Tamara was beyond speech. She fell into his arms and held on tightly. When she finally stepped back she punched him in the arm with all her strength.

"You big jerk! Flowers and chocolates work a hell of a lot better than rubber snakes."

Everyone finally relaxed and released a collective sigh of relief. Cord quickly cleared the house, sending Tamara and the boys outside to talk. Savannah sat in a spent heap on the couch. Her nerves were shot.

Cord locked the door and began moving toward her, roughly pulling his shirt over his head. She stared in shock as he quickly dispensed with his jeans and briefs. Moving to the couch he sat next to her and gathered her into his lap. Then he began removing her clothes.

"You have to learn to trust me to do my job. Handling the hands is up to me. That's why you hired me, sugar."

She stared into his eyes for several moments. "If you ever do something like that to scare me again, I'll kick your ass." The seriousness of her expression made him chuckle.

"Damn, but you are one feisty filly. Taming you and this ranch is going to be one hell of a challenge."

Her mouth hung open as she stared at him with shock. "Taming me," she repeated with indignation. "First of all, what makes you think you're man enough? Second of all, who the hell says I need to be tamed?"

His hearty laughter was music to her ears, relaxing her tightly stretched nerves.

"I say you need to be tamed, and I'm more than man enough to do it."

He quickly flipped her over so her abdomen rested across his broad thighs, her legs and upper body hanging down. Savannah struggled to get free of his grasp. With little effort he held her in place with one beefy forearm across her lower back. The other hand stroked gently over her bare ass. A shiver of anticipation coiled through her body.

"You should not have gotten between me and that cowboy, sugar. Now I have to punish you."

A startled gasp escaped Savannah. "Punish me. What the hell. You let me go, Cord, before I kick your ass."

His hand stilled in its soothing motions on her bottom. "Now see, it's that wild streak that we have to work on taming."

Wham.

His large hand landed with a loud smack on her ass. She moaned as her pussy throbbed and flooded with thick juices. The next blow sent a combination of fiery heat and pleasure through her body. She jerked, rubbing her sensitive, weeping flesh over his roughened thigh. The coarse hairs abraded her sensitive labia, creating stunning sensations through the tender tissues.

The next slap landed lower on her cheeks. She felt a cool rush of air a split second before his hand connected to her heated flesh, creating a blissful agony.

"You have a gorgeous ass, sugar. It turns so nice and pink under my hands."

His big hand stroked soothingly over her tender flesh sending heated pleasure/pain to every nerve ending. The stinging blows still vibrated through her body sending dangerous heat to her pussy. She couldn't believe she was enjoying this.

"Oh God," she moaned. She was going to explode. It would not take much. Savannah was riding a razor's edge. "Please,

Cord." Whether she was pleading for him to stop or continue, she wasn't sure.

They were both breathing heavily now. He gently parted her thighs, his cock jerking at the sight of her bare pussy glistening with thick cream. His fingers ran along her slit, gathering the moisture. With obvious joy he brought his fingers to his mouth and greedily sucked them clean.

Damn, that was so hot.

"You taste so good, sugar. Hot, sweet and spicy. I could eat you for days and never be satisfied."

His fingers returned to her slit to gather more of her juices. His explicit words had her vaginal muscles contracting, her body bowed as she pushed back against his too light touch. She needed more. So much more.

"Please, Cord." Pleasure and frustration were evident in her strained voice.

With swift movements, Cord stripped off her remaining clothes and positioned her straddled over his legs. He moved her as easily as if she weighed no more than a feather.

"Damn, sugar. You are burning me alive."

Her lips latched onto his, opening for his tongue, twisting and tasting the heat of his mouth. His hands cupped her full breasts, twirling her nipples the way he knew she liked. She ground her pussy against his erection. The broad head of his cock pressed against her weeping slit, seeking the heat radiating from her core.

His cock was hard and demanding against her sensitive flesh. Her bountiful juices covered him with a searing heat. Each movement sent more thick juices dripping down to coat his balls. His heated blue eyes, almost completely black from desire, stared into her very soul.

She rose up onto her knees. Reaching between their bodies she took his hard shaft in her hand, rubbing the head over her clit, soaking him further with her hot response. His pulse beat rapidly in the thick, blue vein that ran the length of his shaft.

More than her next breath, Savannah needed to hold that pulsing life force deep within her body. She slowly worked the head of his cock into her vaginal opening, strong muscles clamping down over the hard flesh.

"Oh yeah, sugar," he moaned.

Tightening her muscles, she milked his cock while slowly working it into her body inch by inch. His hips jerked as the molten lava heat of her sheath covered his shaft. The slow impalement was driving them both insane. His hands held her hips in a fierce grip as his control began breaking.

Sweat slicked their bodies and popped up in a line over his brow. His jaw clenched tightly as his entire body trembled beneath Savannah. Her moans of pleasure seemed to be driving him closer to the edge.

When she finally had him fully sheathed in her hot pussy, she held her body still while contracting her vaginal muscles over his thick cock. She rolled her hips against him, anticipating the moment he would let go, giving himself to her completely.

"Yes, Cord. Give me everything. I need all of you. Don't hold back," she urged.

Her sensual words snapped the last of his control. His fingers tightened on her hips, his pelvis bucking wildly. He slid her upward then slammed her down on his thrusting cock. She screamed as his head reached all the way to her womb, filling her so completely.

Still it wasn't enough. She could not impale him deep enough into her hungry body. She couldn't pound herself down hard enough. She wanted him to be completely enveloped inside her heart and soul. Wanted him to meld into her, become inescapably part of her, forever.

Leaning forward he took one taut, rosy nipple between his lips, laving and suckling. Savannah arched her back, pressing her breast firmly against his attentive mouth. Her fingers threaded through his hair, holding his head close to her needy flesh.

The intensity of his thrusting had her screaming as her muscles milked his cock, fighting to hold him deep inside. Powerful movements of her hips brought her slamming down to meet each hard thrust.

"Ahhhh…fuck, Savannah. Fuck yes! Take me. Take it all," he growled. His dark, muttered words sent electric sensations pulsing through her body, straight to her clit.

With each deep thrust the tight bundle of nerves ground against his pelvis. She froze for a split second before her orgasm took control of her trembling body. Very clearly her mind saw his naked cock in her vagina. His hot seed jetting against her womb as she greedily sucked up the fluid. She saw her waiting egg and the sperm reaching its goal. Then she saw a baby growing inside her body.

The vision hit her like a blow to the chest, taking her breath away. She felt sweat sliding down her back, but was racked by cold chills. In the intensity of their need neither one of them had thought about protection. But in that instant she knew it was exactly what she wanted, needed.

When he came they would make a child, joining their lives. Their child would be a part of both of them that she would forever cherish.

"Cord! I need you to come…NOW," she screamed. Gathering every bit of her inner strength, Savannah clamped down on his shaft.

His cock jerked, swelled, then throbbed in release. Joy spread through her as she felt his hot seed erupting inside her body. She screamed out her orgasm as they created a child. Love exploded from her heart as their souls combined, creating a new life.

Tears streamed down her cheeks unnoticed. They had not talked about the future, only about their present needs. Their conversations had always been light and easy. She had no idea how he would feel about what had just happened between them.

No matter what happened, she would not regret a moment shared with Cord. It was in that moment she realized how much she loved him. With everything in her, she prayed for their future and the future of their child.

When he finally came back to himself, Cord wiped the tears from her face. He assumed they were the result of the earth-shattering climax and melding of their souls. No matter what, she was his now.

As soon as his climax had begun, Cord realized with sudden clarity that he had not put a condom on. He felt every delicious slide of flesh against flesh, the heat of her pussy nearly burning the skin off his cock.

He didn't regret it for a second. She would be his now, no matter what. He had marked her body, branded her with his sperm. She could deny him no longer. She belonged to him.

"Mine," he growled against her neck possessively.

While they'd made love he couldn't get deep enough, couldn't pound hard enough. He'd wanted inside her, totally inside. He wanted to inhabit her heart, her mind, her soul. He wanted to own every inch, touch every centimeter, melt into her very being.

Their frenzied mating had been more intense than anything he had ever experienced.

Chapter Eight

&

Okay, now the pushy cowboy was really starting to piss Savannah off. Every time she tried to have some fun, he was there to spoil things. It was getting downright aggravating. She really needed to burn up some of the restless energy that plagued her.

Today she was being sneaky. After Cord had dispersed the boys to start working, she'd rounded them up. They'd jumped into the packed Hummer and headed off to play.

When they arrived at the lake, the boys stared at Savannah for several moments in silence. Okay, racing the jet skis over the various jumps she'd had built in the lake wasn't really crazy play. Their problem lay in the fact that the water was still damn cold.

"Come on you wussies. The water is not that cold and the sun is strong enough to keep you warm. You won't even notice it after the first few minutes."

Still, they just stood there, silently staring at the lake.

Savannah sighed deeply. "Come on boys, the wet suits are in the back of the truck." She watched them hopefully.

It was Riley that finally got them moving. Slowly a devilish smile spread across his sensuous lips. "Last one in has to clean the stables for the next week."

They raced around the Hummer, grabbed up the wet suits and charged into the small cabin near where she'd parked. Laughter bubbled up in Savannah. It was about time they had some fun.

Knowing her boys wouldn't turn her down, Savannah had put her wet suit on under her clothes. She stripped off the outer layer and moved into the boathouse. Riley was the first one to join her.

They made quick work of lowering the skis into the water and filling them with gas. Savannah was the first one out onto the lake. Wearing a stopwatch and whistle around her neck, she anxiously waited for the boys to join her. They hadn't been able to play any water sports since last summer. Although the water chilled her, she knew that the boys' antics would soon warm her up again.

Jumps of several heights were anchored at different points around the lake. She'd also had buoys placed to set up a racecourse. They rode the course a few times slowly to reacquaint themselves with the twists and turns. Once everyone was ready, Savannah timed them as they played with reckless abandon. So far, Jesse had the time to beat. She could see the determination to do just that in three pairs of intent eyes. Her boys took winning very seriously.

Savannah had an incredible time. She had not laughed so much in the past few weeks. Slowly her restless energy was replaced by sheer joy. Playing with the boys was almost as good as making love with Cord.

She became a little apprehensive when they started trying stunts they had seen on an extreme sports show. A niggling feeling in the pit of her stomach told her someone was going to get hurt, but she couldn't tell who or how.

Savannah argued until she was blue in the face trying to get the boys to call it a day. Nothing worked. It had simply been too long since they all let off some steam.

Riley sped out onto the lake and performed a tailstand that got the other boys whooping and hollering. After getting up some speed, Riley spun the ski one hundred and eighty degrees with the trim wide open. Near the end of the spin he shifted back on the ski and pulled back the handlebars. The front end of the ski lifted skyward. He used the throttle and steering to ride it out.

Jesse was next. He sped out onto the lake and positioned his ski for one of the jumps. He hit the gas and rapidly gained speed. Savannah gasped and began rubbing her pendant. The ski soared up the ramp and flew into the air. Jesse got the ski into an almost vertical position then kicked his legs out while gripping the handlebars. He performed an incredible high-speed, superman stunt, barely repositioning himself in time before landing.

Okay, this was getting out of hand. What the hell was she going to do? The boys were really worked up now, ready to try and top each other. Where was that big party pooper, Cord, when she needed him?

Zeke headed out next. He got the ski going at a good speed then extended his legs forward, feet hooked under the handlebars. Somehow he managed to hold down the throttle with his foot. Taking his hands off the handlebars he lay down on his back, extending his arms backwards.

A shrill scream escaped Savannah as she watched him head straight for the opposite shore, unable to see where he was going. At the last minute Zeke righted himself and went into a sharp one hundred and eighty degree spin.

She pleaded with Brock not to do anything stupid. Hell, he was normally the most sensible among the cowboys. But her intuition was screaming at her that if anyone got hurt, it would be Brock.

Her heart pounded painfully against her ribs. All she could hear was the roaring of her blood rushing through her body. Brock headed out with a confident smile. Her heart stopped when she had a vision of his riderless ski slowing to a stop with Brock nowhere in sight.

Everything in her mind screamed for Savannah to clamp her eyes tightly shut. She did not want to witness Brock hurting himself. No matter what signals her brain sent they shorted out somewhere along the way. Her eyes remained stubbornly wide open, staring out onto the lake.

* * * * *

It was incredibly peaceful in the barn where Cord worked hauling bales of hay up into the loft. The physical exertion quickly had his shirt sticking to his torso. Before long he took it off to relieve some of the heat.

Hauling hay did not require a lot of concentration. Cord's thoughts turned to Savannah. She had become very important to him in such a short amount of time. The strange bond they shared never failed to astound him.

Somehow he sensed when she was getting one of her crazy ideas. He didn't know why she was trying to kill herself. Yesterday she had wanted to wax up snow skis to traverse down a muddy hill after a torrential rain shower. He shook his head wondering where the hell she came up with the wild ideas. Worrying about her had become a constant state of mind. He'd kept a close eye this morning, sensing a buildup of restless energy flowing through her.

After a while the peace and quiet began to grate on his nerves. Things on the ranch were never this quiet for so long. Eventually you would hear shouts between the men as they worked. As his apprehension grew, Cord decided to take a break and check on things. Grabbing a bottle of water from the small refrigerator in the barn, he began to make a circuit of the ranch yard. The first thing he saw was that Brock was not in the corral working with Star Gazer. Moving to the bunkhouse, he looked for Zeke, who was supposed to be fixing the rotted front step. Tools and supplies lay in scattered disarray, but no work had been completed.

Cord's anxiety heightened as he walked to the stables looking for Jesse and Riley. It had been their turn to muck out the stalls. When he entered the structure the only sounds that greeted him came from the horses.

"Shit, I never should have let her outta my sight today." Working quickly he saddled and bridled Stormy. As he raced past the house he noticed that the Hummer was not in its normal parking spot off to the side.

It would take entirely too long to search the whole ranch. He had to focus his thoughts and quickly determine where they would have gone. The north meadow was a typical site for their games, so he headed there as fast as Stormy could move.

Finding the meadow empty sent cold shivers down his spine. The hairs on the back of his neck stood on end. Something was wrong. He could feel Savannah's building anxiety reaching out toward him. An image of her rubbing the rose quartz pendant, as was her habit whenever something bothered her, popped into his mind.

"Where are you, sugar? Come on, you've got to help me. I can't get there unless I know where you are."

In his mind she was wearing some kind of dark, formfitting material. Focusing all his concentration on the image of Savannah, he tried to expand his view to include her surroundings. The only result of his intense focus was the beginnings of a fierce headache.

Unaware of his actions, Cord's hand went to his chest. He rubbed his fingers near his breastbone as he'd watched Savannah do so many times.

"Damn it, Savannah. Where the hell are you?"

A distant sound broke through Cord's concentration. Without thought he headed Stormy in that direction. Dropping down close to her neck he urged the horse to go faster. Something told him he did not have much time to spare.

Before long he realized the sound was the whining of motors. His course would take him across gently rolling open fields and eventually to the lake. All at once the image of Savannah made sense. She was wearing a wet suit.

Stormy began to grunt with each breath. No matter what, the mare would give Cord everything she had. He just hoped it would be enough. His fear rose with every pounding hoofbeat.

* * * * *

The jet ski sped over the water. Savannah watched as Brock moved his entire body onto the left side of the speeding vehicle. Leaning slightly he put his left foot into the water. For several moments he zoomed on that way before quickly stepping off with his right foot. He seemed to teeter for a moment before steadying himself. The move was similar to barefoot waterskiing, but infinitely more dangerous.

Not even realizing she had been holding her breath, Savannah finally sucked in a large lungful of air. She felt Zeke's hand on her arm in an attempt to offer reassurance.

Just when she began to relax, the unthinkable happened.

Brock shifted his foot sending up a large rooster-tail spray of water. He was grinning like an idiot when he lost his balance and seemed to bounce like a stone skipped across the water. In the next moment he disappeared beneath the surface, bringing her vision to life. The ski slowed to a stop, sitting riderless in the water.

Oh God. They were too far away from him. They would never get to Brock in time. Already the boys had surged off, headed for the last place they had seen Brock on the opposite side of the lake.

Distantly she was aware of Cord galloping on his big gray mare toward the dock. He jumped off Stormy before she even stopped. With quick movements he pulled off his boots and jeans, then dove cleanly into the water.

She could not move. The frantic signals from her brain were still short-circuiting somewhere along the way. She couldn't breathe and she no longer felt her heart pounding in her chest. She was vaguely aware of the fact that her vision began to close in, narrowing to an even smaller focus regardless of how hard she tried to focus on what was happening. With a feeling of dread, she watched the water's surface for any sign of either man.

Oh please Cord, get to him in time, she silently prayed. *Dear Lord, bring him out of this alive and I'll stop this craziness. No more wild games. I'll settle down and be a good girl.*

Time lost all meaning for Savannah. Everything moved in slow motion. She felt the trail of every hot tear that burned a path down her cheeks.

Suddenly, Cord surged up past the surface of the water. He took in a great, gasping breath, hauling Brock up with him. Brock's body sagged lifelessly. Cord pulled the other man against his chest, holding him close as he treaded water.

Jesse made it to the two men first. Reaching out he hooked an arm under Cord's shoulder and hauled them to the shore. Jumping off the jet ski, he helped Cord drag Brock up out of the water.

Savannah could barely see. Her vision had narrowed down to a pinpoint of light. She tried to call out Cord's name, but found she had no voice. The last thing she heard was her name shouted in Cord's anguished voice, echoing over the too still lake.

* * * * *

Once he was sure Brock was breathing, Cord looked for Savannah. For some reason he still felt there was danger. While the hands tended to their friend he peered out across the now still lake.

Finally spotting her, he watched in horror as Savannah swayed drunkenly atop the ski. She seemed to right herself for a moment, but immediately began to teeter again. Her name was ripped from his throat as he helplessly watched her topple over limply into the water.

Without thought, he grabbed one of the discarded jet skis and headed out across the lake, full throttle. Savannah seemed to bob lifelessly in the water next to her ski. Cord did not even realize that he continued to scream her name as he dropped off the ski next to her.

She'd only been in the water a matter of seconds, but he was still terrified beyond belief. He pulled her up against his chest and slowly swam to the nearby boathouse, his heart hammering a haphazard, disjointed rhythm. It was in those long, drawn out moments that he realized how much he loved Savannah.

He hauled her effortlessly up onto the dock. Dropping his head to her chest, Cord listened to her breathing while his fingers measured the pulse beating steadily in her wrist. The steady rise and fall of her breast beneath his cheek finally allowed him to breathe again. Relief washed over him, leaving him feeling physically and emotionally drained.

After carrying Savannah to the Hummer, he drove around to pick up the hands, leaving Zeke behind to ride Stormy back. He kept her in his lap, held securely against his chest. It made driving difficult, but he was unwilling to let her go.

Brock was now sitting up on his own, wearing a sheepish grin. It was obvious he knew that Cord would be kicking some ass over what had happened. He leaned on Riley as they climbed into the big vehicle.

Once they were underway, Jesse began to utter apologies. Cord simply held up his hand for silence. He was in no way ready to deal with the hands until Savannah fully recovered.

* * * * *

Feeling exhausted, but warm and sheltered, Savannah stretched languidly. Cord's arm tightened against her back as he pulled her in more securely against the shelter of his large body. His softly spoken words fluttered the hair lying over her cheek.

"Never again, Savannah. You won't put me through that hell again. No more crazy games. No more tomboy antics with the hands."

She lay silently, head resting on his chest, listening to his heart beat. No matter how strong her stubborn streak she would not fight him on this issue. She had already decided to call an end to the wild play she shared with her cowboys. She would not put their child at risk.

It struck her that she now kept two major secrets from her lover. Soon she would have to find a way to tell him about the first. Dependent on his response, she would decide whether to seek his response to the second.

Holding anything back from him was difficult. She loved him more than she'd ever known it was possible to love another person. He made her feel complete in ways she'd never contemplated. It would be hard to give him up, but if he reacted poorly to her abilities that's exactly what she'd have to do. The boys would help her raise her child.

Cord propped himself on an elbow and stared down into her eyes. "Promise me, Savannah. No more."

She stared into the sparkling, blue-gray depths of his eyes. Doubt flooded through her. Regardless of her intentions, how could she promise not to do something so essential to her survival? She knew that eventually she'd once again get antsy. While she would take every precaution to protect their baby, could she make that promise?

"I'll try," was all she said.

Anger and fear flashed across his handsome face. It tormented her not to be able to give the man she loved everything he desired. This was just a promise she could not honestly give him.

"You'll have to do better than that, sugar. I won't compromise on this. Give up the games or I'm gone."

Now there's a catch twenty-two. She was damned if she did and damned if she didn't. Regardless of the wild games, Cord would most likely leave anyway once she told him about her abilities. Then add their child in to the mix and she did not know how much longer Cord would be by her side anyway.

Savannah chose to answer him with action. Wrapping her fingers behind his head she pulled Cord down for a searing kiss.

They made love, achingly slow, and full of tenderness. She prayed it wouldn't be for the last time.

Chapter Nine

ജ

After the near tragedy at the lake, Cord had become her constant shadow. The cowboys became very serious about their work. Playtime was over. Yet with each passing day, Savannah's restlessness grew.

She played small pranks on the cowboys in an attempt to liven things up. It surprised her when Riley started to get snippy about her antics. The fun loving cowboy had become very mellow and serious since watching his friend nearly die.

Cord seemed to have no sense of humor whatsoever. She'd thought sealing the toilet bowl with cling wrap was hysterical. She'd been the only one laughing, though. Riley had to hide a grin behind his hands.

The most elaborate prank was played on Jesse. After finding a website for pranks, she downloaded a program to be sent in an e-mail. When the e-mail was opened it displayed a message telling the reader that their computer had just been infected with a deadly virus. The screen then showed the computer desktop as all its icons were being dragged to the trash bin. No matter what combination of keys that were struck, nothing could stop what was happening. The trash bin icon then opened up revealing its contents, which included the computer's hard drive. Then it showed that the trash was being emptied. Eventually the screen faded to black.

Jesse was the ranch computer geek. He spent a lot of his free time surfing the Net and playing computer games. He even had ideas of starting an internet business. Watching his expensive, high tech computer crash nearly put him into heart failure. After several moments of panic the screen flashed a smiley face and displayed the statement, "You've been punked!"

Savannah had laughed so hard she'd nearly wet her pants. The look on his face had been priceless. She was the next most experienced computer literate person on the ranch. When Jesse had raced into the house in a panic she'd literally rolled on the floor laughing, holding her belly.

"Oh, Jesse James. If you could only see the look on your face," she'd said between fits of laughter.

Jesse had been very upset by her prank. To make it up to him she'd promised to buy him a new computer game in town. That was how they all ended up shopping in Target.

Savannah had not been surprised when Cord insisted on going with them. Then the other cowboys decided taking a break was a good idea, especially when Cord offered to buy everyone dinner at the local steak house. The rare treat was enough to entice the most stubborn cowboy off the ranch.

Somehow, being in town only made her restlessness worse. While she was accustomed to being noticed by men, something strange was happening. It was as though she had become a man magnet. Every guy in the store seemed to want to smile at her and flirt. The only thing that stopped them was the very large, unsmiling cowboy at her side. Cord was a natural deterrent to anyone wanting to flirt with her.

He was really starting to get on her nerves. Savannah felt like she was being stalked. Even when she managed to lose him by quickly slipping around a corner within moments he was back on her heel. She felt cornered, trapped and in need of an escape route. It was time to get the big, stubborn jerk off her back. She needed some freedom back.

Strolling around the store she began to get an evil idea. Wouldn't the store's security force be interested in a stalker? And with her newfound magnetism the security men would go to extra lengths to protect her. Oh, what a delicious, devious, hysterical idea.

Putting on her most seductive smile, Savannah moved in close to Cord. "Hey stud. I want to go try on this bikini. Why don't you go across the aisle and pick me out some new panties. I'm starting to run out since a certain he-man keeps ripping them off in his haste."

Tilting her chin down, she looked up at Cord from under her long, thick lashes. She could tell her ploy was working by the way his eyes darkened with desire.

"Mmm, well if you didn't tease me so much I wouldn't be so hungry."

Stroking her hand along his muscular arm she purred seductively. "I think maybe dark blue would be nice. Ooh, or maybe something with some lace."

Cord's eyes glazed over. Savannah rubbed against his side like a cat seeking a good scratching. "Maybe if you're a good boy we'll go swimming without the bikini tonight." For added effect she sent him a visual.

The image that popped into Cord's head had his cock lengthening and swelling within his jeans. He saw Savannah and himself naked and soaking wet under the silvery light of the moon. She clung to his body as he thrust hard and deep into her wet heat.

"Alright, sugar. I'll meet you back here in about ten minutes." He gave her a quick kiss before wandering off toward the lingerie department sporting a big, goofy grin.

Savannah casually strolled in the area of the fitting rooms for several minutes before picking up one of the red courtesy phones. In a sweet, naïve voice she told the store employee about the big cowboy who was stalking her around the store. With painstaking detail she described Cord, his clothes and hat. She told the employee that he was carrying around silky unmentionables, stalking her every move through the store. After listening to their assurances that the store's security guards would see to her safety, Savannah hung up.

Moments later she was idly looking through clothing racks as Cord approached with several slinky pairs of panties dangling from his big fingers. He wore the sexy, devilish smile that always made her heart beat faster.

Right behind him were two plainclothes security officers. They stepped up just in time to hear Cord's seductive words.

"If I buy you this red thong, will you let me rip it off your body?"

Savannah turned with a look of horror on her face. Looking past Cord she addressed the security men. "That's him. He won't leave me alone."

Confusion wiped the smile from Cord's face. He turned abruptly to face the two men.

"Sir, step away from the lady," the larger of the two commanded.

"What the hell's going on," Cord demanded.

The security men stared at him sternly. "We don't take kindly to stalking ladies through our store. You'll have to come with us now," said the smaller man.

The men closed in on him, each firmly grabbing one of his arms and pulling them behind his back. They began pulling him away with forceful intent. They were such a mismatched pair. One was a huge, hulking mass. The other was small and willowy thin.

Speaking from between his clenched teeth, Cord's voice was strained. "Savannah, what the hell are you doing. Tell them right now that this is one of your crazy damn pranks."

His eyes shot daggers at her over his shoulder as the security officers dragged him away. Cord looked mortified. The other shoppers stared at him with knowing looks as he was led away to the offices. Savannah struggled to keep her laughter under control until the odd-looking trio was out of sight.

* * * * *

"How many times do I have to tell you this? Savannah Thompson is my employer. I'm the foreman at her ranch, the

Shooting Star. She likes to play wild pranks. That's what's going on. She's playing a nasty prank on me."

Frustration built inside him until Cord was ready to strike out. He sat in a small security room with the store manager and the two security officers. He'd silently begun thinking of them as Mutt & Jeff, the classic, oddball comic pair.

The store manager hesitated again with her hand on the phone. "I'll have to call the police and let them sort this out."

Cord bit the inside of his cheek to keep from lashing out. "Look, if you will just find Miss Thompson on the security cameras, I can tell you exactly what you're gonna see."

"Go ahead, I'm listening," she said.

"Okay, she will be near the front of the store. Four big cowboys will be with her. They will all be standing there laughing their stupid faces off."

The manager turned toward Mutt & Jeff. "Go ahead, Mike. Find her on the cameras."

Flipping through several monitors they spotted Savannah standing close to the entrance. Jesse, Riley Zeke, and Brock stood there with her. The five of them were obviously laughing heartily. They could see that Savannah even had tears streaming down her face.

The manager turned toward Cord once again. "I don't find this situation to be the least bit funny, Mister Black."

Cord struggled to relax his jaw. "I assure you, neither do I. If you still don't believe me, go talk to Miss Thompson. I'm sure by now she'll be willing to confess to her antics."

She stared at him for several more moments. He could tell she was trying to decide her best course of action. "I should still call the police and let them handle the whole crazy bunch of you." Turning, she addressed Mutt & Jeff. "Please bring Miss Thompson and her cohorts here."

"We can't leave you here with him," the big one complained.

"I will be fine. I really don't think Mister Black will try anything stupid. Just go get Miss Thompson, please."

* * * * *

Oh, this one would go down in the annals of all-time great pranks. Savannah could not contain herself. She laughed so hard her ribs hurt. It felt so good to get out her restless energies and pull one over on her big guard dog all at the same time. Tears streamed down her cheeks. She hugged her self tightly trying to keep from falling apart.

At first her cowboys had looked bothered when they'd approached her. They thought she was upset by something. With halting progress due to her extreme laughter, Savannah had explained what she'd done. Soon the boys were all laughing hysterically right along with her.

"Damn, Van. He's gonna be so pissed off. I don't wanna be around when he sees you again," Zeke informed her.

The other cowboys were all looking at her as if she were a lunatic.

"Yeah, that was a great prank, but shit. That man is gonna be madder than a wet hornet," Brock stated.

"I don't care. The look on his face was well worth it," Savannah was saying as the two security officers approached the group.

"Excuse me, ma'am. We'll need you to come with us for a moment," the small one stated.

Immediately the four cowboys crowded in protectively around Savannah.

"And just who the hell are you?" asked Jesse.

"Store security, sir. The manager needs Miss Thompson to help sort out a little problem for us." They stood waiting, clearly impatient.

Savannah moved out from behind the boys. She began walking in the direction they had just come from, but Riley stopped her with a firm hand on her biceps.

"Uh, Miss Thompson will not be going anywhere without us," he stated. The look on his face left no room for argument.

The shorter man looked at the big one questioningly.

"That's fine. Let's go."

When they reached the security office the manager and Cord had to come out into the hall. The room was far too small for the now large group assembled together.

The cowboys kept a protective distance between an obviously angry Cord and Savannah. She was touched by their sweet gesture, but anxious to face his wrath. Knowing her reasons for her actions did not make the confrontation any less volatile. She wanted him severely riled. She wanted to effectively assert her freedom and drive him away. That would prevent her from having to see the look of horror on his face when she told him about her abilities.

One look at his clenched jaw and angry face told her that she'd accomplished her mission.

After listening to the manager's stern lecture, Savannah smiled sweetly. "Look, I'm sorry about upsetting everyone with my little joke." Her expression revealed everything except apology. "I really need you to let him go now though. He's buying dinner tonight."

The cowboys all had to hide their smiles behind their hands. Riley coughed to cover up his laughter. The manager looked at them all with anger brimming in her eyes.

"Just stay out of my store. Go play your games at the DollarMart, okay?"

Savannah was somewhat irked over being told to shop elsewhere, but she took the lecture in stride. Without another word she turned on her heel and casually walked out of the store. The cowboys were right on her heel, staying between her and Cord, yet out of his reach.

The sense of having messed up big time hit Savannah as she walked toward the exit. Cord's feelings and intentions hit her like a blow to the gut, sparking a small pull of regret. He was beyond angry. He was leaving mad.

She'd take the time to hate herself for it later. But right now, she only wanted to have this whole episode finished. She felt confident that she'd done what was required to accomplish her goal. It would be much easier to never have to face telling him her secrets.

Everyone was silent during the drive back to the ranch, dinner out totally forgotten. The tension hung thick in the air, making the large vehicle feel small, almost claustrophobic. After the truck was parked they all watched as Cord silently walked to his cabin shutting the door quietly behind him.

Zeke let out a deep sigh. "Well, at least he didn't freak out."

Savannah stood shaking her head. The small thread of regret continued to grow into something overwhelming. She'd taken the easy road, but was it the right thing. "No, but this is worse. I've never seen Cord go quiet like that. It surely can't mean anything good."

Brock put an arm protectively around her shoulders and guided Savannah into the house. "Come on, I'll help you make dinner." It was obvious to everyone he did not want to leave her alone.

While Brock and Savannah cooked, the other cowboys set the table. They settled down to watch TV in the house while waiting for dinner. No one wanted to leave her alone to face Cord's anger.

Brock was not one for being anything less than blunt. "Why are you trying to drive him away, Van?"

"What are you talking about?" Her innocent act didn't fool him.

"Look, I know you well enough to know what you're doing. You're afraid of getting too close, of having to tell him your secret."

Savannah turned quickly, her mouth hanging open in shock.

"Hell, Van. Your secret isn't a secret to those of us that are close to you. We all know that you see things. We accept it as part of you. You're pushing Cord away because you're afraid that he won't, aren't you?"

The self-assured, knowing look in his eyes stole her last stitch of confidence. Could it be true? Did everyone close to her know what she fought so hard to keep a secret? Not just know, but accept her anyway? No, that was impossible.

* * * * *

Frustration and anger coursed through Cord's veins. He'd had all he could take. After everything that had happened, she still wanted to play games. Even after he'd asked her to stop, warned her he'd leave.

Through the haze of his anger, Cord could admit the obvious. She had intentionally pushed him, trying to get a reaction. All he saw was her defiance and his failure to tame the wild woman who was obviously more important to him than he was to her.

He couldn't feel his own pain. He hid it below the seething feelings of betrayal. Since he didn't own much it didn't take him long to pack and load his truck. After hooking up the trailer he drove over to the stables. Stormy was not happy about being loaded up into the trailer. She had become quite attached to Moon Dancer and was acting stubborn.

"Come on girl, we've got a long drive ahead of us."

Cord coaxed her into the small trailer, quickly getting her settled in for the trip. After shutting Stormy in he saw movement in his peripheral vision. Looking over at the house he noticed Savannah standing in a window watching him. Silently he turned his back and climbed into the truck. Without looking back, he drove away from everything he desired, everything he'd come to love and care about.

* * * * *

Ugh, how infuriating. Nothing could hold Savannah's attention. She'd tried watching a movie, reading a book, working, but it was all useless. Her restlessness grew greater by the moment. Pacing the house, she thought again about what she had done.

Really there was no other option. The longer Cord had stayed on the ranch and in her bed, the more Savannah had come to lean on him. Every day she fell deeper in love, became more addicted to his presence. Driving him away was the least painful option. Certainly better than watching the revulsion cross his handsome face when she finally admitted to her abilities. She could not stand the thought of watching his reaction to that revelation.

From experience she knew that he would close himself off to her. He'd be afraid that she would always know what he was thinking and feeling. Trust would go out the window. He'd worry that she would be able to read every private thought. It would slowly drive a wedge between them.

Then there was the baby.

Absently she rubbed her still flat abdomen. Cord was the kind of man who would feel honor and duty bound to marrying her. He would do so out of a sense of responsibility. That was the last thing Savannah wanted. If she ever married it would be for love. But she would never marry. No one would be able to accept her abilities and still be able to feel love.

Life on the ranch had become rather sedate. Everyone fell into a quiet routine. Savannah no longer sought the risky games that had given her so much pleasure. She would not do anything to put her child at risk.

No one mentioned Cord or her ability to see things. It still amazed her to think that the close-knit group knew about her visions, but were not put off by them. It just couldn't be. There was no way they realized how much she could see.

The boys all seemed to know something was going on. They tried to tempt her with wild ideas. The craziest was their idea to take two trucks and go four-wheeling in the mud.

That in itself was pretty tame. But what the boys had in mind was to blindfold the drivers and have the navigators give verbal instructions. Savannah had visibly shivered at the thought of crashing.

Riley had stopped his crazy pranks ever since the confrontation with Cord. He didn't need to scare Tamara any more to get her attention. The four cowboys had gained her undivided focus. She now spent a great deal more time at the ranch and the boys took her out on the town every Friday night. Savannah wondered which one would finally win her affections.

The day Zeke's letter came from the university was bittersweet. He had been working in the stables. She handed him the envelope with unshed tears burning in her eyes. He'd opened the envelope with trembling fingers then proceeded to whoop and holler with joy.

He would start school in May, but was already busy making plans. She could sense his reluctance and fear of leaving the ranch, but these emotions were overridden by his need to prove himself and his joy over being accepted into the program.

He was leaving in the morning to get settled in. She would miss his shy, sweet smile. He had become part of her family. She now understood the empty nest feeling mothers had when their children moved away to begin their own lives.

Mostly she felt smothered. The men had become even more overprotective. Every time she attempted to complete even the most menial task one of them was there gently taking over. There was always someone by her side throughout the day. While she enjoyed the attention, she craved some time alone.

Savannah had made up a fictitious cousin to go visit for a few days. She needed to get away from the men and think. In the morning after seeing Zeke off, she would drive to Billings.

She had already booked a room in a bed and breakfast. It would be nice to eat out, shop and be alone.

Her emotions had become unstable from the pregnancy hormones surging through her system. She found herself tearing up over sappy commercials on TV. Small acts of kindness or courtesy, like one of the boys holding a door open, would hit her with a tidal wave of feelings.

Yes, a few days to calm her emotions and find her center were just what she needed. Then she could come back to the ranch relaxed and in control again.

As always her thoughts turned quickly back to Cord. Where was he? What was he doing? Did he miss her? No matter what she did, thoughts of him haunted her every waking moment. They had become very close in such a short time. They were totally compatible in bed, and in the stables, the back of his truck, in the hot tub, under the stars. They had fucked like insatiable teenagers in heat, but hadn't really talked much. She didn't know his goals and dreams, his fears and desires. All she really knew was his body.

Her abilities lay like an albatross between them. She hadn't told him about this essential part of her soul. How could he love her when he didn't even really know her? True, they shared a deep, tangible connection. Anyone close by could feel the electrical energy that arced between the two of them whenever they were close together. Still, regardless of how little they had verbalized, Savannah felt that she knew his soul.

It struck her then what a giving man Cord Black was. He unselfishly gave his comfort, warmth and support. When they made love he had always ensured her pleasure before taking his own. And that's what it was, making love. She could call it fucking all she liked, but that didn't change the facts. Every time they came together they shared every part of their beings.

Memories of their frantic mating after the intense confrontation between Cord and Riley swept through her mind. That had not been fucking, or even making love. They had been marking each other, trying to tie themselves permanently together. Heat coursed through her body at the memory of how primal their needs had been and the ultimate result.

That had been when they had created their child. Cord had succeeded in joining a piece of them together, forever. No matter what happened, she would always have a big part of Cord in their child.

Savannah had never been able to read her own future. She pushed away useless thoughts of what would be and concentrated on preparing Zeke's farewell meal. She wanted everything to be perfect his last night on the ranch.

Sure, he'd promised to come back to visit often, but it just wouldn't be the same. Silent tears slid down her cheeks, splattering in big drops against the countertop. Damn it, she'd told herself she wouldn't cry tonight.

Turning to the counter, she picked up the dishes heaped with steaming food. Tamping down her emotions, Savannah was determined to enjoy their last meal with Zeke. Afterwards they would roll up the carpet and dance the blues away.

Chapter Ten

❧

Morning came all too quickly for Savannah. She would have stood in the ranch yard holding tightly to Zeke forever if Brock had not gently pulled her away. Then the big, tough cowboy tenderly wiped away her tears as she watched her young friend drive away.

She had never felt so alone on the Shooting Star before. After kissing each of the boys goodbye, Savannah got ready to leave. Tamara pulled her off to the side to talk.

"Why are you running, Van? We all know who you are and we love you. Cord loves you. You have to trust him enough to tell him. He would not walk away, especially if he knew about the baby."

Savannah gasped. The casually dropped comment hit her like a bomb. "What are you talking about?"

The ferocious look in her friend's eyes pierced through Savannah's barriers.

"Damn it, Van. I know you better than you think. You are literally glowing. And when you think no one's looking, you rub you hands over your abdomen." She pulled Savannah into a fierce hug. "You have to stop hiding, Van."

Savannah stepped back from her all too perceptive friend. "I won't be back until the weekend. Take care of the boys for me."

Tamara just shook her head in frustration, but a wicked smile crept across her lips. "Don't you worry about the boys. I know exactly how to take care of them. You worry about taking care of yourself." Deep worry lines creased her delicate forehead.

Climbing into her big Hummer, Savannah headed out. Miles of beautiful scenery passed by her windows unnoticed. Absently she stroked her belly while her mind drifted. They all seemed to know the secret of her visions. Tamara had also figured out about the baby. How could it be possible?

A gentle smile curved the corners of her lips. If anyone would know her deepest secrets it would be the boys and her best friend. Tamara was the first person she had felt so close to since her grandmother had passed on.

Tamara's words rang in her head. *"Why are you running, Van? We all know who you are and we love you."*

It was so hard for her to comprehend. She was used to being shunned when friends learned of her abilities. But not Tamara and her boys. They didn't seem to be put off in the least.

She couldn't take that chance with Cord though. It would kill her to be rejected by him. She loved him so much. It was better to live without him than to face him not trusting her or turning away in disgust.

Thoughts swirled through her mind as she drove on automatic pilot. When she pulled up at the bed and breakfast she felt utterly lost. Savannah had no idea how she had arrived at this juncture in her life. Was Tamara right, was she running away?

She shook off her lingering doubts, and stared into the beautiful suite in amazement. In the center of the enormous room stood a king-size, four-poster bed. The thick mattress was covered with hand-crocheted, ivory bedding with a multitude of matching pillows. An elegant crystal vase of fresh flowers graced the nightstand.

The comfortable sitting area was bathed in sunlight from large bay windows. Savannah ran her fingers over the smooth polished mahogany wood. If you were going to get lost for a few days, the extravagant B&B was certainly the way to go.

In the center of the large bathroom stood a huge, clawfoot tub. She could picture herself sinking down into that tub filled with fragrant bubbles. After unpacking she decided to head out and do some shopping, which in itself was a luxury.

Regardless of how wonderful the room was, for some reason it made her think of Cord. Of course, everything made her think of Cord. In such a short time he had become her main focus. Now, even when he was not near, Savannah felt his presence, smelled his distinctive masculine scent.

Even walking through the quaint nearby shops she was overwhelmed with thoughts of Cord. He was so much a part of her, felt so close even now. How was she ever going to get him out of her head?

In one shop she stopped suddenly, certain that Cord was there. She could smell him, feel him. Carefully scanning the room only revealed another woman shopper. Something about the woman was very familiar. Her thick, wavy, deep brown hair cascaded over an elegant neck and slender shoulders. If only she could see the petite woman's eyes, then she would be sure.

Savannah moved casually closer until she rounded the end of an aisle and came face-to-face with the woman. Large blue-gray eyes sparkled with warmth and intelligence, stealing her breath away. Hell, she was further gone than she'd thought. Now she was seeing Cord's eyes in complete stranger's faces.

They passed each other without a word. Although certain now that they'd never met, there was something innately familiar about the woman.

Alright, you've officially lost it Van. How the heck could some pretty stranger make you think of Cord? Sure, her hair, eyes and coloring are shockingly similar, but please.

Feeling unnerved, Savannah headed back to the B&B. The walk only put her nerves more on edge. The small hairs on the back of her neck stood on end. She kept looking over her shoulder, expecting to see Cord standing nearby.

* * * * *

"Cord, you're not listening to me. Cord?"

Shaking his head, Cord fought to focus on his sister's words. It was hard to pull his thoughts away from Savannah. And every time he looked at Stephanie, he saw his mother's face. It brought on a disconcerting feeling.

"What did you say, honey?"

Taking his much larger hand in hers, Steph stared into his eyes.

"You've really got it bad, big brother. Question is what are you going to do about it? Hanging out with me is not going to solve your problems."

He knew she was right. Regardless of how much he enjoyed spending time with her, he needed to take some action. He couldn't let the woman who held his heart drive him away. He didn't care what her big, dark, hairy secret was. He had every intention of spending the rest of his life with Savannah Thompson, whether she realized it or not.

There had been times when he'd been certain she was on the verge of telling him everything. She would get this look in her eyes, giving him a vague glimpse of something. The walls would slip, and her mouth would open then close soundlessly. She'd seem to contemplate her words.

He could always tell the exact moment when her walls slammed firmly back into place, shutting him out. He was damn sick of being left on the outside, trying to get a glimpse through a chink in her armor.

"Yeah, I know. I was hoping you'd help me do some jewelry shopping. I'm gonna head back to the ranch on Friday and make her talk to me."

One hand flew up, clasping over her mouth, stifling her scream of joy. Cord studied his sister's familiar features. In the candlelit restaurant her dark hair shimmered. Emotions swirled through the depths of her expressive eyes.

"Oh Cord. Are you sure? I'd hate to see you get hurt."

Pulling her hand to his lips, Cord brushed a soft kiss across her dainty fingers.

"I'm sure, Steph. She won't turn me down if I can just get her to listen."

He'd known that eventually he would go back to the ranch and force Savannah to tell him everything. Today he'd decided that he would not go back empty-handed. His love for the wild little filly was not something that would go away. He'd given her enough time to stew. Now it was time for action.

While he'd walked around the shops this afternoon, Cord felt Savannah's presence surrounding him. Goose bumps had covered his body as he strolled casually along the sidewalk. She held his heart and soul. He wanted her in his arms for at least the next sixty years.

"Wow, good luck," Steph said. "It sounds like you have your work cut out for you to get her to listen. But if she's half the woman you've described, it will be worth the effort."

Cord nodded his head. "She's priceless!"

Once again he was drawn into his own thoughts about the beautiful woman who had so quickly captured his heart. Nothing else mattered to him now. He'd given her space, let her run. It was time to put a stop to her craziness. He'd make Savannah see that he wasn't going anywhere without her.

It amazed him how quickly his dreams had changed. Sure he would still like to have his own ranch, but now the most important thing was that Savannah be there with him. She had more spunk than any other woman he'd ever known. Tough as nails and such a hard worker. Yet she had a soft, gentle, caring side too.

He'd finally gotten used to her casual, loving nature. Hell, she treated all her employees like family. Seeing their happiness made her happy. And the woman had the patience of a saint when working with the animals. They were so responsive to her gentle voice and touch.

Even her wild, playful nature appealed to Cord. Sure, at first it had made him crazy. He'd never seen a ranch run like the Shooting Star. Somehow though, it worked perfectly. The

Shooting Star was in his blood now, right along with its owner. Her crazy antics made him smile, even though they scared the hell out of him at the same time.

The land felt like home and damned if he was going to give up either the ranch or his woman. Yes, after some shopping it was time to go home.

* * * * *

"Is it a full moon or something?"

"I don't think so, Van. Why, what's going on?" asked Millie.

The sweet, older woman cooked an enormous breakfast buffet every day for all the B&B guests. The pleasantly plump cook reminded Savannah of her grandmother in ways. They had quickly become friends.

"All the men in this town have gone girl crazy. I just walked over to Johnson's Market and had construction workers whistling at me. Almost every man I run into is a shameless flirt. What is up with this town?"

Millie's cackling laughter filled the room. "It's not the town, Van, it's you. You're in love, glowing and those wonderful feelings radiate out to everyone near you. It makes them want to be close to you."

Savannah stared at the other woman, her mouth hanging open. If she didn't know better, she'd think Millie had a little second sight going for her.

Men in the town had certainly noticed her newfound, sexy confidence, burning physical hunger and raging hormones. They'd felt the vibes rolling off her and the primitive animals inside them sat up and took notice. Millie was right.

"Honey child, no matter how you try to deny it, you're in love. Isn't it about time you went home and faced the man who captured your heart instead of hiding out here?" Millie stood with her hands fisted on ample hips waiting for a response.

Savannah sank down into her chair in defeat. "If only it were that simple, Millie."

The other woman harrumphed. "It's only complicated because you're making it that way."

Savannah shook her head before dropping it into her hands. "You just don't understand, Millie."

Pulling out a chair, Millie perched on edge. Taking Savannah's chin, she tilted her face up so she could see her eyes. "Why don't you try me, honey child?"

Well, what did she have to lose. She'd already lost the man she loved. Savannah spilled everything that had been weighing on her mind. She told Millie about her abilities and how everyone turned away upon discovering them. She talked about how much she missed her grandmother, the one person she'd ever been able to discuss everything with and not fear her pulling away.

By the time she finished talking Savannah was exhausted. Millie remained quietly contemplative for a long time. Finally, she took Savannah's chin in her work worn hands. "You've got to go to him. Tell him everything. Honey child, if he loves you it won't matter. He will accept you and everything that makes you the unique woman you are. And if you love him as much as you say, then you owe him the chance."

Millie's fingers stroked lightly over Savannah's cheek. "You have to stop running and keeping everyone at a distance. Cord Black sounds like a man worth loving. Give him the chance to prove it to you."

Later, lying on the big bed, Savannah's mind churned endlessly. Could she really trust Cord enough to tell him everything? She would trust him with her life, but could she trust him with her heart?

At least she was sure of one thing. She'd run far enough and long enough. Although she'd like to hide away forever, it was time to face her life. The words of a popular song echoed through her head.

Sometimes I'd like to hide away somewhere and lock the door
A single battle lost but not the war
Cause tomorrow's another day
And I'm thirsty anyway
So bring on the rain

Yeah, I might feel defeated,
I might hang my head
I might be barely breathing – but I'm not dead

Yeah, it was time to go home. Time to face who she is and trust in the man she loves.

Once she'd made the decision, Savannah was anxious to get moving. Just thinking about Cord had her slit covered with hot cream. Why the heck hadn't she packed her vibrator?

Picturing the sexy, long, cool drink of water that was Cord Black had her groaning with need. Everything about the big cowboy radiated sex, from his turbulent stormy eyes, to all the glorious muscles that made her want to trip him then beat him to the ground.

She loved feeling the play of his muscles from head to toe as they came together. God, just thinking about running her hands over his broad back while he thrust hard and fast into her pussy was enough to drive her insane with aching desire. She felt so empty without him.

The man had an innate, devilish sensuality that rolled off his hard body in waves. Mmm, it felt so phenomenal to feel his muscled body envelop her in his warmth and his long, thick cock filling her so completely.

Somehow, he was blocking her. No matter how hard she concentrated on reaching out to him, she ran into a brick wall.

Jumping up from the bed, Savannah began tossing her clothes into her suitcase without a care for the wrinkles that would result. All that mattered now was getting back to the ranch, tracking down Cord and convincing him to stay. Somewhere on his application paperwork was an emergency contact number.

Briefly she considered calling the ranch and having one of the hands look up the number, but she needed to get home. She needed her land, her friends and her damn vibrator. Although, not necessarily in that order.

Millie hugged her goodbye and wished her luck. Savannah made the long drive in record time, a new determination pushing her forward. She would lay herself bare before Cord and pray that he could accept her, faults and all.

Chapter Eleven

❧

Hot need coursed through every cell in her body. Savannah felt like she was on fire. She was going to have to make quick work of finding her cowboy again. She needed him more than her next breath. Wanted him so badly she'd do whatever it took to get Cord back onto her ranch and into her arms.

It felt so good to be home. Just driving down the dirt drive toward her house was like being drawn into a welcoming embrace. The rugged land had become a part of her flesh, part of her very soul. Her heart soared to life just looking over her splendid piece of heaven.

While climbing out of her truck she noticed Tamara's car parked at the bunkhouse. Savannah was overwhelmed with the desire to see her friends. They would help her find Cord and bring him home where he belonged.

Moving with quiet grace came effortlessly to Savannah. It was not something of which she was even consciously aware. Soundlessly she slipped through the door expecting to find her friends watching a movie or playing cards. What she found instead stole every thought from her mind, every bone from her body, leaving her a brainless blob.

Somewhere a neuron fired, trying to send a signal to her body. It all but screamed, "Close your eyes and quietly walk away." But that was impossible. Savannah no longer had control over anything as simple as closing her eyes. There was no way on Earth she could not watch the erotic manifestation taking place before her eyes.

Thick quilts had been laid out in the center of the floor. Tamara was on her knees, totally naked, facing three equally naked cowboys. Brock, Jesse and Riley stood close together.

With her hands, Tamara stroked Brock and Riley's cocks as her mouth was stretched around Jesse's thick shaft.

The striking tableau was more sensual than any scene in the hottest erotica books Savannah had ever read. The foursome's moans and sexy noises struck her body like lightning, collecting with searing heat in her abdomen. Her pussy clenched with aching need, saturating her panties with hot juices.

As she watched, Tamara let Jesse's hard cock out of her mouth with a pop, then replaced it with Brock. Now she stroked Jesse and Riley in her small hands, while sucking Brock's big shaft into her mouth. Savannah's body shivered at the sound of his deep, rumbling moan. She barely halted her own cry of response.

Thankfully no one would be able to see her in the shadowed entry area. Her legs gave out, and Savannah sank to her knees. Her cream was flowing past the thin barrier of her panties, coating her thighs. Damn, they were making her so hot.

Jesse moved around Tamara, spreading her thighs further apart. He slid between her legs, stretched out and began licking her pussy. Tamara's hips rocked against his mouth as she alternated between sucking Brock and Riley's cocks deep into her mouth.

While Jesse's tongue fucked Tamara's pussy, two of his fingers teased her puckered anus. Brock and Riley moved closer and reached around Tamara, spreading her ass cheeks wide. Using her own copious juices, Jesse coated his fingers and began moving them within Tamara's ass. He worked her body relentlessly, stretching her back entrance enough to take a third finger.

Savannah's empty pussy clenched. Her swollen clit throbbed. She let her fingers move up under her skirt, pushing her soaked panties to the side. Sliding two fingers into her pussy, the sensitive tissues clamped down on the invading digits. God, she was so hot that she expected to see steam rising up from her drenched folds.

Biting her lower lip was all that kept her from crying out. Adding a third finger to those thrusting inside her heat, she used her thumb to stroke her engorged clit. She was so close already.

Not even an earthquake swallowing up the ranch could make her take her eyes off the scene in that room. She knew that the erotic images would play through her mind and drive her own fantasies for many years to come.

She watched as Riley dropped down onto the blankets, stretching out on his back, his cock standing straight up like a pole.

"Fucking ride me," he growled.

Tamara let Brock's cock slide from her mouth. Jesse moved out of the way, then settled in behind Tamara as she impaled herself on Riley's shaft.

Turning her head to the side, Tamara once again took Brock's cock into her mouth. Jesse knelt behind her, between Riley's outstretched legs. After positioning the broad head of his cock at her anus, Jesse began to work his thick erection into the small hole. Tamara held rigidly still on Riley's dick.

Savannah stroked her own body, watching her friends fuck. Briefly she considered joining in, but rejected the idea. What she needed was Cord. No substitute would be acceptable.

The two men, now filling Tamara front and back, began a coordinated thrusting. She screamed around Brock's cock, which filled her mouth. Riley massaged both of her small breasts with his big hands. Jesse reached around her body and began stroking her clit.

Savannah could see Brock's hands clenched in Tamara's dark hair. His hips were thrusting forward, fucking her mouth, while Jesse fucked her ass, and Riley fucked her pussy. The overwhelming, multiple stimulations made the petite woman come undone. Every inch of Tamara's tiny body appeared to be racked with spasms.

Shaking with the need for her own release, Savannah fought to find the strength to sneak out of the bunkhouse. She did not want to be discovered, embarrassing her friends and herself. On wobbly legs, she weaved drunkenly across the ranch yard toward her house. Her fingers trembled so badly that she was barely able to open the front door. Once inside she wasted no time turning on lights, instead just moving as quickly as possible toward her bedroom.

Every inch of her body was sensitized, quaking with need. What she had just witnessed had been too much. Electricity hummed through every nerve ending. Her empty pussy still cried out to be filled. She moaned restlessly, feeling an enormous void engulf her senses.

Leaning over to the nightstand she removed a large silk pouch. Dropping it onto the bed, she opened the zipper and removed her trusty jackrabbit vibrator. The seven-inch pink shaft was packed with beads. The bulbous head and textured sheath felt sensuously real.

With one quick thrust she buried the jelly cock inside her aching pussy to the hilt. After several deep thrusts she turned on the controls to a pulse pounding speed. The head of the cock wiggled as the plastic balls ground against her G-spot. Another touch of the controls had the bunny ears tickling her clit.

Normally Jack was all it took to send her into an earth-shattering orgasm, but not tonight. No matter how she manipulated the delectable phallus, she needed more.

Searching in the pouch again, she found her rotating stud anal vibrator and a tube of lubrication. Using her right hand to control Jack, Savannah lubricated the fingers of her left hand and worked two into her anus. The tight muscles clamped down, sending searing sensations shooting up her spine. She worked the tight channel until it stretched to accept three invading digits.

After removing Jack from her pussy, Savannah staggered from the bed. She secured the anal vibrator to the floor by its suction cup base, turning the vibrating balls toward the wall. She spread a generous amount of lubrication over the six-inch shaft, and turned the dial to a gentle hum, setting the controller close by.

Positioning herself in a squat, Savannah braced her back against the wall. Her fingers spread her ass cheeks wide. With slow movements she worked the thick vibrator into her oh so sensitive channel. When her ass cheeks met with the floor she turned on the gyrating feature, increasing the speed of the vibrating wonder. Her tight muscles flexed and clenched, milking the amazingly tireless device. The balls vibrated sensuously against her perineum.

Once she had the shaft gyrating just right and the balls at the perfect vibration speed, she picked up Jack again. Sliding the thick shaft over her slit, she coated it in her slick juices. Using her right hand, she manipulated the ingenious pink cock in and out of her aching pussy.

Oh, dear God. It still was not enough. She desperately needed Cord. Easing the ache had always been simple thanks to her battery operated friends. But Savannah knew that now nothing but Cord's cock would be able to quench her burning need.

She screamed his name in her mind, over and over again, frustration riding her hard. Slowly she slid up and down the wall while continuing to thrust Jack. With her left hand she massaged her breast, twirling the aching nipple between her thumb and finger.

The stud gyrated in her ass, balls vibrating against her perineum. Jack plunged deep into her pussy, spinning balls creating a mind-numbing friction against her G-spot, ears tickling her clit. Bending her head down, her warm tongue flicked over her pebbled nipple before she sucked the peak deeply into the hot cavern of her mouth.

Not enough, her mind screamed. The multiple stimulations kept Savannah on a razor's edge, failing to push her over the precipice into blissful release. It would never again be enough. She desperately ached for Cord.

* * * * *

Stormy was fit to be tied. The normally agreeable horse had had enough. What Cord wanted was unimportant. All she wanted was to continue lazily grazing in the tall, sweet grass along the roadside.

"You're being stubborn as a jackass," Cord gently scolded, all the while stroking her with the currycomb. Nothing could convince Stormy that it was time to get moving. He'd even tried to entice her with her favorite treat, peppermint candies. His patience was wearing thin. The short pit stop had turned into a long rest.

"Come on, girl. We don't have that much further to go now."

She just swung her big, gray head around and glared at him, then returned to slowly chomping.

His erect cock pressed painfully against the stiff confinement of his jeans. The unruly organ had grown impossibly large. Somehow he sensed Savannah's growing need. Picturing her beautiful face, Cord whispered, "Hold on, sugar."

Invisible hands pulled at him, making Cord desperate to be on the road, desperate to be with his woman. Unbidden, erotic images continually flashed through his mind.

Using brute force, he finally got Stormy into the trailer once again. By the time he finally arrived at the ranch and got Stormy settled, it was late. Cord felt both mentally and physically exhausted. All he wanted was a hot shower, a firm mattress and his wild woman.

The entire ranch was dark and silent, but a feeling of sexual need filled the air. He moved through the house quietly, assuming that Savannah was asleep. As he walked down the hallway toward the bedroom, Cord stopped dead in his tracks, nostrils flaring.

The heady smell of sex permeated the air. A dark, murderous rage coursed through his veins, tightening his muscles. He would kill the bastard that had been stupid enough to touch his woman. His gray eyes turned icily intense, focused.

With fierce determination, Cord kicked the bedroom door open, driving the knob through the wall. Savannah's tortured screams rang in his head. His fists were clenched tight, ready for action. What he saw nearly brought him to his knees.

"Jesus H. Christ," he growled.

Savannah looked up, meeting his passion-filled eyes, a frustrated whimper escaping her lips. She squatted against the wall, long golden waves of hair pushed over her right shoulder. Her swollen, red lips sucked at her own breast. Never in his life had Cord seen such an erotically charged sight.

His eyes traveled lower, watching in awe as she violently thrust a vibrator between the swollen, pink lips of her pussy. Something thick and dark peeked out between her ass cheeks.

Leaning casually against the doorframe, his big body hummed with energy. The sensual, erotic images would haunt him for the rest of his life. "Fucking son of a bitch!"

That deep, sexy voice sent electric sensations straight to Savannah's straining clit. She let her nipple slip from the suction of her mouth. "Cord...I need you...help me," she pleaded. She watched him move across the room with that incredibly sexy, slow, rolling-hipped gate. Squatting down before her, he stared into her eyes for what seemed to be an eternity.

"Suck your nipple again for me, sugar."

His voice was a velvety caress that sent shivers down her spine. Helpless to refuse, she once again drew the turgid peak into her mouth. The intensity in his passion darkened eyes held her gaze. She sucked her nipple for his pleasure now.

"Let me see you flick it with your tongue," he ordered.

As she complied, Cord reached between her legs and took control of the thrusting vibrator. Each time he drilled the toy into her clenching pussy, he twisted his wrist. The invading phallus scraped against her sensitive inner walls, causing her to cry out.

"Come for me, sugar."

That was all it took. That sensual demand finally plunged her over the brink into a mind-blowing orgasm that curled her toes. She barely heard his words as the Earth shook beneath her feet.

"Damn, woman. Why the hell didn't you ever show me your toys before? I would've enjoyed being invited to play."

With a primal growl he pulled Jack from her pussy, then lifted her off the still rotating stud. Cord stood stock-still for several heartbeats staring at the thick device.

"Holy shit, you're killing me. I would've filled your sweet little ass. All you had to do, Savannah, was let me know."

He continued to stare for several frantic heartbeats longer before carrying her to the bed. She could feel the barely restrained need coursing through his body, his cock lengthening within his jeans.

Leaning forward he took her lips in a savage kiss. Their tongues danced and twirled together. He plundered the deepest recesses of her mouth. Cord kissed her more thoroughly than Savannah could have imagined was possible.

With savage motions he yanked his shirt off. In mere seconds he'd stripped off his jeans, briefs and boots, standing gloriously naked next to the bed. Without a word, he flipped her over. Savannah automatically caught her weight on her hands and knees.

Climbing up between her widespread legs, he pumped his cock several times within his fist. Finally, he thrust the hot, silky shaft between her legs, parting her saturated folds. His chest heaved against her back with his strained efforts to breathe.

"Damn, you're so wet for me. So hot and tight around my cock," he praised.

Savannah trembled with need, cried out his name. She needed him plunging inside, filling the empty ache. Regardless of her orgasm, she still needed to feel his thick length buried deep within her body.

His voice was a harsh, raspy exhalation against her neck. "First I'm gonna fuck that beautiful pussy, hard and deep, while you bathe my cock with your burning cream. Then I'm going to drive it so far up that sweet little ass that you won't know where you end and I begin. After that, as soon as I can move again, you're gonna suck me dry." He growled possessively. "I won't let you up for air again until you come for me so hard that you nearly shake yourself apart."

"Ohmigod," she cried out.

His dark words stroked her emotions, while his hands stroked her nipples and his silky cock stroked over her clit. An unexpected, shockingly intense orgasm hit her out of nowhere. Savannah cried out his name as her body shattered.

True to his word, Cord gave her no time to breathe. In one hard thrust he slammed his cock balls-deep into her still convulsing pussy. Her scream ripped through the room as he pounded into her aching flesh.

"Oh God...yes. Fuck me...harder," she called out.

It felt so good to feel him, skin to skin, no barrier between them, thrusting so deep. She would have sworn that she could feel him all the way up to her tonsils.

Cord's control snapped. He mindlessly slammed deep into her body with relentless need, fingers sinking deep into her hips. His pelvis slammed against her ass, balls smacking against her pussy. Their bodies created wet, rhythmic slapping sounds. Wild, animalistic sounds exploded from deep in the back of his throat.

Savannah had never experienced anything so intense. She lost track of how many times she'd come. He thrust into her as if their very lives depended on each powerful joining. She was amazed to feel his cock swell inside of her seconds before pulsing in release. Just feeling the hot jets of sperm shooting into her womb threw her over the edge once again.

With frantic motions, Cord pulled out of her grasping pussy, quickly putting on a condom. He pushed her chest down onto the bed, raising her ass higher. Without pause, he positioned the broad head of his still erect shaft against her nether hole and drilled deep inside. The tissues were stretched, lubricated and ready for him, granting easy entry.

A trail of fire blazed through that narrow channel, sending flames shooting from the top of her head, all the way down to her toes. Her head tossed wildly as her hips hammered back against his hard body. His devilish fingers pulling at her nipples had pleasure thundering from her aching breasts, through her belly and bursting in her pussy.

Cord was a wild man, a creature of primal need. His guttural cries driving her insane. Just when she thought the sensations were too much, his hand moved between her legs. With smooth motions he plunged Jack deep into her clenching flesh. It hadn't even registered on her lust fogged mind that he'd brought the vibrator into the bed with them.

Savannah was stretched on a sensual rack of pleasure. She was filled to overflowing. Her own wild cries joined in with Cord's.

The pink vibrator stroked his cock through the thin tissue that separated them. The swirling beads driving him over the edge. Her muscles clamped down tighter than a fist against his cock, milking his flesh, drawing him deeper.

"Oh shit," he moaned. "I'm not gonna last, sugar. Come with me, *now*!"

The climax ripped through his body, tearing him apart, binding them together. They collapsed together in a sweaty, sated heap, panting for much-needed oxygen.

* * * * *

Oh God, he was paralyzed. He couldn't breathe, couldn't move and couldn't think.

"Cord," Savannah gasped between harsh breaths. "God…get it out…hurry…please," she stammered.

It took him a minute to figure out what the hell she was trying to say. Gathering what little strength he could find, Cord toppled them over onto their sides. Holding her spooned against his body, he slid the vibrator from her trembling flesh, dropping it to the bed.

His eyes fluttered opened, his nostrils flared, drinking in the scent of their passionate fucking. The sweat had dried and his fevered body cooled, leaving him feeling chilled. Tapping into his last reserves of strength, Cord rose and went to the bathroom. He filled the big tub with hot water and scented oils after discarding the used condom. The pleasing aromas of apples and cinnamon rose on the heated air.

Ignoring her mumbled protests, he scooped Savannah up in his arms, carrying her to the bathroom. All complaints ended as her tired body slid into the warm water, small murmurs of appreciation now escaping her lips instead.

Cord slipped in behind her and proceeded to gently care for her body. They soaked in the tub until the water turned cold. When she began to shiver, he tenderly dried her limp body then tucked her into bed. He pulled the covers over them both, holding her within the shelter of his body. Together they plunged into a deeply contented sleep.

Several times during the night they woke up and made love again, even sharing an intense sixty-nine session. She seemed totally unaware of having cried out, "I love you," during one particularly intense orgasm. She didn't hear the same words whispered back against her neck as she fell asleep once again.

Cord had wanted to talk and settle things between them. When he had seen her frustrated masturbation session, all thought had quickly fled his mind. Any conversation would now have to wait until morning. They were both too exhausted for anything other than sleep.

Chapter Twelve

ဆာ

Shivering in the inky darkness, Mandy curled into a tight ball, hugging herself tightly. She had never experienced a darkness so complete and encompassing. It felt as though she had fallen into a place where light did not exist.

"Momma," she cried out. Her hoarse voice sounded as soft as butterfly wings to the tired girl. "Momma, help me."

Although she heard no noise, Mandy felt that someone was near. Tentatively she questioned, "Is–is someone there?"

Holding her breath, she waited for a response. When none came, she finally breathed again. The only sound she could hear was the furtive noises of some small, night animal. She prayed that it would stay away and that it was not a rat. Mandy hated their beady, little red eyes, which seemed to stare right through her.

She felt so cold and dirty. Her normally shiny brown hair was a knotted, tangled, dirty mess. The new, pretty pink outfit Momma had given her was torn and covered with filth.

Time was not a concept that her young mind embraced very well. She had no notion of how long she had been in the cold, dank, dark hole. Hunger pains knotted her stomach into a tight, hard ball. Her mouth was so dry that she wasn't even able to swallow.

"Momma, Daddy, please. I'm here. Please come help me. I wanna go home. I'll be a good girl. I promise!"

Her silent pleas went unanswered. Hugging herself fiercely, Mandy fell into a fitful, restless sleep.

Struggling for air, Savannah sat straight up in the bed, clutching at her throat.

"Mandy," she cried out softly.

The vision had been exceptionally powerful. Her stomach was clenched tight as a fist with hunger, regardless that she had eaten dinner only several hours before. Her throat felt as dry as the Sahara desert.

With immense care, she untangled herself from Cord's body. Quickly, she donned jeans, sweatshirt, socks and sneakers. Deftly, she wrapped a bandana over her hair. Wasting no time, Savannah moved through the dark house and out to the stables. While she would like to take the Hummer, she knew it would not get her into small places.

Normally she enjoyed the peaceful beauty of the ranch yard under the night sky. Walking under the stars typically relaxed Savannah, bringing her a sense of inner balance and calm. Tonight, nothing could calm her soul. She had to get to Mandy quickly, before *he* came back.

She had no idea who *he* was. All she had received from the girl was a deeply shadowed silhouette, resembling that of a large man. Mandy had not seen him clearly, but he frightened her badly.

The horses nickered a greeting as she moved quietly through the stables. With nimble movements she quickly saddled and bridled Moon Dancer. After mounting, her agile steed made his way across the dark ranch. Instinct guided their way. She knew that Mandy was not on her property. There were no caves such as the girl was trapped in anywhere on the Shooting Star. Heedless of potential dangers, Moon Dancer made his way rapidly across the darkened land. Soon she found herself on Bar B land, Wyatt's property.

Briefly she wondered how the girl had ended up on the neighboring ranch, but dismissed it as trivial. What mattered was finding Mandy and bringing her to safety. Certainly her parents would be near frantic with worry.

At the base of Shadow Mountain, Savannah dismounted. She let Moon Dancer's reins drop to the ground. The well-trained horse would remain close to that spot while grazing on the sweet grasses, awaiting her return.

Fear clutched at her heart when Savannah could not reach out to the girl. No matter how hard she concentrated on the huddled image she'd received, she could not establish contact. Silently she prayed that the girl be deeply sleeping. No other possibility was thinkable.

Without caution, Savannah began scaling the gentle rise of the mountain. She did not care what happened to her as long as she reached Mandy. Every facet of her being was focused on that single goal. Nothing would distract her from her mission.

Here she was, once again risking it all to save a child. The potential results of people once again discovering her abilities briefly flittered across her awareness, but she shoved those thoughts away. Even if her life became a living hell nothing mattered except helping Mandy. If she had to give up the ranch and move again, so be it.

Making her way over a particularly rough piece of terrain her foot twisted in a small hole. Crying out, she fell hard. With her fingers and the toes of her shoes, she frantically grabbed at the rocky earth, desperate to find purchase. She felt the soft flesh of her palms being torn open, her body abused by several rocks as she slid haphazardly down the sheer, rocky mountainside.

Eventually she was able to stop her rapid descent by catching hold of the thick roots of a scrubby plant. Lying perfectly still, precariously hanging off the side of the mountain, she struggled to regain her breath. Pain lanced through her body. After taking several deep breaths she began to shore up her footing. Finally, feeling once again sure of her balance, Savannah began to climb again.

Her hands had taken the brunt of her slide. The skin was deeply torn, with dirt caked into the open wounds. At least the dirt helped stem the flow of blood.

Wasting no time, Savannah began moving steadily back up the mountain, pausing only briefly to let her instinct guide her in the right direction. Her senses told her that she was drawing near and that the shadowy male figure was not close by.

Haphazardly, she moved headlong in the direction her intuition led. The terrain became more even, easier to traverse. Idiotically, she let her guard down, relaxing her aching muscles.

A shrill scream cut through the peaceful night as the Earth disappeared from beneath her feet. Her body was thrown helter-skelter into a deep, black chasm. Savannah's last thought was to wonder how deep the fissure could possibly be when her head struck a rock and the world went pitch black.

* * * * *

Sitting up, Cord gasped for air. A sudden sense of danger woke him from a deep, contented sleep. Something was very wrong.

"Savannah," he called out.

Groping among the blankets he found the bed empty. Without a care for his state of undress, Cord moved through the eerily still house. His senses told him she was in trouble.

Dressing quickly in the jeans, T-shirt and boots he'd discarded earlier in a heap on the floor, he headed out into the night. The ranch yard was quiet and peaceful. Almost too peaceful.

Looking around, he noted all the vehicles were still parked in the same places. Moving to the barn he counted the ATVs. He quickly accounted for all the ranch vehicles. As soon as he walked into the stables, Stormy's distressed neigh broke the silence. Moving quickly to the mare's side he noted the empty stall next to hers.

"Looks like we're going for an early morning ride, girl."

Cord did not have to think about the steps required to saddle and bridle his horse. They came as second nature. His mind wandered with thoughts of Savannah. Although he did not want to admit it, he felt that she was somehow in danger, possibly hurt.

"That damn, wild woman is going to be the death of me," he grumbled.

Stormy rubbed her muzzle against his broad chest, seeking comfort and warmth from her master. Absently, he stroked her long snout reassuringly.

They headed out across the land at a breakneck speed with the sun just beginning to rise on the horizon. He pushed the mare at a reckless pace. Something told him that he did not have much time to find his wild little cowgirl.

* * * * *

Groggily, Savannah struggled to sit up. Her body protested even the slightest of movements. She felt battered and bruised. What the hell had happened? Her head throbbed painfully, preventing her from collecting her thoughts.

Lightning bolts of pain shot through her left arm from fingers to shoulder when she tried to support her upper body. With a groan, she dropped back to the cold, damp earth. Darkness swam at the edges of her mind, but she could not give in. Everything in her said she had to stay alert if she was to survive.

Slowly she struggled to work open her eyes. Allowing time to adjust to the light, stabbing pain shot through her skull. She'd never experienced such a painful hangover before. She must have gone out drinking and dancing with Tamara. That would explain why she felt so sore.

Why the hell was she lying in the dirt? Going out on a bender did not explain why she was lying on the cold ground. Mentally she took stock of her aches and pains. Her arm and head throbbed painfully. No, a simple bender could not explain what was going on.

Clamping her jaw, Savannah fought to tamp down the pain. She had to know where she was, and what was going on. The pain in her head made her want to slam her eyelids shut again, but she resisted the insistent urge. Something was unmistakably wrong. She had to assess the situation and figure out a course of action. At least that's what her rational mind said. The rest of her wanted to just shut down until the pain went away.

Without moving, she concentrated on her surroundings. She appeared to be in a cavern. That made no sense whatsoever to her foggy brain. How the hell had she ended up in a cavern?

Clandestine noises caught her attention. Something or someone was moving up behind her. Fear washed over Savannah, stealing her breath. Remaining as still and quiet as possible, she waited. Before long more tentative noises reached her ears. They were too soft to have been made by an adult. It was either an animal or a child cautiously sneaking up on her. With a flash the vision returned, clarifying her situation.

She had taken off in the dark searching for Mandy. The last thing she remembered was making her way up the mountain until the Earth disappeared from beneath her feet. A fall would certainly explain the pain she felt.

Slowly, Savannah lifted her throbbing head and turned it to face the opposite direction. The cavern grew narrower and darker in this direction. She barely made out the small shape hidden in the shadows.

Her voice came out as a hoarse, unrecognizable croak. Clearing her throat, she tried again. "Mandy, its okay. I'm here to help you, sweetie. Are you all right?"

The girl moved slowly closer. Her fear was palpable. Talking in what she hoped to be a reassuring voice, Savannah continued. "My name is Savannah Thompson. I own a horse ranch near here. I came to bring you home, sweetie."

In a trembling voice, the girl whispered. "The man. He won't let us go."

Savannah struggled to remain calm. "What man, sweetie? Did you see a man here?"

Mandy vigorously nodded her head. "He chased me. Dropped me down the hole."

Savannah shivered visibly. Good God. They were in a heap of trouble. "Do you think you can climb back out, Mandy?"

"No, I tried. It's too high. I just fall again." She began to quietly cry.

"Come here, sweetie. It's okay now. I'll get us out of here. I won't let anything hurt you." Savannah prayed that her words would come true. Right then she had no idea how to manage getting them both out of the dark cavern.

The girl scooted up next to Savannah. Her shadowed eyes held fear, pain and a small glimmer of hope. She wished there was a way to wipe away the fear and pain, but knew on a deep level that she could only provide small comfort.

Reaching out with her right hand, Savannah lovingly stroked Mandy's cheek, then down over her shoulder-length hair. The small girl curled up against her side, seeking warmth and shelter. "That's right, sweetie. Let me hold you and make it all better."

They lay that way for what seemed like hours, but was most likely only minutes. They each drew warmth and comfort from the other as Savannah worked to gather her strength. Her body felt abused and uncooperative. "Mandy, sweetie. Help me sit up, okay. I want to get a good look around."

Supporting her left forearm with her right hand, Savannah struggled into a sitting position with Mandy's help. The small exertion had her gasping for breath. Concentrating fiercely, she put her remaining energy into getting to her feet.

Mandy rushed to her side as she swayed drunkenly. Her head felt like it was being crushed in a vice. Her stomach rolled with nausea. Taking slow, deep breaths, Savannah gained her balance. With great effort, she moved to the edge of the cavern and looked up into the early morning sunlight. She had no idea how far up the lip of the fissure was from where she stood. What she knew, with heartbreaking certainty, was that there was no way she could scramble up the nearly vertical chasm wall.

Backing up to the cavern wall, Savannah let herself slowly slide down until she was sitting. Emotions swirled tumultuously around in her head. She prayed that her baby had not been hurt during her fall. Working to calm her frazzled nerves, she searched for a way out of this situation.

It took several moments before she could focus her thoughts again. This was no time for weakness. She had to come up with a plan. Sheer determination gave her clarity and strength.

First things first. She had to do something to stabilize her forearm. Just looking at the obvious deformity made stomach acid rise in her throat. Peering around the dark cavern, she could see nothing useful. "Mandy, is there anything flat and hard I can use to hold my arm straight?"

Happy to have a task to perform, the girl jumped up. She moved into the narrow portion of the cavern. Soon Savannah lost sight of the girl as she was swallowed up by the inky darkness. Fear surged through her heart. She didn't want Mandy out of her sight.

Just when she was ready to call out, Mandy appeared carrying a piece of wood. It appeared to be the slat from a crate. "That's perfect, sweetie. Good job," she praised the girl.

After resting her forearm against her thigh, Savannah pulled the bandana from her head using her good hand. She held the cloth out to Mandy. "Okay, sweetie. Now I need you to find a sharp rock that will tear the cloth. We need two pieces."

It took several minutes for the girl to find a rock she felt was sufficiently sharp. She gave the task serious concentration. With great care she made a small cut in the material. Grasping with both hands, she ripped the material in two.

Taking several deep breaths, Savannah tried to prepare herself for the pain to come. Finally, she explained to Mandy what needed to be done. It took several minutes to reassure the girl that the arm had to be splinted.

Not wanting to scare the girl, Savannah clenched her teeth tightly, taking deep breaths through her nose. It took a supreme effort of will to keep from screaming when Mandy stretched her forearm out straight over the piece of wood. Following

Savannah's instructions she secured the board in place using the torn pieces of her bandana.

She fought valiantly to remain conscious. Her vision narrowed down into a small tunnel. Her jaw began to ache from the pressure she exerted. Her breath came rapidly through her nose, her chest heaving with the effort.

Giving Mandy a small half smile she leaned back against the cavern wall and passed out, once again giving in to the darkness that engulfed her senses.

* * * * *

Cord rode in endless circles around the huge property having no idea where to look. Eventually he gave up and returned to the ranch yard. The hands stood in the center of the yard looking confused and anxious.

"What the hell's going on? What are you doing here?" questioned Brock.

Dismounting before responding he told them what they had already surmised. "No time for questions! Savannah took off on Moon Dancer at some point during the night. I've been searching since before dawn. I haven't found any trace of them."

Jesse ran a hand through his hair, giving voice what they all were thinking. "What the hell has she gotten herself into now?"

The men quickly divided up into two search groups. Brock and Jesse would go on ATVs. Cord and Riley would go on horseback. They took long-range radios to stay in touch. Not knowing what they would find, each group also took a first aid kit and large bottles of water.

After discussing what areas of the ranch each group would cover, the grim-faced men headed out. One way or another they would find Savannah and bring her home. They all silently prayed that she would be in one piece.

Chapter Thirteen

ଚୈ

The light coming in the chasm seemed to have intensified from what she remembered. Savannah had no idea how long she had been out. If the worried look etched across Mandy's face was any indication, it had been quite some time.

Her body was stiff, sore, battered, bruised and broken. Her hands felt numb from the deep cuts. It took a great effort of will to concentrate on her relaxation exercises. She had to focus on a way out of this mess. No one knew where they were. It was up to her to figure something out.

Maybe if there was something they could use to climb up they could reach the top. "Mandy, is there anything else lying around in here? Any more boards? Maybe something we can use to help us climb up the wall?"

She forced her voice to be light and cheery, but the effort was wasted. Mandy did not seem the least bit comforted.

"No, there's nothing else in here. Just us."

Tears welled up in her big hazel eyes. Her lower lip trembled with trepidation.

"That's okay, sweetie. Come over here. I need a hug." She pulled the girl into a one-armed embrace. "Tell me about the man, sweetie. How did you get here?"

The tiny body trembled in her embrace. It took several moments for the girl to respond. When she did, her tale chilled Savannah to the bone. What kind of monster would terrorize and trap a small child?

Mandy talked wistfully about camping with her parents. Somehow she had gotten separated from them during a storm. She had walked around endlessly searching for her parents, probably in the wrong direction. After what she assumed to be two days, a man on a big black horse had chased her through the wilderness. From Mandy's description he had herded her like cattle toward the chasm. When she'd crouched at the top in the darkness, he had loomed over her tiny body. With a swift push Mandy fell down the opening, hearing his laughter trailing behind.

Savannah's body shuddered hearing the girl's tale of trauma. How frightened the poor child had been. This adult had not been there to rescue Mandy. His intent had been to torment the girl.

The next day he'd stood at the top of the cavern and tossed down a small brown paper bag. Inside was a small bottle of water and a flattened peanut butter and jelly sandwich. Each day the man came and dropped down a bag of water and food. Not enough to give her energy, but just enough for the girl to survive.

Mandy had no idea how long she had been in the cavern. What little concept of time she possessed had quickly fled. She expressed unwavering certainty that Savannah would get them out of there safely.

If only she shared in that certainty.

Tucking the small girl against her side, Savannah urged her to take a nap. She would need her strength. Fatigue and hunger pulled at the girl. Eventually, her breathing slowed as she slipped into a restless sleep.

They needed help. Savannah knew she could not do this alone. The pain made her thought process disjointed. She struggled to relax her mind. She had to find Cord. If she could reach him, she could direct him to their location. It had been pitch black, but she had a pretty good idea of where they were.

One of the techniques she often used was to picture a control room similar to an airplane cockpit, representing her body's control center. The small room contained a wall full of switches, dials and buttons. A chair sat before the panel where she could sit and adjust the different settings.

It took great effort to tamp down the pain enough to concentrate. Using all of her abilities, Savannah immersed her thoughts with pictures of the control room. It took much longer than normal until she finally found herself in the small room. Several warning lights flashed in shades of yellow, orange and red. The room wavered around the edges as she fought for control until it stabilized at last.

She could not touch anything here with her hands since she was just a misty apparition. Instead, everything had to be done with her mind. Prioritizing what needed to be done, she first concentrated on the pain meter. The black needle was stuck at the top of the dial.

Reaching out with her mind, Savannah worked at slowly lowering it to the bottom. With each trembling motion downward her body relaxed a little more. Tension and pain melted away, allowing her focus to become sharper.

Searching the panel she found what she needed, a silver toggle switch, which was neatly labeled "Cord". With all her mental strength, Savannah pushed on the switch, but it refused to budge. She applied more force. Soon sweat broke out on her brow, her body trembling with the effort, but there would be no giving up. Allowing other parts of her senses to shut down, she diverted more power to her task. Her muscles trembled.

Oh, God. Please help me. I have to reach him. It's the only way.

Abruptly she felt the slightest give in the switch. Sweat dripped down her face and into her eyes. With the tenacity of a pit bull after a bone, every part of her being focused on this one menial task. With a mental grunt the switch finally flipped upward, opening their link.

A vivid image of Cord's handsome face filled her mind. His turbulent eyes were darkened with emotion. Fear rolled off him in palpable waves. While she wanted to reassure him, Savannah knew she couldn't.

"*Cord,*" she cried out.

"*Thank God. Where are you, sugar? Are you okay?*" His powerful voice filled her mind, allowing the smallest spark of hope.

This would be the most difficult part. While she needed Cord's help, she did not want him to know how dire her situation was. They needed him calm and in control. "*No. I'm in some kind of chasm on Shadow Mountain. It's on Bar B land. One of the cowboys should be able to show you how to get here. I need you!*"

Silent tears of relief streamed down her face. Just seeing, feeling and sensing Cord reassured her, gave her hope. Somehow he would get to them, and bring them out of the cavern.

"*Savannah, are you okay? Are you hurt?*" he questioned impatiently.

"*Yes, I'm fine,*" she lied. "*Just a little banged up. Please hurry, Cord. There's a little girl. She's so afraid.*"

Relief washed over her with the assured tone of his next words.

"*I'm coming, sugar. I will bring you both home.*"

* * * * *

The men rode the ranch land in vain. There was no sign of Savannah. None of them had any experience as a tracker. The hoof prints they found could have been made during the night or last week for all they knew.

The immensity of the Shooting Star's land mass weighed heavily on Cord's mind. How the hell would he ever find Savannah? There was just too much ground to cover.

Looking over at Riley, he saw the man's face held a grim expression. Most likely the younger man's thoughts shadowed his own, but the determination in his eyes reassured Cord that Riley would not give up until they found Savannah. In a small way, seeing that helped ease his mind.

Sudden pain slammed into the side of his head. A mixture of fear, pain and exhaustion rushed through his body. He had no idea what was happening until a murky image of Savannah popped into his mind. Her dirty, tear-streaked face was a sight for sore eyes. She looked more beautiful to him than ever. Feeling her pain, he struggled to determine its source. Somehow she was blocking a great deal from him, refusing to let him see her injuries.

Keeping her image in the periphery of his mind, Cord turned to Riley. "Do you know how to find Shadow Mountain?"

Riley looked at him in surprise. "Sure, it's on the Bar B Ranch. How do you know about it though?"

"We don't have time for explanations right now, Riley. Savannah is there and there's a young girl with her. We have to hurry."

The other man looked at him with a shocked, deep blue gaze, not quite believing his words. "How the hell do you know that?"

Cord growled his impatience. "We don't have time for this. I just know. Radio the others to meet us there."

It took several moments for Riley to respond. Finally, he snapped into action. He passed the word on to Brock and Jesse. Taking the lead, he headed out rapidly over the countryside.

Relief flooded through Cord. Savannah had become too precious to him. There was no way he would lose her now. And there was another life at stake. He would not let them down.

* * * * *

Savannah's groggy mind was slow to wake up. Some unseen threat tickled at the back of her consciousness. As she slowly swam up from the depths of sleep, memories crashed down. Her left arm had become blessedly numb but her head still throbbed.

Stiffness had settled into her muscles from lying in the uncomfortable position. She could tell from the quality of light coming in through the chasm that time had moved on to late morning. The small weight nestled against her side made her wonder about her own child again.

Looking down at her jeans she was thankful there was no blood. Of course that didn't mean the baby was unharmed. *Please, God. Let my baby be alright. Give its injuries to me, just spare my child.*

Feeling a presence moving closer she reached out mentally to Cord. "*Is that you? Are you here?*" She tried to keep the fear out of their link but was certain she had failed.

"*What's going on, sugar? Is someone there?*"

Just hearing his voice in her head helped relax her stiff body slightly. "*I'm not sure. I feel someone close by. Where are you?*"

He didn't cut off his curse quickly enough. The terse obscenity rang through her head. "*Cord?*"

"*We're coming, sugar. Hang on for me. Be strong.*"

The link abruptly shut down when she heard someone moving over the ground near the chasm opening. Shading her eyes with her good hand, Savannah searched for the source of the noise.

Mandy whimpered next to her when a shadowy figure loomed above them. It was impossible to visually identify who was there since he was backlit by the sun but Savannah knew instantly.

"Wyatt?" she whispered.

His whiny voice grated on her already frazzled nerves. "Well, what do we have here? Looks like Alice fell down the rabbit hole." Maniacal laughter shattered the quiet.

Savannah tried to calm her raging emotions. "Wyatt, we need help. We're trapped down here."

He stared down at them silently for several moments. Mandy curled into a tight ball, rocking slightly. Savannah would give anything to spare the child this trauma.

Something was dropped down into the cavern. The package landed with a splat. "You'll just have to share for now. I didn't know I'd captured another little girl. I have to go, but I'll come back shortly. Then the three of us are gonna have a real good time."

His maniacal laughter sent cold tendrils of unease down her spine. The bastard was going to leave them trapped in the chasm. Hell, she knew with sudden clarity that he was the despicable piece of shit that had chased the scared little girl who lay curled up in the fetal position.

She could feel Cord tugging at their link, trying desperately to reestablish contact. The fear he felt for her was a powerful force but she held him back.

"Yes, I do believe it's time for us to get much closer, Savannah." With that, Wyatt disappeared as quickly as he'd arrived. She pointlessly screamed his name, but no other sounds came from above as she felt him moving further away.

The fear in her voice when she called his name scared the hell out of Cord. Then there was absolutely nothing. He mercilessly pushed Stormy to move faster. They had to reach Savannah quickly.

His mind brought thoughts to the surface that Cord would rather not have in his head. He wondered how he would survive if the unthinkable happened. Screaming at himself to focus on Savannah, he tried to reach her again. All he received was a strong sense of fear.

When they finally reached the blasted mountain he vaulted off Stormy's back, leaving her to graze with Moon Dancer. Taking the lead, he rushed up the steep slope. "We're looking for some kind of fissure, or chasm," he called over his shoulder.

It seemed that they climbed endlessly. The terrain varied greatly. When possible, he rushed headlong forward. His determination drove him steadily upward. Savannah was here somewhere and she needed him. He'd find her somehow.

* * * * *

With Mandy's help they moved further back into the chasm, out of sight of the rim above. Each slight movement sent sharp streamers of pain through her abused body. Nausea rolled through her stomach with each step.

She knew that moving away from the opening would not prevent whatever Wyatt had planned for them, but it made her feel better. She didn't want Mandy to experience looking up at their tormentor again.

It wasn't long after they were settled that they began to hear noises from above. Wyatt was back and this time it seemed he would be joining them in the cavern. Savannah pulled Mandy close to her side. "No matter what happens, I want you to keep your eyes closed, Mandy. If you get the chance to get away, run."

The girl began to protest, but Savannah cut her off short. "Don't worry about me. I can take care of myself. I want you to promise me, Mandy."

They did a pinky promise. Both of them looked up when something dropped down the cavern wall. Staring hard, Savannah finally was able to make out a rope ladder hanging along the wall. Shivers racked her body. She tried to be strong for Mandy, but it was nearly impossible.

Turning Mandy's face into her side, Savannah tried to provide what little protection she could. Mentally she sent an image to Cord of where she had been before she fell. That was all she could do. There was no time for anything else. When she opened her eyes, Wyatt stood at her feet.

"Well now, Savannah. It would appear that I finally have you where no one can interfere."

Disgust rolled over her in waves, threatening her sanity. She'd always known Wyatt Bodine was sick, but she'd thought him harmless. Savannah no longer had the luxury of that illusion. It was clear in his beady eyes that he meant her harm.

She sent a final, brief message to Cord. "*I'm sorry, Cord. I will fight hard, but I can't win this one. I love you!*" She did not give him time to respond, quickly slamming a mental door. She did not want to chance him receiving any images of whatever happened now.

"Don't hurt Mandy," she pleaded.

Wyatt stared at her for a moment—that strange, lopsided grin curling up one end of his mouth. "Well, maybe we can make a deal. If you're really nice to me and cooperate, I'll let her go. If you fight me, then you'll watch as I fuck her tight, virgin cunt."

He cackled wickedly at the look of horror that claimed Savannah's face. In her mind she flipped the switch to connect with Mandy. "*Don't listen to his words, honey. Everything will be fine. Just do as I say.*"

The girl did not respond, she just remained tightly curled against her side.

Wyatt pulled a long, wicked looking knife from his belt, then moved forward. "You're wearin' way too many clothes."

Grabbing a fistful of her sweatshirt, he cleanly sliced it down the middle. The remarkably sharp blade found little resistance. Moving to her feet he ran the blade up each leg until her jeans fell away from her body. She shivered as the cold steel cut away her panties, brushing over her skin in an icy cold caress.

"Wyatt. Let Mandy move out of the way."

He nodded his approval. Savannah spoke to the girl through the link first. "*No matter what you hear, do not look, Mandy.*"

Out loud she said, "Mandy, move over to the other side of the cavern."

The girl obeyed without a word or glance.

Thankfully, Wyatt ignored Mandy. He was too busy devouring Savannah's naked body with his eyes. Silently, Savannah said, "*Good girl. When he stops paying attention, I want you to go quickly up the ladder. Then I want you to run far away. There are some nice cowboys nearby who will help you, Mandy. You can trust them."*

She sent Mandy a mental picture of the five men so she wouldn't be afraid of them when they found her.

Wyatt roughly kicked her legs apart with his booted foot. She let out a small yelp, which he seemed to enjoy. Dropping to his knees he stared at her bare pussy lips, practically drooling.

As promised, to protect Mandy, she did not fight when his calloused hands began to manhandle her tender breasts. Savannah had done what she could to facilitate Mandy's escape. Now she would have to endure Wyatt raping her body to give her time to get away. She bit her lip to keep from crying out in revulsion, knowing it would only fuel his lust.

In her mind, Savannah went to another place. She pictured herself floating on her back in the lake. The water was warm and the sun shone down, heating her skin. The surface rippled occasionally as a fish jumped at flies.

Peace and serenity filled her every sense. Nothing but the water and sun existed for Savannah. She no longer felt Wyatt's nasty hands. All she could feel was the welcoming embrace of the cool water safely enveloping her mind and body.

* * * * *

Cord was distantly aware that Jesse and Brock had joined the search on the mountain. His entire being was focused on finding that damn fissure. The picture Savannah had sent was burned into his brain.

He almost ran right past the entrance when he approached from a different angle than she had shown him. A small noise made him stop and look around. Suddenly a small girl appeared out of the nearly camouflaged chasm rim. She whimpered and shrunk back upon seeing him.

Speaking as gently as possible, Cord tried to coax the frightened child forward.

"Honey, its okay. I'm a friend of Savannah's. My name is Cord. You can come out. Everything will be alright now."

A little head peeked out once again. The other men had moved up behind Cord. It was Riley who was finally able to gain her trust.

"Hi Mandy. I'm gonna take you home now, honey. It's okay. I'm a good cowboy. How about we get you a nice big hamburger and some french fries. Then we'll call your mom and dad and I'll drive you home." He crouched down to make himself less imposing, held out a hand and smiled brightly at the skittish girl. "Nothing can hurt you again, honey. Come on now. Let's get you home."

With a whimper, the girl surged up from the fissure and ran into Riley's outstretched arms, wrapping her legs around his waist, arms around his neck. With soothing words he held her close and began moving back down the mountain. "Have you ever ridden on a horse before, Mandy?"

The girl only shook her head.

"Well, you are going to like Star. He's a sweet horse who loves to give little girls rides." The big cowboy spoke in a poor John Wayne imitation.

Riley's constant chatter drifted away as he moved further down the mountain. Cord focused on the opening and moved forward. A rope ladder hung down the wall of the chasm. A muffled groan sent him into action.

He moved quickly down the ladder. It was making him crazy that he could no longer feel Savannah. When he reached the bottom, Cord let his eyes adjust to the dim light for a moment.

Movement at the far end of the cavern caught his attention. Killing rage coursed through his veins. Wyatt Bodine knelt between Savannah's legs, fumbling with his zipper. Savannah lay motionless, her clothes cut away.

Chapter Fourteen

۵

"Prepare to meet your maker, Bodine," he growled, then surged forward.

With a primal, animalistic cry, Cord sprang into action. He knew it would take a miracle to keep him from killing the no-account son of a bitch, and didn't hold out much hope of said miracle happening. Wyatt Bodine had dared to touch his woman. Big mistake. He would not receive any merciful, quick death. No, Cord would insure the bastard suffered severely, for a long, long time.

He was barely aware of Brock and Jesse moving behind him as a thick, blinding haze of rage took his mind. With superhuman strength, Cord grabbed the fat man under his arms, hauling him up and tossing him clear across the musty cavern.

The fact that Savannah still had not moved fueled his rage past reason. The killing instinct boiled within his blood, stoking his savage, primitive side. He became a wild animal protecting one of his pack. Blood would be shed.

Dropping on top of his prey, Cord began landing brutal blows to Wyatt's head and face. Seeing the man's blood begin to flow threw his surging hormones into a wild frenzy.

Brock and Jesse stood back watching the scene unfold. Any previously misconceived doubts about their foreman's feelings for their boss instantly evaporated. Make no mistake about it, Cord Black would kill for the woman he loved.

As they pulled him off the other man, Cord's fists still swung destructively with murderous force. Finally, Jesse shook him hard to bring Cord out of his primal state. "You can't kill him, cowboy. We want to see Wyatt rot in jail, not you. Besides, Savannah needs you."

At the mention of her name, Cord frantically sought out her still, lifeless form. He covered her naked torso with his T-shirt, being remarkably careful of her crudely splinted left arm and then checked for any other obvious injuries.

He found a knot on the back of her head where her hair was matted with dried blood. The assorted bruises and scrapes he found took nothing away from her beauty. With amazing tenderness, he scooped her limp form into his arms. The other men watched as he cradled her like a child within the shelter of his body. He would accept no assistance as he made his way slowly up the ladder.

Brock raced ahead on his ATV to call for an ambulance. Cord carried Savannah on the other vehicle. Their progress was slow as he tried to avoid the rougher, jarring terrain. Jesse rode Stormy, observing the two other men and their charges.

It became noticeably evident that Mandy had big, tough Riley wrapped around her little finger. During the entire trip back to the ranch house, Riley gave his undivided attention to her constant chatter. The precocious, eight-year-old princess regaled them with stories about school, friends and family.

Two bored-looking paramedics were waiting in front of the house. They foolishly attempted to remove Savannah from Cord's arms when he pulled up next to them. Following Brock's advice they allowed Cord to carry her into the ambulance and remain by her side.

At the hospital, the ER physician ordered multiple x-rays, a CT scan and various other tests. The broken arm was aligned and set in a fiberglass cast. The wounds in her hands were cleaned, stitched and bandaged. A nurse tried once again to run Cord off in order to bathe Savannah, but he turned the tables on her and took over the job.

When all the tests results were back the physician returned to the small cubicle. "The CT scan results were good. She has a mild concussion, but will recover fully. I will give you a referral for an orthopedist to follow up on the broken arm."

"Wait a minute," Cord said. "Why the hell hasn't she woken up yet if she's okay?" He nervously fingered the small velvet pouch in his pants pocket.

The physician nodded his head and seemed to consider the issue for a moment before speaking. "With a head injury we have to allow the patient time to heal while we keep watch. She may wake up in two minutes, two hours or two days. You must be patient, Mr. Black."

He looked over several of the papers attached to the clipboard he carried. "The blood work all came back normal. I'm going to order an ultrasound to check on the baby, but everything appears fine."

All four men stood staring, mouths hanging open at his last statement.

After the harried man left, Brock stepped forward. "I don't know if you have realized it, Cord, but Savannah is very intuitive. She also has a way of escaping into her mind when something causes her great emotional pain."

Riley nodded in agreement. "Talk to her, Cord. If anyone can pull her back, it's you."

Cord considered the men who had become her adopted family. Their love and concern for Savannah was clearly visible on their faces, but they were right. The only person she needed right now was him. He stood in quiet contemplation for only a moment. Ever the man in charge, he began issuing instructions to the others.

"You boys go back to the ranch. Wait with Mandy for her parents to arrive. Better call Zeke and Tamara to let them know what's going on too. I'll call later and let you know how Savannah's doing."

The look on his face left no room for discussion. Reluctantly the other men left Savannah in Cord's capable hands and headed home.

Cord remained lost in deep thought as he weighed the other men's words. Could that possibly be her big, dark, hairy secret—that she had some kind of premonitions? Why would something like that bother her so much? And why had she kept their baby a secret? Did she even realize she was pregnant when she went running off in the middle of the night? Why was she so terrified of telling him?

He had an abundance of questions. Unfortunately there were no answers forthcoming. His lip trembled slightly. God, he'd come so close to losing her. The urge to possess and protect her nearly overwhelmed Cord. Seeing her lie lifelessly on the stretcher held his heart in a painful, tight fist of fear.

When Savannah was being settled into a private room, the orderly refused to allow Cord to carry her from the stretcher to the bed. Instead four employees lifted her with the sheet, efficiently moving her over.

Pulling a chair up next to the bed, Cord took her right hand in his. With innate tenderness he caressed her sweet face, tucking long, golden strands of hair behind her ears.

What the heck? Stranger things have happened. Using a hushed tone, Cord began speaking to Savannah. He leaned in close, continuously stroking her face. The softly spoken words brushed across her pale skin.

"It's time to come back, sugar. Everything is okay now. Wyatt is gone, locked safely away where he can't hurt you again. Come back to me, Savannah. I need you. Our baby needs you. I love you, sugar!"

The litany of words was recited countless times. He pleaded for her to listen, to come back to him. Not once did he stop speaking or tenderly stroking her face. Nurses came and went unnoticed. Day moved into night. Eventually he fell into a light, twilight sleep, his head resting on her undamaged arm, still muttering affirmations.

* * * * *

"Riley," Mandy whined. "Star's hungry. He needs some apples. Pllleeeaaassseee, can I give him s'more apples?"

Looking down into that sweet, angelic little face, sparkling hazel eyes brightened by laughter, there was nothing he could deny her. "Sure, honey. Go grab another one from the house."

Riley watched as she skipped off happily across the yard. Thankfully, it didn't seem that there would be any lasting effects from her ordeal. Maybe Wyatt Bodine would get to live after all. Although, Riley would do everything possible to insure that his life was spent looking out from behind thick steel bars.

A car coming up the drive drew his attention. A tight fist wrapped around his heart at the realization that this must be Mandy's parents come to take her home. He hated the idea of watching her leave. The ranch would never again feel the same without her angelic presence.

Mandy walked out on the porch, dropping the apple with a squeal upon seeing her parents. She raced forward as they were getting out of the car and jumped into her mother's open arms. There was no mistaking the resemblance. Mandy Morton was the spitting image of her momma.

Mandy talked a mile a minute about Star, the ranch and Riley. He walked forward, pasting a big, welcoming grin on his face. "Howdy, Mister and Missus Morton. My name's Riley…"

Before he could react, Riley was swept into a fierce hug.

"Call me Sandy, please. Oh, God. Riley, I can't thank you enough for saving my baby…"

He stopped her words with a shake of his head. "Nothin' to thank me for, Sandy. Your daughter is a bright, wonderful girl. It has been my pleasure to have her company for a little while."

Mandy's father reached out a hand, which he firmly shook.

"Craig Morton, nice to meet you. There is no way I can ever repay you for what you've done." Holding up a hand, he effectively silenced Riley's protest.

"If there is ever anything, and I mean absolutely anything that you need, I want you to call me."

"Thank you, Craig. There is one thing…"

"Name it and it's yours."

He didn't hesitate for a second. "Well, Mandy really likes the ranch and the horses. It would be nice if y'all could come up once in a while and spend some time here. We'd all really like that." Riley gestured to the other cowboys who had crowded near. The men all nodded their agreement.

Craig gave Riley an assessing look, then broke into a broad grin that split his face, reaching all the way to his deep brown eyes. "She got to ya, didn't she?" He looked down at his daughter lovingly. "What do you think, Mandy Pandy? Would you like to visit the ranch and your friends again?"

She hopped up and down excitedly. "Pllleeeaaassseee, Daddy. Can we please? And can we bring apples for Star and the other horses? Can we, Daddy?"

"If you'd like to, angel, then I think we should drive up as often as possible."

Mandy squealed with delight and raced away. "I've gotta tell Star."

Brock ushered all the adults onto the porch where he'd set out a carafe of coffee, and some pound cake. They learned that Craig and Sandy loved the outdoors, hiking and camping. At least once a month they went to a nearby park, which is where Mandy had become separated from them.

"Riley, what about the cabin near the lake?" Jesse asked. "That would be perfect for weekend outings, don't ya think?"

Pushing the pesky, stray locks from his forehead, Riley nodded his head. "I think that's a wonderful idea. You'd have privacy there, but be close enough so Mandy could come over for her riding lessons. That is, if you approve, of course?"

"Oh, Riley. That would be wonderful, if it's not too much of an imposition. I know Mandy can be somewhat... overwhelming," Sandy said.

"I would really like to teach her to ride."

They talked and got to know each other as long as Mandy would permit. Before long she dragged her parents off to meet Star. They took a tour of the ranch in Jesse's truck while Brock ordered pizza for supper.

The Mortons fell in love with the little cabin on first sight. After dinner they settled in for the evening. Everyone was having such a good time they decided to wait until the following afternoon to drive home. They wanted to have a chance to hear about Savannah's condition and possibly meet the woman who had so selflessly risked her own life for their child.

* * * * *

Cord woke up with a start. Pale streaks of moonlight shining through the window cast Savannah with an ethereal glow. She appeared so small and fragile tucked into the hospital bed. Thankfully some color had returned to her face, but her normal healthy sparkle was painfully absent.

Lovingly, he rubbed a big hand over her soft belly. His child lay within the shelter of her womb. Their baby. He was going to be a father. Love swelled up through his body, pushing his heart up into his throat.

Please, God. She's got to be okay.

He'd finally found the woman of his dreams and she was going to give him a child. Emotions swirled through Cord. He was awestruck, amazed and totally, completely, one hundred percent in love with his sweet, wild cowgirl. Nothing would ever change that. His love would only grow stronger.

Cord pictured the two of them sitting on the front porch in rocking chairs, old and gray-haired, watching their grandchildren play in the yard. The Shooting Star Ranch would be the perfect place to raise a family and watch them grow. Having Savannah by his side for the rest of his life was the sweetest thing he could imagine.

A single tear drifted down his rugged cheek, turned silver in the moonlight. It trembled and clung to his chin for a moment before falling onto Savannah's hand.

"Come back to us, Savannah. We need you," he whispered.

Cord lowered his head to the mattress, lost in his thoughts. At first the feel of fingers threading through his hair didn't register. When short fingernails massaged his scalp he let out an anguished cry.

Savannah watched his head slowly rise until she could see his beautiful gray eyes, shimmering with unshed tears. Panic clutched at her heart. Something must be terribly wrong for her strong cowboy to feel such a depth of emotion.

"Cord? What is it? What's wrong?" she asked in a soft tone.

For the first time in his life, Cord found himself struck mute. He had no words to adequately express his feelings.

"Nothing now, sugar," he finally said in a raspy voice. "Everything's perfect."

"You seem so sad?"

He shook his head, setting the chocolate brown waves in motion for a moment. "I've never been happier in my life. Just seeing those big brown eyes again is a wonderful sight, sugar."

Climbing up onto the bed, he pulled her into the shelter of his body. "I was so terrified that I wouldn't see them again. Tomorrow we'll talk about you stealing off by yourself into the night on some crazy whim. Right now I just want to hold you."

"Is Mandy all right?"

"She's fine, sugar. Got those cowboys of yours wrapped around her little finger." He tenderly stroked her cheek, reveling in how perfect it felt to have her tucked up against his chest. "Go to sleep now, Savannah. You need to rest."

Sometime later he remembered his promise and called the ranch. The boys were ecstatic to hear that Savannah was awake. They promised to visit the next day and bring the Mortons to meet her.

Cord held onto her through the night as she slept peacefully in his arms. He felt a new determination that Savannah Thompson would soon be Savannah Black and would never again be far from his side.

Chapter Fifteen

ജ

After eating breakfast and showering in the morning, Savannah felt much more human. The nurse told her that as long as she continued to do well they would let her go home in the afternoon. While Cord showered, she called home and talked to her boys. She felt better just hearing their voices.

Riley had spoken in great detail about the Mortons. From what he said, Savannah was sure she'd like the couple. She was thankful to hear how well Mandy was doing. It seemed that the girl suffered no ill effects from her ordeal.

Sitting in a chair near the window, she became quickly frustrated with trying to tug a brush through her knotted hair. When the coarse bristles hit the swollen area of her scalp, she cried out in pain and irritation.

Cord rushed out of the bathroom. For a few moments he just stood stock-still and stared at the picture she made. Golden rays of sunlight played over her hair, making the thick strands shimmer. A pale glow surrounded her silhouette, giving her an angelic appearance. Her quiet curses and rough tugging were anything other than angelic.

He went to her when she slammed the brush down on the table and muttered a curse. Picking up the offending instrument, Cord gently began working the tangles out of the silken tresses. After a few silent moments of reflection he asked, "Are you ready to talk yet?"

Here we go, she thought.

"Um, sure."

Expecting to receive a lecture about her wild ways, Savannah was taken back by his question.

"What is it that you've been hiding from me?"

Oh, God. Okay, you can do this. It was bound to come up sooner or later. Might as well just spit it out.

She wasn't ready for this. Wasn't ready to watch him turn away from her, but she couldn't think of any way to stall other than playing ignorant. She knew that wouldn't work with Cord.

"Whatever it is, it doesn't matter. It can't change the way I feel about you, but it's driving a wedge between us. So just tell me. What's your big, scary secret, sugar?"

Taking several deep breaths, she worked to calm her chaotic nerves. Going through her relaxation techniques helped somewhat. By the time she began talking it was in a detached, uninflected tone.

"I guess it's best to start at the beginning."

Cord just nodded.

She told him about her confusion as a child when other people did not see the things that she did in her head. It had thrown her young mind for a loop how she could know things before they happened. She related stories of preventing friend's injuries and finding missing objects. Leaving out no details, Savannah related everything to Cord. She told him about her talks with her grandmother and how the wise old woman was the only person with whom she could talk freely. Her feelings of isolation, loneliness and not fitting in were all spoken of without emotion.

The possible power of her abilities was an unknown factor. They were not anything she had ever tried to develop or learn how to utilize. Her "second sight" had always seemed more of a curse than a tool.

Cord felt pride when she told him about helping to rescue the abducted child by using her visions. When she talked about the aftermath of that selfless act he wanted to punch someone. How could people be so cruel? Her friends had ostracized her because of their stupid fears and her hometown had driven her away with their morbid curiosity.

His heart melted for the confused girl she had been. He understood now why she was so terrified of telling him about her not so well-hidden secret. She didn't know that the cowboys all suspected she had some type of extraordinary, intuitive capacity.

It made him crazy to watch her shut down, become so mechanical. How could she think he would be like those narrow-minded people? He'd never turn away from her like her so-called friends had.

When she finally finished, he dropped to one knee before her chair. Her hands were clasped in tight fists, her knuckles had turned white. With great tenderness he took her hands, slowly working them open. God, they felt so cold. It felt as if telling her secret had taken the life force right out of the normally larger than life woman.

Cupping her hands in his own, Cord rubbed and blew on them until they began to warm. He stroked his hands over her arms, giving her some of his warmth, but it was no good. He had to reach her on a deeper level.

Effortlessly, he scooped her up into his arms and leaned back against the wall, sitting on the floor. Cord held her tightly across his lap, then tilted her face toward his own. "Savannah. It's okay, sugar. I'm not going anywhere. Your visions don't scare me. I'm not afraid of your abilities. They're part of what makes you who you are and I love everything about you."

He could tell by the spark of hope in her big brown eyes that he was getting through her protective barriers. A little of the tension left her body but she was still unsure. Her feelings were clearly visible on her heart-shaped face.

"I love you, Savannah. I love your wild lust for life, even though it makes me nervous. I love how we can feel each other even when were not together. I love your playful side and when you get very serious. I really like the images that flow from you into my mind when you are turned on. I love it that your visions let you help people and that you do so without a thought to yourself. I love everything about you, sugar!"

Love shone in her eyes. Silent tears sluiced down her cheeks unnoticed, as hope brightened her watery gaze.

"You're not afraid that I can read your thoughts? Not worried that I will see your deepest secrets? Don't you feel like your privacy will be invaded?"

Her question pulled at his heart. Cord shook his head slowly. While he spoke, he brushed away her tears. "Savannah, I already told you. You are everything to me. I'm not afraid, or worried. I have no secrets from you, but I also know you'd never invade my privacy."

She looked absolutely stunned and incredibly gorgeous. He couldn't hide a smile when he asked his next question. "Is there something else you need to tell me, sugar?"

Unconsciously, Savannah's hand stroked her abdomen in a protective gesture. She gasped and sputtered, but was unsuccessful in forming any coherent words.

"Its okay, sugar. I love you!"

Reaching into his shirt pocket, Cord pulled out a small piece of paper. A dark shadow of ink was visible through the glossy white sheet.

The vision of a baby's profile filled her mind. Then she saw their son as a towheaded toddler with brilliant blue-gray eyes and a beautiful, cherub face. He would have her spirit and his father's strength, the perfect combination of the two of them.

With a gasp she said, "He's beautiful. Looks just like you. How'd you know?"

Cord turned the sonogram picture so that Savannah could see their son's image.

"The doctor assured me the baby was unharmed. The girl that did the sonogram gave me his first picture."

He was silent while Savannah studied his eyes.

"How do you feel about this?"

"Damn, woman. Haven't you been listening? You shouldn't have to ask, but I guess I haven't really expressed my feelings. Right now I don't know how to describe what I'm feeling. Pride, elation, joy, love. There are no words that can do justice to explain my emotions."

Looking into his expressive eyes, Savannah saw everything he couldn't formulate the words to convey. Like magic, the heavy weight she'd not even realized was her constant companion for longer than she could remember lifted away. For the first time in her life, the visions that haunted her did not crowd her when she relaxed. She felt free, light, elated and truly loved.

Cord Black loved her, visions and all. She'd trusted him to answer her call and come to her rescue. How had she ever survived without feeling such unconditional love and acceptance for so long?

"I love you, Cord. I didn't fathom just how much until this moment."

His tempting lips spread into a dazzling grin.

"So, does that mean you'll marry me?"

Savannah stuttered, unable to believe what she had heard.

"W-Was...th-that a proposal?" she stammered.

The room tilted and swirled as she was lifted and placed back into the chair. Cord knelt on one knee at her feet. "Let's make sure there's no mistake."

He took her left hand, brushing a brief kiss over her knuckles. "Savannah Thompson, I love you more than life. You're everything that's precious to me. And you're as close to heaven as I'm ever gonna get. You're my every prayer and desire fulfilled. Will you do me the honor of becoming my wife?"

A small, deep blue velvet pouch appeared in his hand. Opening the drawstring top, he upended the pouch over his open palm. The sunlight streaming in through the window refracted colored shards of light across the room from a large marquise diamond ring.

Savannah gasped. Her good hand flew up to stroke the pendant nestled between her breasts.

"Oh my God. It's a beautiful ring and a beautiful proposal, but I won't marry you just because I'm pregnant. I want more than that."

He raked his fingers through his wavy hair, clearly frustrated.

"Damn it, sugar. I had this ring in my pocket before I knew about the baby. The whole reason I came back to the ranch was to ask you to marry me. The baby is an added bonus."

Sinking to her knees, she threw her arms around Cord, almost knocking him out with the cast. She buried her face in his neck, holding onto him fiercely.

"Should I take that as a yes?"

Leaning back, Savannah began raining loud, smacking, open-mouthed kisses all over his face in between words. "Yes…yes…yes. Oh God…yes. I've waited so long, dreamed so long. I'm not letting you get away."

He cradled her close while his hot, eager tongue explored the depths of her silken mouth. She was his now and he'd let nothing come between them.

* * * * *

Zeke paced around the cold, sterile waiting area. The mint green walls, with their thick, plastic wallboard were depressing enough. Add in the geometric pattern of blue, green and peach, it became enough to make you sick. But that was not the end of the offensive assault on the senses. The uncomfortable chairs bolted to the floor were covered with purple vinyl cushions.

If you weren't already feeling sick when you came to this hospital, you sure would be after spending any amount of time in the hideous waiting room. The vending machine coffee was acidic enough to eat a hole through the toughest stomach lining. Before long they would have to drag him into the ER to stop the internal bleeding. And the strong smell of antiseptic was making his throat close up.

He looked up with the sound of the automatic glass doors swooshing open. The ragtag group of friends walking together was a sight for sore eyes.

"'Bout time y'all got here. The Nazi nurse at the desk won't tell me a damn thing and this room is about to make me sick, not to mention the coffee."

Tamara rushed forward and launched herself into his arms. He caught her easily. Holding her close, Zeke took comfort from her familiar form pressed tightly against his body.

"Quit your bitching, cowboy." She gave him a sultry smile. "Damn, but I've missed you."

Before he could respond, Tamara had seized his mouth in a hot, needy kiss. In his peripheral vision, he could see the other boys shifting restlessly. When they finally broke apart she turned to face their friends.

"Now don't go getting all riled up. Come on. Let's go see how they're treating our girl."

One of the nurses was stupid enough to try to stop them. She'd said only two visitors were allowed at a time. There were eight of them, including the Mortons. And none of them was willing to stand around the abysmal waiting room.

They found the room easily enough. The door stood wide open. Zeke was the first one in. When he stopped suddenly, Tamara crashed into his back.

"What the hell?" she asked.

Peeking around his broad back she saw Cord and Savannah kneeling on the floor, wrapped tightly around each other. She cleared her throat loudly and stepped around Zeke.

"We interrupting something?" she innocently asked.

The pair pulled apart. Cord stood, helping Savannah to her feet. Only after wiping away her tears did he turn his attention to the large group filling the doorway.

"Yeah, you are. But don't let that stop you."

He laughed as the tenacious, little pit bull marched boldly forward. Tamara didn't stop until she had Savannah locked in a protective hug.

"Damn it, woman. Just look at what a mess I am. Dark circles under my red, puffy eyes. You can't go making me worry about you like that."

Savannah just shook her head, too choked up for words.

"And why are you crying? Is this big, knothead upsetting you?" She gave Cord a stern frown.

Smiling brightly, Savannah merely held up her left arm. The hot pink fiberglass cast held her friend's attention for only a moment. As soon as she noticed the big diamond on her third finger, Tamara squealed with delight.

"Oh, hell no. This means we're going to have to put up with his sorry ass for a while. Well, you're gonna have to teach him to relax a little," she teased.

Leaning in to her friend, Tamara whispered, "Congratulations, sweetheart. I'm so happy for you."

Before she knew what had happened, Savannah was being passed from one tight embrace into another. Finally, she found herself standing in front of Mandy. She started crying again as she hugged the little girl close.

"I'm so glad you're alright."

Mandy broke out into seemingly endless chatter. She told Savannah about riding Star with Riley and feeding the big, sorrel gelding apples. She talked about sleeping in the lakeside cabin and how Riley had invited them to come and stay as often as possible.

Quickly, a picture formed of how taken she had become with the prankster cowboy. When Mandy finally stopped for a breath, Savannah introduced herself to Sandy and Craig. They couldn't stop thanking her for everything she'd done to save their daughter.

Craig shook her good hand. "It appears that congratulations are in order. I wish you every happiness the world has to offer, Savannah."

Everyone crowded around the small room. The talk was light and happy. Savannah sat looking over the large group. This was her family. They were a rather eclectic group, but they all belonged to her. No matter what else happened, she knew they would only grow closer over the years. They all belonged together.

She glimpsed visions of their future. The group would grow over the years as they married and children were born. One thing would remain constant, however. They would always be together at the ranch. If they left, it would only for short periods of time. She knew then that she had to find a way to make the Mortons a permanent part of her family.

Tuning back into the conversation she was given the answer. Craig Morton was a certified accountant. He loved his work, but hated his job. *Perfect.*

"Then you ought to quit," she said with authority.

All conversation in the room ceased. Her boys could all tell something important was about to happen.

"That would be nice, but I can't just quit. I have to support my family," Craig said with a chuckle.

"No problem. I need someone to manage the ranch finances for me. It's become too much of a job for me to handle myself as the ranch grows. There are the financial accounts, payroll and taxes. You'll work with us. It's obvious how much you all love the ranch."

Everyone remained silent, so she continued. "You can start out in the lakeside cabin, but the ranch is huge. You pick the site.

My cowboys are right handy with building things. And you'll need a bigger place once the twins come anyway."

Sandy stared at her in amazement. "Twins?"

"Uh huh. But that's a year off yet. The boys will have plenty of time to finish the house first."

Mandy hopped up and down looking like she had to pee really badly. "Daddy, say yes, pllleeeaaassseee. Oooooh, please say yes."

Craig looked around in a daze of confusion. "I, well…"

He looked at his wife. "What do you think, honey."

Sandy interlocked her fingers with his. "I think it's a dream come true."

"Um, well then I guess we accept," Craig said.

Cord smiled brightly at the obviously overwhelmed man. "Don't worry, you'll get used to it," he stated, earning the riotous laugher of all the men in the room.

"Zeke will be back during school breaks and then permanently when he graduates. That just leaves Tamara we have to work on," Savannah said with a bright smile.

"Wh–what?" Tamara gasped.

Savannah gave her friend a stern look. "I need all of my family close. And I'm gonna need your help when the baby comes. I certainly can't rely on the boys to help take care of my son."

Tamara just continued to stare. A stunned look had settled over her delicate features.

"You don't spend much time at the bookstore. The manager you hired does a great job. The foreman's cabin is perfect for you. Of course, you'll want to redecorate though."

As she surveyed the people gathered around her, Savannah saw confusion from most of them. "It's simple. You all are my family. The ranch is huge. There's plenty of room for everyone. I want you all there."

Chapter Sixteen

∞

God, it felt so good to be home. Tamara and the boys had set up elaborate decorations and the welcome home party lasted well into the night as the margaritas flowed like water. The Mortons ended up staying the night again. In the morning they'd head home so Craig could quit his job and they could get ready to move.

Looking around the room, Savannah reveled in how right this felt. This is how it was supposed to be. Everyone she loved laughing happily together. She still felt someone was missing, but she'd figure it out.

Strong arms wrapped around her waist from behind. She was pulled up against the broad expanse of a warm chest. When he kissed her neck, shivers of anticipation coursed down her spine.

"You look tired, sugar. Ready for bed?" Cord asked, while brushing kisses along her neck.

"Mmm. Ready for bed, but not to sleep," she replied.

She grinned as his cock jerked to attention against her back. Cord raised his head. His voice boomed out through the room, drawing everyone's attention.

"Party's over everyone. Savannah needs her rest."

She had a difficult time suppressing her laughter. The house cleared quickly. Everyone headed off for the night after hugs and kisses were shared.

They made their way through the house turning off lights as they went. She felt content just knowing they would all remain close by. She also felt content from sharing such a mundane nightly task with Cord. All too easily she could picture them going through the same routine every night for the rest of their lives.

"I know you didn't bargain for all this, but it feels so right to me, Cord."

He brushed a kiss across her right hand. "Then it is right, sugar. Whatever makes you happy makes me happy. I kind of like having our friends close. That way I know there's always someone to watch out for you and the kids."

Her musical laughter filled the air. "Kids, huh. Just how many kids were you thinking about having?"

"Hmm, at least four. By the time they grow up, it's gonna take at least that many to manage this growing ranch."

She laughed lightly. "Planning ahead are you. What if they don't want ranch life?"

It was his turn to laugh. "Savannah, you're not the only one who sees things. I just know they will want to stay close. And I know they will all love the ranch. If they want something else, that's fine too, but I just don't see it happening."

They spent several hours lying in bed, talking about everything and anything. They had so much to catch up on, so much to learn about each other. Savannah told him about her time at the bed and breakfast and her friend Millie. She told him how lost she'd felt without him.

When Cord talked about his sister, Savannah surprised him by suggesting that she move out to the ranch. Since Stephanie's work hosting websites was all done on the computer, it didn't really matter where she lived.

They talked about the scene she had walked in on in the bunkhouse and her concerns for Tamara. Savannah had hoped she'd pick one of the cowboys and settle down. She'd never imagined she'd start some wild group thing with all of them.

"Come on, you can't tell me you've never fantasized about having a ménage a trois," Cord teased. "Being pleasured by two or three men. Having all your erogenous zones stimulated at once."

They shared their fantasies, dreams and realities with each other. Savannah could not remember ever having felt so close to anyone. It was wonderful to be able to finally tell someone everything without fear of rejection.

"You know, maybe I should try a ménage," she teased. "We could get one or two…"

Her scream cut through the quiet night, followed closely by her musical laughter. Cord flipped her over with lightning speed, pinning her to the bed with his body.

"No way, sugar. Let's make sure there's no mistake here. This body belongs to me and only me. No other man gets in here," he said, cupping her mound in his hand.

"Hmm, what if I brought another woman into bed with us?"

A contemplative look settled on his handsome features. "Now that has some possibilities."

Suddenly, his head snapped sideways when a pillow forcefully hit him on the side of his head. They played for several minutes until Cord ended up between her legs, his erect cock nestled against the warmth of her mound. Then they both became serious, intense heat burning through their flesh.

Every time he touched her, tasted her, the same intense electrical current passed between their bodies. And it still amazed him how perfectly they fit together as if made for each other. They were supposed to be together. Cord had never been more certain of anything in his life. This was his woman, forever.

Savannah wondered what put the contemplative look in his eyes.

"Penny for your thoughts." His mouth curled up in the devilish smile that never failed to make her heart beat quicker. Looking down between their bodies to where his cock nestled against her hip, she clarified, "And not that thought."

"Hmm. If I really think hard about something, form an image in my mind, can you see it?"

Savannah's whole body tensed. Here it comes. He was worried about her reading his thoughts. Then the worry would become worse no matter what, and he'd begin to pull away. She wasn't ready to give him up, not when they'd come so far.

She couldn't keep things from him any longer. She wouldn't do that to him. She loved him too much. Taking a deep breath she braced herself for the inevitable.

"That depends on a few things. First of all, I can't just invade your mind. If you want me to see something, I should be able to, but not unless you allow it to happen."

His response shocked Savannah.

"Okay, well I want you to see this, and you asked what my thoughts were. Look at what I'm picturing, sugar. Share this with me."

Closing his eyes, Cord rested his head against her breast. He focused his thoughts, and hoped she saw the pictures that went through his mind.

He started with a sunset scene. All the people important to them were gathered to witness their wedding vows. After being pronounced man and wife, they climbed up onto their horses and rode away into the setting sun.

In the next image, Savannah sat in a rocking chair, a pale-haired baby nestled to her breast. She hummed softly while their child nursed. Cord stood behind the chair massaging her shoulders, a look of intense pride on his face.

Then he saw the two of them working side by side in the corral with a horse. In the ranch yard, several children of varying ages played together with reckless abandon.

Finally, he saw an aged Savannah and himself sitting on the porch swing. They watched their children working the land they all loved so much. They sat with their fingers intertwined and shared a passionate kiss.

Love surged through the unique link they shared. Everything Savannah had seen through his eyes entwined her heart more firmly with Cord's. Their lives would be a patchwork of shared experiences, happiness and joy. Sure they'd have their trials and tribulations, but the strength of their love would see them through anything.

"Oh yes, Cord. That's what I see too."

* * * * *

The days became a blur for the three women working diligently to plan the wedding. Savannah was thankful to have Craig handling the financial accounting. Having that very tedious, time-consuming task out of the way allowed her to become consumed with planning.

Her dress was being custom-made in Billings, requiring multiple trips to the city for fittings. Tamara usually came along during these trips for company and for her own fittings of her bridesmaid dress.

On one such trip, Savannah expressed her concern for Tamara and the four cowboys. She was worried that all of them would end up hurt. The future was unclear for the group of friends. She was careful to make sure her friend did not realize she'd witnessed one of their sexual sessions.

"You have no idea what an incredible experience it is to be loved by four men," Tamara stated, unashamed. "There is no erotica book out there that can do justice to the decadence of four tongues, eight large hands, four big cocks seeing to your every pleasure. I don't know if I'll ever be able to achieve satisfaction with just one man again."

Savannah could somewhat understand her friend's raging desires. Over the past year her favorite fantasy had been to walk naked into the bunkhouse while the boys were all showering and initiate a group encounter. She hadn't entertained any of her fantasies since Cord had become part of her life. Although the experience would certainly be incredible, she was content just being with her sexy lover.

Images of the night she had walked in on the group of friends pleasuring each other roamed through her mind. Her body tingled from scalp to toes with sensations generated by the forbidden images. She envied Tamara, and the incredible pleasure her friends found together, but still she worried.

Just the thought of that night made Savannah hot. The bare lips of her pussy were soaked with hot cream. She prayed the scent of her sex would not reach her friend. Thankfully the warm summer weather rushing through the open windows should quickly dissipate any smell. Dealing with her soaked panties during her fitting would be a whole different problem.

Thankfully, they had arrived in Billings early. Tamara suggested some shopping while they waited. Never one to turn down a chance to hit the mall, Savannah headed toward the large complex of shops.

A trip to Victoria's Secret solved her immediate problem. A small fortune later she had a new wardrobe of bras, panties, teddies and sleepwear. She even picked up a very racy garnet-colored bikini. The little, triangle top provided easy access to her full breasts with ties in the front, back and neck. A devilish grin settled across her lips every time she considered how Cord would react to the sexy, little swimsuit.

Tamara had also indulged in some new, seductive garments to entice the cowboys. Savannah did not want to think about the boys drooling over her beautiful little friend.

As had become their custom, the girls ended the trip with dinner out. Tonight they chose a local steakhouse for their dining pleasure. It was a favorite with her cowboys and coming here made her think again of her close-knit group of friends, her adopted family.

A busboy was busy lighting tiki torches surrounding the front entrance of the restaurant as the girls drove up. Valet parking attendants quickly opened the door of the huge Hummer, lending the girls a helping hand down from the high seats.

Savannah noticed the appreciative glances they received as they were led through the large restaurant to a table at the center of the room. The two attractive friends were accustomed to drawing male attention when together. Add in that they were dressed to the nines and that attention drastically increased.

Savannah's long, curvy body and golden blonde hair contrasted perfectly with Tamara's petite body and dark mahogany tresses. They exuded sexual confidence and grace as they walked to the chairs held out for them. Neither paid any heed to the lustful looks they received.

Before they had even finished perusing the menu, drinks had been sent to their table by three men seated across the room. With a bright smile the girls held up their drinks in a mock toast to the men before tasting the crisp white wine. Savannah figured one glass of wine wouldn't hurt the baby.

They laughed deeply, enjoying the simple pleasure of the shared meal while silently soaking up the male attention like rays of sexual power. By the time they left both women were anxious to get back to their men.

It was late when they finally got back to the ranch. Walking up the porch steps, Savannah heard familiar female laughter coming from inside. Throwing the door open she raced inside, immediately catching the comforting scents of vanilla and cinnamon.

She found Cord seated at the kitchen table finishing off a piece of fresh baked coffee cake. The stern look she attempted to give him was effectively negated by the sheer joy in her sparking brown eyes.

"Cord Black, I'm ashamed of you. My friend comes over to visit, and you put her to work in the kitchen. What is wrong with you?"

Millie jumped up, a bright smile lighting up her sweet face.

"Now, leave the boy alone. You don't think a skinny, little thing like him could stop me from doing what I want?"

They shared a brief hug. Savannah pulled back with a questioning look in her eyes. "What are you doing here? How did you find me? Are you here for a visit?"

The words came out rapid fire from her with barely a breath in between. Mille laughed heartily. "Slow down, honey. Give me a chance here."

She waited a moment until she had Savannah's full attention. Millie looked up at Tamara, nodding in greeting. "From the looks of all the skinny people around here, I've come just in time. How's anyone supposed to have energy without the proper fuel."

Crooking her finger at Tamara she said, "Sit down over here now, gal. We need to fatten you up some."

Tamara smiled and did as instructed. Mille served both women large chunks of the warm coffee cake with large, cold glasses of milk. The plump woman patted Cord's shoulder as she put another huge serving of the confection on his plate.

"Growing boys need to eat well," she instructed.

After she seated herself, Millie looked toward Savannah. "Your sweet man here tracked me down and offered me a job cooking for the growing ranks here at the Shooting Star. Besides, you're gonna be busy taking care of that babe when he comes."

She looked deeply in Savannah's eyes. "I reckon that works for you, honey?"

Cord watched as her face took on a whole new light. There was nothing in the world that could compare to the radiance of Savannah's face when she was happy. He would do whatever was necessary to keep that look in place for the rest of her life. He'd do anything to make sure his incredible woman had everything she ever wanted, everything she ever needed, regardless if the need were realized or not. There was nothing he would deny her. He almost lost her once, now he'd do anything to ensure she remained his.

"That's a wonderful idea," she enthusiastically agreed. "It will be so good to have you here with us, Millie." In that instant, Savannah knew that's exactly what had been missing. Millie belonged with them on the ranch, part of her expanding circle of family. She didn't think it was possible for things to get any better. Cord was so sweet and considerate.

The brilliance of her smile bathed her face with a warm glow. She moved around the table and straddled his lap, wrapping her arms around his neck.

"You are incredible, Mister Black. I am in awe. Thank you!"

Savannah poured the great depth of her feelings into a hot kiss. Neither one came up for air until Mille began forcefully clearing her throat.

Leaning back, Savannah shot him a questioning glance. "You realize she's gonna try to keep us in line, don't you?"

"She may try, but that doesn't mean we have to cooperate, sugar."

They all laughed heartily, basking in the warmth of friendship.

Chapter Seventeen

જી

Need was eating her up inside. She needed to be fucked, and soon. There was no sense sugarcoating the issue. She needed a big, hot, throbbing cock slamming fast, hard and deep into her dripping wet, aching pussy.

Hot. It was so hot, Savannah felt like an ice pop in the core of a burning furnace. Sweat trickled heatedly between her breasts, soaking into the waistband of her shorts. Summer had certainly arrived. She couldn't stand the added heat of wearing a bra. Instead she was suffering when every time she moved, her sensitive, neglected nipples brushed against her sticky tank top.

As soon as Millie arrived she'd declared it improper for Cord to be staying in the house and sent him to the bunkhouse. She'd stood there and said she strictly forbid any "hanky panky" before the wedding. At first Savannah had been amused. The woman Cord had hired to cook for all of them stood there telling Savannah she could not sleep with her fiancé in her own house.

All humor she'd felt for the situation had quickly evaporated. Millie stuck to Savannah closer than a second skin. Every time she tried to even sneak a kiss with Cord the infuriating woman would be there shooing him away.

It was just so hot. She couldn't take the heat. Giving up any pretense of working with the young filly between her otherwise empty thighs, Savannah dismounted and turned the animal out into the pasture.

The heat melted away her energy. Finding a shady spot under a nearby aspen, Savannah sank to the ground, leaning against the thick trunk. The cowboys had been keeping Cord busy, but maybe they could sneak away to the lake.

She could clearly visualize the two of them floating naked in the crisp, cool water. Clear, fat drops would glisten on Cord's tanned skin. Mmm, and she would relish slowly licking every one from his magnificent body. She would drink him in like a cold glass of water, quenching a thirst that had nothing to do with hydration.

Raised masculine voices drew her attention to the barn. A fresh wave of heat surged through her body like a fever, threatening to melt her skin away. Cord stood in the middle of the roof like a Grecian god, wearing only a pair of cutoff denim shorts. Sun glinted off his sweaty, bronze skin creating a surreal glow. Rivulets of sweat sluiced over rippling sinew as he used his shirt to dry his face.

Savannah licked her lips, following the path of a pregnant droplet as it glided down the center of his six-pack abs before disappearing into his navel. With a groan she pulled her mind away from the lovely little orifice. Slowly she began to notice the other shirtless boys.

Jesse climbed a ladder propped against the side of the red barn. He balanced a stack of shingles on one shoulder as he moved effortlessly under his burden. She watched the flex and play of muscle as his body moved smoothly upwards.

On the ground, Brock and Riley worked stacking supplies for the roof repair. All moisture left her mouth watching Riley as he picked up a bottle of water and tipped his head back, draining its contents. The muscles in his neck worked as his throat took in the clear fluid, a small trickle skating down his flesh.

This was crazy. "I need to be fucked hard!"

Tamara's laughter pulled her out of her thoughts. Oh shit, had she said that out loud? "Well then quit staring and go get you some," Tamara said, confirming her worst fear.

A pink flush heated Savannah from cheeks to breasts. "Didn't anyone ever tell you it's not nice to sneak up on people?" she teased.

Tamara just laughed. "Honey, if you need some then set up a midnight rendezvous. Think about it. Millie gets up before the sun, so she'll be sound asleep in bed nice and early. Sneak out of the house and get laid."

Returning her attention to the boys, Savannah decided that it wasn't such a bad idea. She'd get Cord to meet her at the pool. Millie would never hear them from her bedroom at the other side of the house. Getting down the stairs without making any noise would be the hardest part.

Just thinking about Cord's body gloriously naked and wet from head to toe had her needy pussy drenched in hot juices. She'd lay him down on one of the padded loungers and lap up each little drop of water. After tasting his balls she'd lick his thick shaft like an ice cream cone before swallowing him down the back of her throat and tasting his clean, masculine essence.

"Huh?" she asked. The only thing that had penetrated her sexual haze had been her name spoken repeatedly.

"Damn, woman. Take my advice and go get that boy tonight. I have to head into the store to take care of my neglected bookkeeping. I'll see ya tomorrow."

The words barely registered. She muttered an acknowledgement and returned her attention to the enticing sight of nearly naked men hard at work. Watching all that scrumptious male flesh was only making her hotter. She had to cool off before she spontaneously combusted.

* * * * *

"Son of a bitch," Jesse mumbled, staring off toward the house.

Cord's eyes followed the other man's gaze and nearly popped out of his head. Savannah stood near the back porch, saturated shorts and a tank top plastered to her body. A look of rapture on her upturned face, eyes closed. Her back was bowed, one arm extended above her upturned head holding the garden hose.

Water cascaded over her head, splashing down over her neck to stream over her flesh. Fat droplets fell from her long hair, shining golden in the sun. Her rigid nipples stood out against the thin material, clearly engorged.

With slow movements she lowered the tip of the hose down into her cleavage, bending backward so far he was amazed she didn't fall. She moved the nozzle down her slightly rounded abdomen, then sensuously slid it beneath the waistband of her shorts. The little crystals hanging from her navel sparkled in the sunshine.

Cord's cock pressed painfully against his pants. Her blissful smile nearly had him coming in his shorts. The water poured from her crotch in a deluge, rushing down her long, slender legs.

Hearing the other men muttering curses finally penetrated the fog that had clouded his brain. "Get your minds back on work," he growled.

Quicker than he would have imagined possible he was down the ladder and moving across the yard, his long gait eating up the ground between them. He shot Brock and Riley a murderous glance as he moved quickly past them.

That damn, sassy woman was going to be the death of him. The forced abstinence was bad enough without her putting on her own little wet T-shirt show.

He could clearly see the shivers of delight that racked her firm, curvy body. Damn, how he wanted to rip off her thin clothes and sink into her hot pussy, right in front of everyone, right there in the yard. His jaw clenched as Cord fought for control.

* * * * *

The chilly water was finally beginning to slake the dry heat from her fevered body, blissful relief pouring through every corpuscle. Savannah gasped in outrage as the forceful jets of water slowed to a slow trickle and ended with a few drips.

"What the…"

All cohesive thought left her mind as she straightened and stared at a red-faced Cord. Anger rolled off him in gale force waves that stole the newfound coolness from her skin. Her breath left her in a whoosh.

"Cord?" she gasped.

"Jesus H. Christ, Savannah. What the hell's wrong with you?"

He couldn't believe it. She just stood there staring at him with a look of confusion. It took all his will power to keep from reaching out and shaking some sense into the sexy, little devil.

"Dammit, Savannah. That was quite a hot little show. If you look closely at the hands, you'll notice they're all sporting raging hard-ons. Not to mention the fact that you're absolutely killing me."

Without any warning he scooped her up, then held her upside down against his side, tucked under one strong arm. He stomped over to the nearby porch steps, sat down hard and settled her squirming body firmly against his thighs.

Savannah screamed as much in surprise as outrage when his hand came down firmly on her backside. The hot sting of the blow radiated through her left cheek, somewhat cushioned by her wet shorts. Moments later his hand landed sharply on the right cheek. Moisture flooded her pussy as a new wave of heat surged through her body.

Each blow had her squirming against the hard muscles of his legs. She needed his big, impressive cock now more than ever. Her pussy ached, her clit throbbed. Each motion had her peaked nipples brushing against the coarse hairs of his thigh. Her breathing came out in sharp pants.

Cord spanked her several more times, watching the other men closely. At first it had appeared they would unwisely intervene until her shrieks of indignation turned into moans of pleasure.

The soft, wet material of her shorts cooled her heated flesh as Cord rubbed the offended globes of her ass. She barely heard his lowly mumbled words over the roaring of the blood in her ears.

"I ought to strip off your shorts right here in front of everyone so I can see how nice and pink your cheeks have gotten."

He was so close to following through on those words. Never in his life had he wanted someone so badly. No, it was more than want. It was pure, undiluted need that was riding him. Why the hell was he denying himself anyway?

The loud slap of the screen door drew both of their attention to the larger than life woman scowling down at them, meaty fists hiked up on her hips.

"That'll be quite enough of that," Millie boldly stated.

Cord looked up into her dark eyes. "Don't interfere here, Millie. Go back inside where you belong while I discipline my fiancée."

His tone and expression brooked no refusal. Seeing the hard look in his eyes the older woman made a wise choice. Without another word, she quietly backed her large bulk back through the door.

With ease born of masculine strength, Cord turned Savannah so that she was now sitting across his lap. He was so hot and bothered it felt like his head would explode. His little, wild filly had no idea what she did to his senses.

Cupping her face in his hands, Cord leaned his forehead against Savannah's. This waiting was ridiculous, and he couldn't stand it anymore. He came to a decision. Tonight they would make love and he would provide a little fantasy fulfillment at the same time. There was no way he could wait another two days until after the wedding. He was amazed his throbbing cock hadn't burst out of the confinement of his shorts, demanding release.

"I can't take this, sugar. I want you to meet me at eleven o'clock tonight out by the pool." He pulled back just far enough so he could see into her beautiful, melted chocolate eyes, where his own need was reflected back tenfold. Yes, tonight he would give her a wedding present she would never forget.

Desire had turned his piercing eyes a dazzling blue. She wanted to lose herself in the ever-changing, deep pools. That sexy, devilish smile had spread across his luscious lips. She just couldn't resist the temptation.

Leaning forward, she teased his lower lip between her teeth, then lightly feathered her tongue over the small hurt. Cord didn't need a second invitation. His lips opened over hers, his tongue pushing past her teeth, sinking into the sweet depths of her mouth.

When the kiss finally ended, both of them were gasping for breath. Cord's warm hands slid sensuously over the curve of her hips, up her sides and settled cupping her full breasts. The heat of his hard cock pressed into her hip had her wiggling to get closer.

"I need you, now. Please, Cord!"

Looking deeply into her eyes, Cord stroked his hand over her wet hair while shaking his head. "Wait for tonight, sugar. I promise it will be worth it."

He stood up and guided her up onto the porch. "Now be a good girl and get that pretty little ass inside. Think about how good I'm gonna make you feel tonight."

Savannah wandered upstairs in a sexual trance. She peeled off her wet clothes and decided some pampering was in order. After a long, cool shower she waxed her legs and mound, then spent extra time stroking her scented lotion over every inch of skin. She gave herself a manicure and pedicure, applying a sexy, shimmery, deep wine color to her nails.

Supper that night was an atypically quiet affair. A feeling of intense anticipation surrounded the sedate gathering. The normal banter and recounting of the day's events was conspicuously absent. A void filled the space where Tamara normally sat. Even normally gabby Millie remained quiet through most of the meal.

Tomorrow everyone would be together. Zeke was scheduled to arrive in the morning to help with final preparations for the wedding. He would be with them for two weeks before his classes started up again.

Savannah kept picking up a strange vibe from the cowboys, but was unable to read their carefully guarded feelings. She hoped they were not upset in some way over the scene in the yard earlier. She did not want her boys to be uncomfortable around her.

As soon as they were done eating, everyone scattered. Savannah had intended to suggest that they all play cards or watch a movie with a big tub of popcorn. It seemed that everyone had their own plans for the evening. She was on her own to find a way of passing the long hours until meeting Cord.

Chapter Eighteen

ဇာ

Reading didn't work. She'd read the same page of the newest erotica novel Tamara had given her three times now. Savannah just couldn't concentrate on the words, so instead she primped.

By the time she headed out to the pool she looked like a wanton goddess. Her hair flowed in golden ringlets, cascading over her shoulders and back. Her skin glowed from the massage oil she'd just finished rubbing all over her body. The skimpy garnet bikini hugged her curves like a second skin. A gold, crocheted cover-up hung over her waist, knotted at one side. Gold high-heeled sandals completed the ensemble, accentuating her long, firm legs.

As she quietly moved down the stairs, Savannah rubbed the pale pink crystal that hung between her breasts. For some reason she felt as nervous as a virginal bride on her wedding night.

Thankfully the neon pink, fiberglass cast had come off her arm two days ago. It would have clashed horribly with the outfit. The skin of her left forearm was much paler than the rest of her body, but there wasn't much she could do about that now. She brushed away the reminder of her ordeal as she set out to meet her lover.

At exactly eleven o'clock she walked down the porch steps and headed out toward the pool. She gasped, her first glimpse of the romantic scene thrusting her heart up into her throat. Hundreds of candles created a warm glow over the area, several floating on the shimmering surface of the water. A blanket had been spread out near the hot tub with a tray of crackers, cheese and fruit neatly placed at one corner. Next to the blanket was a bottle of champagne chilling in an ice bucket and two crystal flutes.

"You look absolutely ravishing, sugar."

Savannah was drawn toward his voice like a moth to the flame. Cord stood at the far end of the pool wearing only deep blue swim trunks. Shadows danced across his sinewy body in the soft radiance of candlelight. That was one sexy hunk of cowboy, and he was all hers.

With her chin tilted down she looked up at him from below thick lashes, giving him a seductive smile. Extending her arm, palm facing up, she crooked a finger at him. Her voice was husky as she whispered, "C'mere, stud."

Without a word he slowly walked toward Savannah as she drank in the glorious sight of her fiancé. She could not believe how lucky she was to have finally found such an intelligent, caring, understanding man to love. He was the one man with whom she could share her thoughts, dreams and visions without fear. Her heart was so full of love for him Savannah was certain it would burst.

Gently she cupped his face in her warm hands, a single tear quivering at the corner of her emotion filled eyes. "This is incredible, Cord. Thank you!"

"Sugar, tonight the world is yours. You want the moon then I'll lasso it and wrestle it down into your hands. You want the sun then I'll convince it to rise at midnight. I love you that much, Savannah."

His lips brushed across hers in a sweet kiss, which slowly built into a raging inferno of passion. A ball of heat started in the pit of her stomach, radiating outward through her body as their tongues intertwined. Her fingers threaded through the soft hair at his nape as she pressed her body in close.

With one hand on the small of her back, the other on her hip, Cord molded them together even closer. The hard length of his erection pressed against her soft abdomen. Heat flowed between her legs like molten lava, soaking the thin fabric of her bikini bottoms.

Both big hands moved to her rounded ass cheeks. His fingers sunk into the smoothly curved globes as he pulled her more firmly against his aching cock. It took all his will to keep from sliding away the thin barrier and sinking deep into her hot pussy.

No, his own pleasure would have to wait. He wanted to ensure her pleasure first. Cord stepped back, looking down into her passion-filled eyes.

"I want to take this slow, sugar."

Savannah had other things in mind. With slow, deliberate movements she untied the gold wrap and let it fall. Her deft fingers moved up between her breasts and made quick work of the tie. Slowly she peeled the dark material away letting the tiny triangles of cloth drop to the ground.

"If I don't taste you soon, I'll die," she boldly stated.

Dropping to her knees on the blanket, she hooked her fingers into the waistband of his trunks. Before he could protest, Cord's pants fell to the ground and his little, wild filly had his cock wrapped in her warm grasp.

She stroked his length firmly in her fist, from base to tip. A small drop of pre-cum glistened in the candlelight. With great relish she slid her warm tongue over the tip, lapping up his salty essence. Her low murmur of appreciation sent vibrations through her lips against his crown.

Just as she'd imagined, Savannah licked his magnificent cock like an ice cream cone, paying great attention to the sensitive slit, crown and ridge. Her eyes were nearly black with desire as she met his gaze over the length of his muscular torso.

Taking great care to not miss any of his silky flesh, she worked her tongue from crown to base and then finally lower to his balls. A deep, rumbling moan rose from his chest as she sucked each one into the warm cavern of her mouth, sliding her tongue over the tightening sac.

She released him from her mouth, gently massaging his balls in her hand. Her other hand gently nudged his legs further apart. Bending lower, she ran her tongue over his sensitive perineum. He gasped as she stretched her warm tongue out and over the thin strip of flesh. She flicked a light caress around the small rosette until it opened enough that she could thrust her tongue shallowly into the narrow channel.

"Savannah," he growled. "I'm gonna shoot off like Fourth of July fireworks if you don't stop that, sugar."

His fingers fisted tightly in her hair. Just the sight of her enjoyment nearly had him shooting his load. She truly appeared to relish giving him head as much as he delighted in receiving her efforts. Once again, he wondered how the hell he'd ever gotten so lucky to catch such an incredible, wild little filly.

Slowly she slid her tongue over his perineum again, bypassing his sac still cupped in her palm. She looked up and smiled at Cord, then wrapped her rosy lips around the head of his cock and worked the delicious muscle deep into the warmth of her mouth.

Soon her head bobbed as she worked his rigid cock, cheeks hollowing with the suction she applied. Her tongue swirled around his shaft as she sucked over the heated flesh and continued to massage his balls. With the other hand her finger found his anus, resuming the earlier caress of her tongue.

Using her own saliva as lubrication, she worked her index finger into the tight hole. Cord's knees buckled and he sank down onto the blanket. Savannah never paused in devouring his delicious cock. She dropped her shoulders and continued to swallow him down her throat.

A deluge of hot cream flooded her bikini, gliding down her thighs. She'd never felt so hot in her life. Her clit throbbed, her pussy ached and her nipples tingled with need. She was dying to feel him sink deep into her weeping flesh. But even more so, she thirsted for a taste of his hot cum.

Vaguely she was aware of some small, furtive noises nearby. Had she heard mumbled words? It didn't matter. All thought left her head when Cord called out her name as his salty, sweet cum blasted the back of her throat in hard jets. She took a deep breath. Relaxing her throat she swallowed the head of his cock as deeply into her body as possible, milking every drop of semen from his balls with her swallowing motions.

Collapsing back onto the blanket, Cord pulled her down on top of him. His handsome face held a look of awed disbelief.

"Damn, sugar. That was incredible. You love sucking my cock, don't you?"

In response she licked her lips with a slow, sensual glide of her tongue. "Mmm," she moaned.

Once some of his strength had returned, Cord sat forward picking something up from the edge of the blanket. "Do you trust me, sugar?"

Savannah did not have to think about her response, it flowed naturally from her lips. "With my life."

His devilish smile made her a little nervous. Reaching out, he stroked his fingers over her cheek. "Good. I want you to trust me with your pleasure too."

With tender care he placed a black silk blindfold over her eyes, tying it securely behind her head.

"Can you do that, Savannah?"

"Umm, yes."

Her senses were reeling. Without sight it seemed that her other senses sharpened. She could clearly hear the ice slosh around in the bucket, followed by paper ripping. The loud pop of the cork leaving the bottle made her flinch.

Cord smiled as three very obviously horny cowboys moved out of the bushes, Riley silently mouthing, "Holy shit."

"Mine," Cord growled, looking at the other men sternly.

"Always," Savannah whispered back huskily, not knowing they had company.

She waited in a heightened state of anticipation for his next move. Her ears seemed to be playing tricks on her. One moment she thought he was on her right, and the next she heard noises to her left. She whimpered softly.

"Shh. Just relax, baby."

He pressed a glass to her lips.

"Take a drink."

Okay, now he was definitely on her right. After sipping the dry champagne, he helped her lay back on the blanket.

"Just lay back and let me pleasure you, sugar. This is just the first of many wedding surprises I have planned for you."

A slight noise to her left had Savannah jerking her covered eyes in that direction. Her nostrils flared as she smelled the earthy scents of evergreen and man. Every muscle in her body tensed. Her head remained facing the left as she addressed Cord. "Is someone else here?"

Savannah gasped as a work-roughened finger flicked first her right nipple, then the left.

"Mmm, just relax and trust me."

Leaning forward, he took her mouth in a heated kiss. He held a firm breast in each hand, gently massaging. Her muscles began to relax as Cord brushed soft kisses across her cheek, working his way to the sensitive area behind her ear. She moaned as his tongue followed the scalloped curves of her ear. Then his teeth sank lightly into her lobe.

Tenderly his tongue and lips worked down her neck, following her thrumming pulse. She relaxed even more, reveling in the sensations as he licked at the hollow of her throat. Somehow his hands never changed position on her breasts as he moved lower down her chest. A chill of anticipation slid down her spine, making her crave the warmth of those big hands all over her body.

Slight little noises still attempted to trick Savannah. She found herself tuning out her hearing and concentrating on feeling every caress of her generous lover. Soon his hand was gone from her right breast, replaced by his talented tongue.

Her nipple tightened as streamers of electrical sensations shot from her breasts straight to her throbbing clit. His warm tongue worked her nipple in a swirling motion before he took the turgid peak between his lips, sucking hungrily.

One thick forearm rested over her upper chest, effectively pinning her to the blanket. Slight pressure was applied by that arm a fraction of a second before her shrill scream pierced the quiet night.

Confusion warred with her sensual need. As the arm pressed her firmly into the blanket, the hand on her left breast was replaced by a warm tongue.

Ohmigod! Her entire body went rigid.

Another strong forearm pressed across her hips as callused fingers began teasing her inner thighs. Cord's voice came as a warm breath exhaled right next to her ear while the two mouths worked her sensitive nipples.

"Its okay, Savannah. Just relax. I'm giving your fantasy to you, sugar. Just lay back and feel. Share this with me. Open yourself up and let me feel what you're feeling, see what you're seeing. Give me this part of you, sugar. Please!"

Her hands fisted in a death grip on the blanket as Savannah fought an internal battle. She knew the only other men Cord would trust with her fantasy were her cowboys. Hell, she had fantasized about this exact event so many times over the past year. Now Cord was giving her the fantasy. She just had to figure out how to relax enough to enjoy it.

He knew how much she had been turned on by seeing the cowboys pleasure Tamara in just this way. But how could she just lie here and let the cowboys pleasure her while Cord watched?

His sultry voice attempted to soothe her frazzled nerves.

"You look so beautiful, sugar. I want to watch you come while we love your exquisite body."

Her senses were bombarded with multiple sensations. The mouth on her left nipple was aggressive, teeth nipping as it sucked powerfully. In contrast, the mouth on the right tenderly laved her nipple. The fingers between her legs gently pushed her thighs apart then began a sensual dance toward the area that most desired attention.

The folds of her labia were tenderly parted moments before a third tongue moved from the bottom of her slit upward to the top, collecting her hot cream. The rumble of an appreciative male moan sent tremors through her body. Cord's hot words gave her permission to enjoy what she was feeling.

"Tastes good, doesn't she? Sweet apples with the spice of cinnamon. Makes you want to spend all night between her pretty legs."

"Hello, laying right here," she complained.

A rough, masculine mumble was the only response.

As the firm tongue stroked over her clit, Savannah's hips bucked upward without her permission, seeking more. Large hands cupped her ass, angling her pussy up to the man between her legs. Amazingly she felt her nipples impossibly lengthen under the hardworking mouths.

Her mouth was claimed in a deep, searing kiss, which swallowed her scream as stiff hairs raked over her clit and firm lips sucked at her. Hot juices gushed from her pussy only to be greedily swallowed down with gentle slurping noises. She could feel a throat working hard to swallow every drop.

The mouth on her lips was Cord. There was no mistaking his kisses. The mouth on her pussy belonged to Brock. Depending on how he moved his mustache felt vastly different, one moment silky smooth, the next prickly, then firmly tickling.

Savannah abruptly ended the kiss.

"Brock," she gasped.

His deep, rumbling voice actually helped to relax her.

"You taste so good, Van."

Finally releasing the blanket from her death grip, she worked her fingers into the hair of each head feeding at her breasts.

"Riley?" she queried.

"Mmm. You're so beautiful, Van."

She felt his words mumbled against her left breast. Her fingers stroked down his sweet face.

Turning her attention to the other side she gasped, "Jesse James."

"Right here, gorgeous."

As she stroked his familiar face Savannah arched her back, pushing her breasts more firmly against their mouths. Both men eagerly returned to their ministrations. Somehow it was a relief to hear those familiar voices.

Her legs were lifted up onto Brock's shoulders, but the hands cupping her ass never moved. She realized that Cord was no longer near her head. He slowly moved around her body making sure her cowboys provided the maximum pleasure.

Two thick fingers thrust deep into her pussy as Brock continued to feast on her clit. Since the hands still cupped her ass, she presumed it must be Cord, though she no longer cared who was where.

Another devilishly thick finger spread her juices from her pussy to her anus. The digit moved in small circles over her nether hole before slowly working deep inside the supersensitive channel. Her body bucked and writhed as Savannah was overwhelmed by delicious ecstasy.

Soon two fingers were fucking both her ass and her pussy. Brock sucked her clit between his luscious lips, twirling his tongue around the throbbing nub, French-kissing her needy flesh.

Warm hands, fingers, mouths and tongues roved over her body sending incredible sensations to nerve endings she hadn't even known existed. She pressed her flesh more firmly against her four lovers as the first tingling sensations of orgasm grew.

Cord's words, repeated by each of her cowboys, drove her over the precipice.

"Come for us, sugar."

Bright white lights flashed behind her eyelids as her entire body was engulfed in a sensual storm. Wave after glorious wave of bliss rolled through Savannah from the top of her scalp to her tightly curled toes. The boys worked frantically to drain every ounce of pleasure from her wildly trembling body as she screamed out in release.

She gasped for air as her body collapsed into a boneless heap. The four men continued to stroke her slowly back into an aroused state, building her up while aftershocks still pulsed through her pussy.

She was beginning to understand how Tamara must feel. It would be incredibly difficult to give up such overwhelming excess once it has been experienced. Yet Savannah knew it would be easy for her. All she really wanted was Cord and his pleasure.

Cord whispered to Savannah, pulling her over on top of his big body, settling her astride his narrow hips. "C'mere, sugar. I want you to ride me."

"Cord," she whimpered. "Take off the blindfold. I want to see you."

Once the blindfold was off, her hands were all over her generous lover. "I love you so much, Cord."

"I love you too, sugar."

Firm hands gripped her hips from behind, lifting her over Cord's huge cock. Cord guided his bulbous head to the mouth of her pussy, then Savannah was lowered once again.

"Ohhh," she gasped.

It felt so good to have him filling her aching pussy. The hands that had lifted Savannah stroked over her hips to the round globes of her ass. Firm fingers began kneading her cheeks, spreading them apart. Looking over her shoulder she smiled into Riley's intense blue gaze. With firm pressure between her shoulders, he bent her down over Cord's body.

Brock and Jesse stood nearby. Mmm, her boys had worked so hard to give her pleasure. Savannah decided it was time to return the favor.

"Come over here boys. Kneel down next to me. I want to taste those magnificent cocks."

They looked briefly to Cord for approval. At his nod, both men moved forward, each kneeling close to her shoulders. She balanced herself by gripping Cord's hips between her thighs. Slowly she rolled her hips in a circular motion. With her hands she stroked the two cocks now positioned at eye level.

Riley's hands continued to explore the deep crevice of her ass, her full cheeks and the tight little hole. As much as she could, without losing contact with Cord, Savannah raised up her ass, giving Riley easier access.

Still rolling her hips, her concentration moved to the two big cocks she held in her hands. She turned toward Jesse, noting the drop of cum shining at his slit. She studied his cock for a moment. While it was discernibly thicker than Cord's, it was also somewhat shorter, but no less magnificent.

With obvious delight she licked off the salty drop of cum. On a hungry growl she stretched her lips around the broad crown. Jesse groaned as she began to suck and lick his thick shaft, stretching her lips almost to the point of pain.

Behind her, Riley licked a wet kiss over her anus. She already felt stretched from the fingers that worked the small channel so recently. His tongue easily burrowed inside, fucking her most sensitive tissues.

She moaned around Jesse's cock, sending vibrations through his rigid flesh. He pumped his hips forward in shallow stabs, gently fucking her mouth. Her hand continued to stroke Brock's cock in her other hand. Cord thrust his pelvis upward, driving his shaft against her G-spot.

"Unnnhhhh," she cried out. "God, yes. Right there."

Jesse's cock slipped from her mouth with an audible pop. She pumped the slick organ in her fist and turned to Brock. His cock was slightly longer than Cord's, but narrower. It would be a challenge to take his whole shaft into her throat.

Savannah loved a good challenge.

She treated Brock to licks and nips before enveloping him in the warmth of her mouth. She sucked him deep and then began a steady, bobbing rhythm while fighting to take his enormous length as deep as possible.

It was hard to focus on anything other than Cord's cock filling her, stroking her G-spot, his pelvis grinding against her clit and Riley's wicked tongue pressing into the tight little orifice. Sensations spiraled through her body.

Soon Riley replaced his tongue with two thick fingers. He worked the digits deep into her ass, stretching the tissues as her moans became constant. Eventually, a third digit joined the others, readying her to receive his cock. Cord must have placed a tube of lubricant on the blanket. She could feel the cold gel begin to warm from her body heat.

With her hands, she pulled Brock and Jesse so close their shafts were almost touching in front of her. Her mouth worked frantically between the two delicious shafts. Seeing Cord watching her with desire darkening his eyes drove her wild. She couldn't get enough of either man into her mouth, and found herself wishing she could suck both cocks at once.

All cognizant thought left her mind when the round tip of Riley's cock pressed against her anus. Her movements on Cord slowed as he gently pressed the broad head past the constricted ring of muscle. Pleasure-pain spread from her ass through her whole body as she was stretched wide open. Every muscle in her body tightened as she screamed.

The boys all stopped moving simultaneously, tensing. Savannah fought for breath to reassure them.

"Ohhh, so good," she panted out. She found it incredibly difficult to speak when she could barely breathe.

As one, a collective sigh of relief came from the four men. Riley's well-lubricated cock began sinking deeper into her ass with small thrusts. Savannah returned to sucking the two cocks she held, but most of her focus remained on the exciting sensations spreading outward from her pelvis.

Savannah quickly became frustrated with Riley's slow motions. She began forcefully fucking both cocks. First she slammed down onto Cord's hips then back against Riley, sinking his cock in her ass to the hilt.

"Ahh...fuck yes...fuck me," she cried.

Each man took turns driving into her, filling every orifice. They fell into a rhythm, Cord and Riley, Jesse and Brock. Savannah chanted continuously, as wave after wave of pleasure rippled through her. "Oh God...oh God...oh God..."

Her body trembled with the ecstasy of being so completely filled and stimulated. Riley's cock in her ass made her much more aware of Cord in her pussy. The two men held her hips as they pistoned in and out of her body with ever increasing speed. Brock and Jesse tweaked her nipples as she sucked frantically.

A mind-blowing orgasm took her with little warning. Her ass clamped down on Riley and her pussy clamped down on Cord. She pleaded with Brock and Jesse.

"Please, come on me. I want your cum on my breasts."

Her fists pumped them at a maddening pace while her tongue laved both shafts. But it was Cord's name she screamed into the night.

"Oh fuck, Van," Riley bellowed as his semen shot into her ass. Brock was next, shooting his load over her breasts as her fist milked him, with Jesse close behind. Cord was last, climaxing long and hard with her name on his lips.

Brock and Jesse massaged their semen into her breasts as Savannah's body continued to be racked by spasms. Small, choked sobs were coming from her lips. Cord and Riley kept moving with her gentle thrusts, helping her wring every ounce of pleasure possible from the overpowering experience.

When she finally collapsed, the boys lowered her gently down next to Cord, who quickly gathered her into his arms.

"So beautiful, sugar. You are so incredible."

The other men collapsed onto the deck, gasping for breath. Savannah had taken everything they offered then demanded more. When they were finally able to move, Brock lifted Savannah into his arms. He planted a gentle kiss on her lips as Cord rose. Riley and Jesse both took their turns leaning in for a kiss before leaving Cord to take care of her.

As he carried her into the house, Savannah basked in the look of pure male satisfaction that curled up the corners of his mouth. Life would be an incredible journey when shared with such a wonderful man.

Epilogue

ഔ

The majestic mountains, ever-present guardians of all that lay below, wore an incandescent patina of amber, garnet and amethyst. Jagged spikes of aged, gray rock soared upwards into the vast, seemingly endless sky. Lush, emerald green grasses covered the valley. It was a picture perfect day for a wedding.

Without question, the Shooting Star ranch lands held majestic beauty. Everyone gathered around the blissful couple meshed with both the land and each other like pieces of a puzzle forming a complete picture.

Everyone excluding Tamara. For some reason she was the only one who saw the apparent truth. They were all blind to the reality that she was a square peg struggling to fit into a round hole.

Just this morning, Savannah had sat down with all of them and calmly explained how she thought of them like family and wanted to keep them all together. Then she had handed sealed envelopes to Jesse, Riley, Brock, Zeke, Craig and Sandy, and Tamara. Inside each envelope was a deed for ten acres of the Shooting Star Ranch.

What the heck Van thought she was supposed to do with ten acres of land was beyond her comprehension. The crazy woman had said they should each build a house, start a family. Tamara had nearly choked on her coffee at that suggestion.

Watching Cord with Savannah reignited a fathomless hunger she'd managed to keep subjugated within the deepest recesses of her soul. An insatiable yearning for some nameless, but vital segment long missing left her feeling incomplete. While her cowboys were able to ease her burning sexual ache, they were unable to fill the void.

In retrospect, moving to the ranch had not been a good idea. Daily exposure to the loving couples in residence slowly eroded her sanity. If only she could put a name to the elusive missing element, she'd be able to embark on a search.

Oh, how she hated weddings, no matter how elegant or tastefully conducted. The wedding of Cord and Savannah Black was certainly divine. A single tear escaped Tamara's bright, jade eye as the blissful couple rode into the dazzling sunset.

Of course, the festivities at the reception would be abject torture. She would silently suffer through the obtuse, jubilant nuptial rites. How laughable that the only other single woman fighting over the bouquet with her would be and an eight-year-old girl. And the implied meaning of catching the flowers made her shudder.

As expected, the available men would then fight over the garter flung over Cord's shoulder. Then the real absurdity would begin as the lucky winner had the dubious honor of sliding his prize as far up the lucky lady's leg as she'd allow.

While the dancing would be enjoyable, in the end it would leave her needing to be fucked. And all the drinking would render the cowboys useless to slake her thirst. Once again she would be left aching.

Maybe she needed a drastic change. Just leave everything behind and set out on an adventure. She'd always wanted to travel, but wandering the world alone didn't appeal to Tamara. Somehow she knew that would leave her feeling even more restless and unsettled.

Damn, what was she thinking? She couldn't leave Savannah anyway. Her friend would need her support during Wyatt Bodine's trial. Cord would be supportive, but she'd need Tamara by her side to face the vile man.

Soon though, her friend would be so wrapped up with the growing ranch, husband and baby that Tamara would not be missed. Then it would be glaringly apparent that she did not belong here. There would be nothing to keep her from drifting away.

She couldn't wait until the happy affair was over. Her cheeks were sore from extended efforts to maintain a counterfeit smile. Would the fabricated cheer be obvious in the pictures? Did it even matter? Most likely no one would even notice if she left the party early.

A black cloud of depression descended on Tamara. Maybe she needed medication. Those commercials with the sad face that ended up bounding after a butterfly always made her wonder. All the symptoms seemed to fit. Feeling sad, anxious, restless, having no interest in activities. At times she felt intense urges to flee, felt trapped, heart pounding, palms clammy, nauseous.

Tamara shook off her mental wanderings. No, drugs were not the answer. No feel good medication could wash away her restless needs and jaded senses.

A large, white tent had been erected to contain the reception. Tamara felt the gently waving material closing in on her. It was time to make her escape. None of the intoxicated revelers were even likely to notice.

Stepping out into the balmy evening air she took a deep lungful of blessedly clean air. Torches provided an amber glow to show the way. The spiked heels she wore sunk into rich earth as she made her way toward her cabin.

She was totally absorbed in her efforts to flee unnoticed. Making her way over the rustic terrain required all Tamara's attention when the torches ended, leaving her in the inky blackness of a moonless night. With determination she moved rapidly while closely watching where she trod, head down.

Turning the corner of the house she walked right into a large, solid wall, driving much needed oxygen from her lungs with a whoosh. Raising her hands, she pressed her palms against the obstacle and shoved. The warm, solid mass never budged.

"Whoa. Hello there, gorgeous. Are you alright?"

If he hadn't already knocked the air from her lungs, the stranger's slow, sexy drawl would have taken her breath away. She looked up into compelling black eyes, which drove all coherent thought from her mind.

Oh God, what was wrong with her? She always had some insolent, cocky remark at the ready. For some reason nothing came to mind other than how dark and dangerous the large man looked. His dark appearance gave her the impression of a rakish bad boy, but there was also something calming about his presence.

Large, warm hands firmly held her hips, providing much needed support. It was a good thing too. Her nostrils flared, drinking in his heady, masculine scent. She smelled leather, sun-warmed flesh and hot man. Tamara swayed dizzily.

The world whirled and dipped wildly. Cold chills raised goose bumps on her arms. Damn it. She wasn't the kind of frail woman prone to fainting. What the hell was wrong with her?

When everything settled again she found herself firmly planted against a wide, hard chest. Muscular arms held her as securely as steel bands around her back and under her legs. Then the big stranger carried her to the porch steps. Instead of putting her down as she expected, he sat with her held captive on his lap.

It would be heaven to just sink into his chest, absorbing his abundant warmth. Tilting her head she looked up into his penetrating black eyes. Rakishly long, raven blue-black hair gleamed in the lamplight. His dark skin held the cinnamon tones of Native American heritage.

She'd been captured by an Indian. Where the hell were her cowboys when she needed to be rescued? Talk about ironic. Tamara pushed ineffectually against the solid wall of his chest again, scrambling to free herself from his grasp.

"Easy now, darlin'," he crooned. "I won't hurt you."

"Wh-who are you? What are you doing skulking around in the dark?"

His smile was a luminous, sexy flash of white teeth that tugged at her heart. She could get lost just drinking in his captivating features. And oh, how she wanted to feel his silky ebony hair slip between her fingers. Heat flooded her pussy at the thought of fisting her hands in the shoulder length strands, holding him captive between her widespread legs.

Luscious, plump lips called out for her tongue to explore their texture and shape. His firm jaw looked as if it were chiseled from granite. Incredibly wide shoulders led to his solid, muscular chest. Without realizing she flexed her fingers, basking in the pure masculine vitality and power she held.

"Dakota Blackhawk, at your service. I was hired last week by Mr. Black. He told me I could begin moving in whenever I was ready."

Tamara stared at him, stunned. Maybe she wouldn't leave the ranch after all. Things could get extremely interesting with Dakota working and living on the Shooting Star. And did she really want the cowboys coming to the rescue? Maybe not.

She wondered briefly if he could hear the racing of her heart, which was beating triple time. Oh the delicious adventures she could have exploring the yummy man who still held her. Just the feel of his thumb stroking over the pulse in her wrist had her pussy lips drenched with hot cream. The sweet pressure and heat of his very large, very erect cock against her hip were divine. And his firm legs beneath her bottom, yum.

"What's your name, darlin'? Do you live here?"

"I…um." Hell, her mind was so muddled she couldn't even remember her name. "Tamara. Tamara Dobbs. Yes, I live on the ranch with my friends."

Oh, God. She was starting to ramble like a total idiot. The way he was looking at her, his sexy voice, took her normally quick wit and sent it packing. If just talking to him, sitting on his lap made her feel like this, what would it be like to have him in her bed? Mmm, or in her Jeep, or the back aisle of the bookstore, or the lake. The delightful possibilities were endless.

Yes, ranch life had just become a great deal more interesting since running into Dakota Blackhawk. Maybe those ten acres would come in handy after all.

Enjoy An Excerpt From:

THE BOY NEXT DOOR

Copyright © NICOLE AUSTIN, 2006.

"What are you up to, Steve?" Cathy's already tense nerves sent anxious tremors of anticipation surging through her body. His smile kicked up another notch, displaying brilliant white teeth. Slightly long chestnut hair hung over his brow, giving him a rakish, bad boy appearance.

Steve guided her with a protective hand pressed against her lower back. He turned her around saying, "I brought an old friend to see you."

The first thing she saw was a broad, solid wall of muscular chest. Slowly her gaze wandered up the thick vein pulsing in a masculine neck. A firm, square jaw was topped off with seductively curved lips, the top one a perfect cupid's bow. His nose was as strong and straight as a knife slash down the center of his face, perfectly dividing the two sides. When she gazed into familiar, exquisite sapphire blue eyes she sucked in a shocked, gasping breath. She felt like someone had just hit her with a two by four.

Those disconcerting, fathomless blue pools had starred in every fantasy she'd ever dreamed up. Cathy had ached for so long to see those eyes staring intently into her own, just like they were now. She had hungered to see emotions swirl within their expressive depths.

His silky, golden blond hair was cut much shorter than she'd ever seen it before. While his body had always been muscular, it was now honed to perfection from hard physical work. And if she wasn't mistaken he'd grown taller over the years. Her gaze drifted briefly down again, noting a trim waist, strong muscular thighs, and a distinctive bulge behind his zipper.

Regardless of the changes that had occurred, she would never forget those deep, twinkling blue eyes. She returned her gaze to those sparkling depths, seeing genuine delight, and if she wasn't mistaken, heated desire.

The paralysis of her shock finally released her from its tight grip. With a squeal of joy, Cathy launched herself into his arms. There was really nothing else she could do. She was so thrilled to see him again, even though in the back of her mind she harbored a little resentment, it was overpowered by her happiness. He caught her easily as her arms clasped around his neck, long legs around his waist. Burying her face in the curve of his neck, she drank in his scent like she was starved for the sandalwood cologne and underlying natural masculine musk.

After a tight embrace she leaned back against the support of the strong arms wrapped firmly around her back. Her hands roamed the chiseled planes of his face like a blind woman studying his features, memorizing with her hands. Was he real, was she actually touching Blake?

"Oh, God. Is it really you? I can't believe my eyes." She stared for several moments, lost in amazement. "Let me hear your voice, then I'll know for sure."

Her intense reaction drew the curiosity of the crowd, but she was too wrapped up in Blake to notice. She was not acting very much like the Cat they were used to seeing, but all she cared about was the fact that she held Blake Carlisle in her arms for the first time in ten years, and she had no intention of letting him go any time soon.

Blake's eyes drank in the changes in the gorgeous woman whose sweet kiss had haunted him for years. The kisses he'd shared with other women had always been compared to that one sweetly passionate kiss with Cathy, and they all were found to be somehow lacking in comparison. There was just something special that had passed between them in that exchange that still managed to touch his soul. Now he discovered that she had been transformed into a stunning woman. He'd never be able to hold himself in check around the amazing beauty he now held close.

"Ah…yeah…it um, it's me." What the hell was wrong with him? He never stuttered. He cleared his throat before trying to speak again. "I'm back in the old house again. Just completed my discharge from active duty. Trying to figure out what to do with myself." He'd be damned if he wasn't running at the mouth, too. His reaction to her was so incredibly strong.

He felt the tremors that coursed through her body as he spoke, along with the goose bumps that broke out over her soft skin. There was no mistaking the affect his voice had on her. Blake took a deep, steadying breath before continuing. The woman in his arms had rocked his world down to the bedrock of its foundation. He watched in fascination as a single fat tear rolled down her cheek.

"Damn, brat. It's so good to see you," he stated in a raspy, emotion-filled tone.

Hearing the nickname snapped Cathy back to their surroundings. She could not show any weakness or vulnerability in the bar. What the hell was wrong with her? With great effort she pulled her Cat persona firmly back into place then slid down his big, hard body with tortuous slowness.

There was no mistaking the long, thick erection that she rubbed against. After several years of having every size and shape dick pressed against her butt, hips and abdomen, Cat was quickly able to size up any man. What she felt now was truly impressive. Far better than anything she'd ever felt before.

She became flushed with heat, awareness setting her nerve endings to tingling. Just the thought that she'd given Blake Carlisle a hard-on made her feel dizzy. How the heck was she supposed to be Cat around him? Conflicting emotions swirled through her head. She still had two more hours to go until the club closed for the night.

Pull yourself together, girlfriend, she silently chastised.

Putting on a show for her audience, she brushed her body against Blake, circling his muscular form. Long red nails scraped over his firm ass, a slim hip, then up to his fascinating, sculpted chest. Casually she drawled, "You sure grew up, sugar."

Okay, you can do this. You have no choice. Cat can't be blown away by a man in public. Get your act together.

Blake was shocked by the change that came over the enigmatic woman who used to be sweet little Cathy. It was similar to watching a chameleon change its colors to blend in with a new environment. What the hell was up with the seductress act? It made his head swim. Who was the real woman? The sweet girl who had greeted him so warmly, or the siren who now circled him like a land-shark ready to take a bite out of his ass?

"Um…yeah. Obviously, I'm not the only one." He watched the practiced, seductive sway of hips as she moved. "Maybe we can get together somewhere outside of here…catch up on old times."

She turned to the bar and filled her tray with drinks. When she turned back he heard her purr.

Holy shit!

"Mmm. Give me a call some time, stud." She glanced down at his crotch suggestively. "Maybe we can work something out."

The double entendre was not lost on Blake. His cock jerked against its confinement, demanding he seize what she was offering, *now*! Thankfully it had been a long time since he had allowed his cock to make decisions for him.

Without another glance, Cathy turned and sashayed away between tables. Blake wanted to rip the arms off the men who dared touch his woman as she passed by. Oh, and make no mistake, she was his woman, even if he wasn't the kind to settle down. She always had been and always would be his. He was home now, and he meant to claim what belonged to him. One way or another he would get her brother's blessing.

Steve clapped him on the shoulder as they both stood watching Cathy expertly work the captivated crowd. "She sure grew up, didn't she?"

Blake turned toward his friend. "Jesus H. Christ. You could have warned me!"

Call Me Barbarian by Liddy Midnight

Princess Cedilla enjoys unprecedented privilege in a society where women are neither seen nor heard. Her life changes when twin barbarian gladiators enter the arena. One glance and Cedilla is irrevocably bound to these Southern warriors — and revealed as half-barbarian herself. Whether in the arena or the bedchamber, Asterix and Apostroph live for the moment — until they find their destined mate. When Cedilla is banished by the Emperor, they devote themselves to satisfying her wildest desires. But the Empire needs Cedilla, and the Empire is intolerant of barbarians...

Dragonmagic by Allyson James

It's hell to be a dragon enslaved. Arys, a powerful silver dragon in human form, is bound to a witch who uses his magic and his body to pleasure her in every way imaginable. When Arys spies Naida, a young woman just coming into her powers, watching Arys performing erotic acts with the witch, he knows that Naida is the key to his freedom. First he must convince Naida she's his true mate and that the power of their sexual play, and her love, will release him.

Fallen For You by Paige Cuccaro

For ten thousand years, Zade's warrior mentality kept him focused on the Watcher's mission — rid the world of the Oscurità fallen angels. And then the witch Isabel came under his care. The Oscurità will be coming to posses her or kill her, drawn by her burgeoning powers. Isabel is a temptation they can't ignore, but neither can Zade. If he succumbs to his feelings, Zade's frozen soul could destroy Isabel. If he resists, his unsatisfied need may cost him everything. To save all he holds dear, Zade must trust that Isabel was born for him, and he has fallen for her.

Spontaneous Combustion by Nicole Austin

Dr. Madailein Flannagan's carnal desires are blazing deep inside, and her best friend Jake Cruise is just the man to fan the flames. But the sexy, bad boy firefighter goes for equally bad girls, and Maddy's afraid she's just not his type. Although lately she has been fantasizing about Jake and a few of his friends… Jake thinks that Maddy is way out of his league, but he knows that she can't refuse a challenge. And he's come up with an irresistible dare guaranteed to send her body up in flames, gain her submission, and maybe even win her heart.

The Ambassador's Widow by Myla Jackson

Chameleon Agent Andre Batello is sent on assignment to "fill in" for an ambassador who died the night before a long-negotiated peace treaty is due to be signed. As part of a special team of individuals with the ability to assume another's identity based on a single strand of DNA, Andre's mission is to infiltrate the ambassador's life and sign that treaty. The one major glitch in his mission: he didn't plan on falling in love with the ambassador's widow.

The Joining by Jory Strong

On the water world of Qumaar, Siria Chaton is a prisoner of her talent. With her credits dwindling, she has few options and little hope for a future. Until Jett and Mozaiic du'Zehren enter her life.

After five years of being a couple, Jett and Mozaiic have gained permission to add a third, a woman, to their joining. They can't believe their good fortune when the woman assigned to them is a water diviner. Now if only she'll accept them as lovers and come home with them to the forbidden desert planet of Adjara.

Why an electronic book?

We live in the Information Age — an exciting time in the history of human civilization, in which technology rules supreme and continues to progress in leaps and bounds every minute of every day. For a multitude of reasons, more and more avid literary fans are opting to purchase e-books instead of paper books. The question from those not yet initiated into the world of electronic reading is simply: *Why?*

1. *Price.* An electronic title at Ellora's Cave Publishing and Cerridwen Press runs anywhere from 40% to 75% less than the cover price of the exact same title in paperback format. Why? Basic mathematics and cost. It is less expensive to publish an e-book (no paper and printing, no warehousing and shipping) than it is to publish a paperback, so the savings are passed along to the consumer.

2. *Space.* Running out of room in your house for your books? That is one worry you will never have with electronic books. For a low one-time c ost, you can purchase a handheld device specifically designed for e-reading. Many e-readers have large, convenient screens for viewing. Better yet, hundreds of titles can be stored within your new library — on a single microchip. There are a variety of e-readers from different manufacturers. You can also read e-books on your PC or laptop computer. (Please note that Ellora's

Cave does not endorse any specific brands. You can check our websites at www.ellorascave.com or www.cerridwenpress.com for information we make available to new consumers.)

3. *Mobility.* Because your new e-library consists of only a microchip within a small, easily transportable e-reader, your entire cache of books can be taken with you wherever you go.

4. *Personal Viewing Preferences.* Are the words you are currently reading too small? Too large? Too… ANNOYING? Paperback books cannot be modified according to personal preferences, but e-books can.

5. *Instant Gratification.* Is it the middle of the night and all the bookstores near you are closed? Are you tired of waiting days, sometimes weeks, for bookstores to ship the novels you bought? Ellora's Cave Publishing sells instantaneous downloads twenty-four hours a day, seven days a week, every day of the year. Our webstore is never closed. Our e-book delivery system is 100% automated, meaning your order is filled as soon as you pay for it.

Those are a few of the top reasons why electronic books are replacing paperbacks for many avid readers.

As always, Ellora's Cave and Cerridwen Press welcome your questions and comments. We invite you to email us at Comments@ellorascave.com or write to us directly at Ellora's Cave Publishing Inc., 1056 Home Avenue, Akron, OH 44310-3502.

THE
☥ ELLORA'S CAVE ☥
LIBRARY

Stay up to date with Ellora's Cave Titles in
Print with our Quarterly Catalog.

TO RECIEVE A CATALOG,
SEND AN EMAIL WITH YOUR NAME
AND MAILING ADDRESS TO:

CATALOG@ELLORASCAVE.COM
OR SEND A LETTER OR POSTCARD
WITH YOUR MAILING ADDRESS TO:

CATALOG REQUEST
c/o ELLORA'S CAVE PUBLISHING, INC.
1056 HOME AVENUE
AKRON, OHIO 44310-3502

MAKE EACH DAY MORE *EXCITING* WITH OUR

ELLORA'S
CAVEMEN
CALENDAR

☥ WWW.ELLORASCAVE.COM ☥

Now Available
from

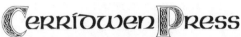

Cerridwen Press

Hocus Pocus

By Teresa Roblin

Shy and quiet Amanda Santorelli is unhappy watching the world go by around her. When her well-meaning but wacky aunt casts an assertiveness spell on her, Amanda's orderly world is turned upside down. Unable to control herself, Amanda blurts out whatever is on her mind every time someone asks her a question. Trying to outwit the spell only makes matters worse. With no control over her own mouth, it's only a matter of time before someone discovers the object of her secret obsession.

Mark Abbott is happy with the way his unassuming assistant runs his office. But all of a sudden she's become a new person—both in attitude and appearance—and he's not sure he likes the effect on his orderly work routine. With each passing day, he finds himself waiting to see what will come out of her mouth next. Before long, he can no longer deny the truth—the new Amanda is seriously making him reconsider his vow never to mix business with pleasure.

Mark doesn't know if it's love—or if he's just a victim of Hocus Pocus.

erridwen, the Celtic Goddess of wisdom, was the muse who brought inspiration to story-tellers and those in the creative arts. Cerridwen Press encompasses the best and most innovative stories in all genres of today's fiction. Visit our site and discover the newest titles by talented authors who still get inspired - much like the ancient storytellers did, once upon a time.

Cerridwen Press

www.cerridwenpress.com

COMING TO A BOOKSTORE NEAR YOU!

ELLORA'S CAVE

Bestselling Authors Tour

UPDATES AVAILABLE AT

WWW.ELLORASCAVE.COM